GYPSY BASTARDS MC: VOLUME ONE

EVERNIGHT PUBLISHING ®

www.evernightpublishing.com

Copyright© 2023

Jade Marshall

ISBN: 978-0-3695-0841-6

Cover Artist: Jay Aheer

Editor: Audrey Bobak

GYPSY BASTARDS MC: VOLUME ONE

DEDICATION FOR *THE WOLF*

This book is dedicated to each and every girl that ever set foot in Rosenhof High School along with the teachers and all the staff working in the hostels. No matter how far we stray from each other, or how often we speak, you will always be my family.
We are more than where we came from but never forget the path you took.

GYPSY BASTARDS MC: VOLUME ONE

THE WOLF

Gypsy Bastards MC, 1

Jade Marshall

Copyright © 2020

Chapter One
Hadley

I hate my job.

It isn't something I say to get people to pity me. I genuinely hate working at Mary's Rib Shack. I hate the mauve one-piece uniform, made of an awful, itchy fabric. I hate that the owner likes us to show off our assets, which means our uniforms are short around the legs and low around the neck. I don't particularly enjoy showing off my barely-there B cups, especially not to *our* clientele. I hate that Mary's is in downtown Gypsy Falls and the people who show up here are sketchy at best, but most are completely creepy. But Mary pays in cash and I need to stay off the grid.

This isn't something I've done out of choice but more out of necessity. Growing up around an outlaw motorcycle club, which I then managed to piss off—through no fault of my own, might I add—means running and hiding to stay alive. If King were to ever get his hands on me, I wouldn't survive. Knowing that death chases me daily and could catch up with me at any moment ensures I always keep my head down.

The area where the diner is located is far from ideal, with drug dealers on every second corner and a nonexistent police response rate. From the linoleum flooring that's cracked and peeling in places, to the faded leather booth seats, and the god-awful music, there isn't a single thing about Mary's Rib Shack that I don't hate.

I work the evening shift until closing time, from four in the afternoon until around midnight. I want to be able to work my way out of this hellhole and provide a better life for myself. I have aspirations and being a waitress isn't one of them.

One day, I want to be able to open my own tattoo parlor. For as long as I can remember, I've loved drawing and through the years, I've honed my craft. Add to that the fact I did an apprenticeship at a tattoo parlor, learning from one of the best, and you have my dream. The only thing I want to do for the rest of my life.

"Hey, can we get some more coffee over here?" the man with the biker's cut sitting in my section all but yells at me.

Earlier, I saw them enter and a chill ran right down my spine. My first instinct was to run, to get the hell out of here as quickly as my legs could carry me. After catching a glimpse of their patches and not recognizing their club, I was able to calm myself.

My hands shake, and my legs feel weak as I make my way to their table. Bikers terrify me. Not some bikers, but all bikers.

The three other guys with him seem rather normal-looking although anyone with eyes can tell that's not the case. One blond and two with dark-brown hair, all of them with protruding beer bellies. The fourth man, the one who just spoke and whom I'm assuming is the leader of this merry band of misfits, gives me the straight-up chills.

He's large, burly, and bald, with a snake tattoo running down his arm to his wrist. It's garish and badly done with absolutely no detail. The man looks me over with eyes the color of mud as I refill the cups. There's no depth to his eyes, just a flat deadness, and I try to avoid eye contact at all costs. I refill all four cups and start to move away when a large hand clamps around my wrist and pulls me back. Again, I feel this crawling sensation running over my skin. It takes everything I have within me not to pull away from his grip.

"Why don't you sit down with us for a minute, darling?" the leader drawls at me.

"I can't. I'm on shift and have to get back to my customers," I reply while trying to pull my arm from his grip.

My breathing becomes shallow and a shiver works its way through my body. The need to get his hands off me is almost overwhelming.

"Well, now, Mary won't mind, and the other waitress can see to your customers while you have a seat with us."

He uses a tone that's supposed to be reassuring but simply serves to creep me out even more. He yanks on my arm and I lose my balance, toppling forward and pouring half the remaining coffee down the front of his pants.

"You stupid fucking whore," he bellows.

Before I can react, he backhands me across the face, causing me to fall. My head connects with the counter and then the floor with a resounding thud. Lying on the floor, all I can think is this is it, my last day at Mary's. I would rather live on the fucking street than work here one more day. Regaining my senses and opening my eyes, I find complete chaos around me. All the guys from the table are on their feet. The two dark-haired men are holding back the guy who just slapped me. He's doing his best to pull away from their grip and has his eyes trained on the front door to the diner.

Storm, my best friend, stands in the doorway. She's a petite Asian woman with long black hair streaked with purple, full sleeve tattoos—courtesy of myself, a small waist, and an awesome set of all-natural C-cup breasts. Storm knows how to defend herself from the time she spent living on the street. She may be a stripper, but she will never let a man get the upper hand again. Apparently, she learned a painful lesson and quickly found someone to teach her how to defend herself.

In three-inch stilettos with her gun pointed straight at him, she stands her ground in front of this monster of a man.

"Viper, why don't you take your little cronies and leave?" She's deadly calm in the face of this man and for a moment, I envy her confidence. I haven't moved from my spot on the floor and simply watch their exchange like the coward I have become.

"You know good and well that your kind isn't welcome around here. Or do I need to make a call?" She appears calm while taking her phone out of the back pocket of her jeans.

Viper tries to charge at her again but the blond man steps between them.

"Time to go," he says, and the other two men start pulling Viper toward the door on the other side of the diner.

"I'm gonna get you. You and your little waitress friend. You're gonna pay. You hear me, Storm? You and that little cock tease!" he bellows as he's dragged out.

"That pussy club ain't gonna save you."

As soon as they are on the motorcycles and roaring into the distance, Storm puts her gun back in her purse and rushes over to me. "Oh, sweetie. Are you okay?" she inquires while pushing my hair from my face to inspect the damage.

"Hurts like a bitch but I'll live. Gonna be blue tomorrow and I'll probably have an egg on my head later, but I'll be fine," I assure her as I push up from the floor. "Thanks for the help."

Storm looks at me with sympathy in her eyes, something I despise more than I can ever explain. I hate being seen for the weak, broken, scared little girl I become once I am faced with something that triggers my past. My past affects me more than I would like to admit, even to myself. So many things can trigger me and have me turning back in on myself. For years, I have secluded myself from people except for a select few. My friendship with Storm often pushes my boundaries and I feel like she is helping me rejoin the world again, one little push at a time.

As she opens her mouth to respond, Mary comes shrieking around the corner.

"You stupid bitches. Do you know what you've done?"

Her face is blood red from the lack of oxygen during her rant and her over-styled, bleach-blonde hair flies all over the place.

"Those assholes are gonna burn my place to the fucking ground because of the two of you!"

"What the fuck is wrong with you?" Storm turns a glare on her. "One of your staff members was just attacked, and all you can worry about is your business? What kind of person are you?"

Mary stares daggers at Storm as I pull myself to

my feet.

"What's wrong with me?" Mary continues shrieking. "Do you know who the fuck those guys were and how bad it can get when you fuck with them?"

"Yes, I do," Storm says calmly. "Those are the limp-dick Mongrels MC and ain't shit gonna happen to anyone. Pope is gonna lose his shit when he hears they were in his territory."

Mary pales when she seems to realize Storm actually knows what she's talking about.

"Now," Storm says, looking back at me over her shoulder, "I am gonna take Hadley home and get some ice on her face. You're gonna cover her tables and still pay her for the hours she's missing. Because that's what a good boss would do."

"Oh, go choke on a dick, Storm. You won't be telling me how to run my goddamn business. Why don't you and Hadley just get her shit and get out because I don't need to draw any more attention."

She calmly turns to me and, looking me in the eyes, says, "You're fired."

Before I can think it through or contemplate my actions, my fist flies out and connects with Mary's nose.

She gives an undignified shriek as she cups her nose. "You cunt! You broke my fucking nose."

I stare at her before regaining my footing. Today may have been my breaking point. I have never—and I mean never—in my life laid hands on another person. "Oh, bite me, Mary. You're a fucking bitch and I quit."

Between hitting Mary, telling her to piss off, and quitting my job, I feel like I'm on top of the world. For the first time I can remember, I stood up for myself.

With what I'm sure is a seriously crazy smile on my face, I turn away from her. I head to the back of the diner where my personal effects are in a locker and change out of my shitty uniform. Taking a deep breath, I realize what I have just done. I stood up for myself but in the process, I've quit the only job I have. How am I going to pay rent, buy food, or pay for my damn car repairs? I am so fucked.

Instead of lingering on that, I square my shoulders and walk out to the front. People are crowded around Mary while Storm is smirking from her spot at the front door. Looking back at Mary, I smile. As I walk out of the diner, I give a single finger salute in farewell, light up a smoke, and walk home.

Chapter Two
Wolf

Sitting at the clubhouse, with a bottle of bourbon beside my favorite ratty green chair and a skinny piece of club ass grinding on my junk, I try to will myself to think about anything else besides today's fuckup. Rock music blasts through the sound system and I let the music flow through me. Staring blankly past her, I try to think about the run we just got back from and how it all went to shit in the blink of an eye.

As the club enforcer, it's my job to ensure the safety of the club members. The fact that Sparrow is lying on a table in the next room while Doc digs a bullet out of his leg gets on my fucking nerves.

Shit shouldn't have happened the way it did. But as usual, the mother fucking Mongrels got in our business and turned shit upside down. What was supposed to be a simple drop off for the Mexican cartel got all fucked beyond comprehension.

Arriving at the warehouse twenty minutes before the drop was supposed to go down is our usual protocol. One of the guys would do a perimeter sweep while the rest of us got the cargo ready to be picked up. It should have been a simple run, one we've made a dozen times without any issues. But the Mongrels decided it was a good idea to try to rob us in the middle of our transaction. They came barreling in on a beat-up truck, all guns blazing probably without thinking anything through. The cartel got pissed, we got pissed, and bullets had started flying in every damn direction.

Luckily, we are still whole and so are the cartel because we for damn sure don't need a fucking cartel war on our street. We did kill two of the Mongrels' lower-ranking members and wounded their enforcer.

What I really want to do is find that fucking vice president of theirs in a dark alley and run a blade across his throat real slow as I watch the life leave his eyes. Viper is a fucking piece of work and enjoys inflicting pain, especially on those who can't defend themselves. I might be a fucked-up motherfucker but I don't hurt women and children. *Never.* That's where I draw the line.

Viper also likes to brag that he'll take any bitch he wants with or without her consent, and that shit grates on every last nerve I have. I'm so exhausted by those pussies constantly fucking around in our business that I'm going to call for full-out war the next time we go to church.

Getting up from my chair without caring about the skinny bitch on my lap, I watch as she falls to the floor in a heap. She has long, bottle-blonde hair that looks like it's lost a fight with a lawnmower. Her dark roots are grown out two inches and it only makes her look cheaper than we all know she is. Her tits are fake and huge and look ridiculous on her skinny ass.

As she sits on the floor, she makes no attempt to close her legs, and with her micro mini pushed up around her waist, there's no mistaking her pussy on display for all to see. The only thought running through my head is I'd lose my mind if my daughter ever disrespected herself that way.

She huffs from her spot on the ground and stares daggers at me. "What the fuck, Wolf? I thought we were gonna have a good time," she whines in her high-pitched, nasally voice.

Rolling my eyes, they go so far back in my head I worry they might get stuck. "Jessie, we've been over this before. There is no way on God's green earth that I am ever sticking my dick in your disease-ridden pussy. Damn, woman, I couldn't even get it up if I tried."

Starting to walk away, I hear her huff behind me. I know she's going to say or do something incredibly stupid, so I wait.

"Fuck you, Wolf. You can't get it up for anyone. Since that skinny bitch figured out she could do better than you and up and left, you've been a limp-dick pussy."

As the last words leave her lips, I circle her scrawny neck with one of my hands, lifting her from the floor and walk her back against the nearest wall. I hold her against the wall with her feet dangling in the air and see the unadulterated fear in her eyes. I lean in and I can almost smell the terror running off her in waves.

I softly whisper in her ear, "Amber didn't leave me, you dumb cunt. She's dead, and if you mouth off to me again, you will be too."

Pulling away, I smile at her, knowing I look like a damn shark because I'm using too much teeth. Slowly, I lower her to the ground. The moment I let go, she scrambles off like a small animal afraid of a carnivore in the woods. Letting loose a loud laugh, I have most of the heads in the club turning my way. I see curiosity in some but from most just amusement. This simply makes me smile even bigger as I give them the finger.

Fuck them. My brothers know me well enough to know I would never hurt a woman. Even though only a select few know me well enough to know what happened to Amber.

She was my high school sweetheart. We met at sixteen and I never have and never will love a woman the way I loved her. At twenty-four, I got Amber knocked up and even though I was terrified, I couldn't have been happier. Bought a house and started getting all our shit straight.

At twenty-nine weeks, Amber went into premature labor and due to massive hemorrhaging, she died on the table. Our daughter was born but only survived a couple of hours before she too passed. I got to hold her for a while and though it almost killed me, I never regretted that experience. I've had real love and I've lost it, and that's fine by me.

I'm a hard and difficult motherfucker. At one point in my life, I've lost everything that meant anything to me. Having loved and lost has made me harder than ever. Now I drink and work and spend time with my club. They are the only things I care about, all I have left. I'll do anything for my brothers and for my club.

Reaching down next to the chair I was sitting in, I grab my bottle of bourbon and head in the direction of where I last saw Doc and Sparrow. I enter the room and see Doc has Sparrow all wrapped up. They're smiling while chatting with each other. This only serves to piss me off. I feel like shit for letting my friend, no, my brother, get hurt because I'm incapable of securing his safety, and the two of them are simply shooting the shit.

"What's the damage, Doc?"

"No damage, Wolf, simply a graze to his calf. Two stitches and he's all fixed up. Didn't even have to numb the area."

Doc smiles at me but my face remains expressionless. I don't care if it wasn't serious. It could have been.

"Wolf." Sparrow stands from his spot at the table he was seated at. He's a tall man of Hispanic descent, with wavy, dark hair and dark-brown eyes. He still speaks with a Spanish accent and when riled up, you can't get a word of English out of the man.

"This isn't your fault, and I'm perfectly fine. You

can't take this all on yourself, brother. Shit happens, you know?"

Usually, Sparrow is one of the only brothers who can calm my ass down, but not tonight. Tonight, I'm riled up and looking for a fight. "No, Sparrow, shit doesn't happen. People let shit happen to them."

With that, I stalk out of the room they were using to patch him up, across the main area of the club, and out the door to my bike. I ignore Sparrow trying to stop me. After jumping on my bike, I gun the engine as I make my way out of the compound and head home.

Chapter Three
Hadley

Lying on the carpet in my living room with a bottle of tequila between us, Storm and I brainstorm ideas on how I can earn a living and survive. As I look around my apartment, I wonder if I should just pack it all up and head back to Louisiana. My people are there, James, Devon, and little Casey. I have a home with people who love me and a great job waiting for me. While I stare at a framed picture of the four of us, my heart aches to see them again.

When I left, I told Devon all about my dream—to own and operate my own tattoo parlor—and she gave me her full support even though she never could understand why I had to leave to accomplish that dream. This's exactly why I left. If I had stayed at home with them, I would always have a safety net. There would always be somewhere safe for me to run, and although I love them and will always be grateful to them, it's time to stand on my own two feet.

It's been four long years since I left home. Four years of struggling to make ends meet and working shitty jobs, and although I would love nothing more than to run home, I won't.

Knowing I don't have a huge skill set and I barely finished high school, I can't afford to be picky about a job. The drunker we get, the clearer my only two options are and neither are very appealing to me.

Option one: Storm can get me a job where she works. Storm strips at a place called From Dusk 'til Dawn but we just call it Dusk. She's really fucking good at her job and earns a mint, especially doing bachelor parties and such. But me? I'm not comfortable enough with who I am and what I look like to actually get my ass naked on stage.

So that leaves me with option two. Waitressing. Again. The problem with waitressing at Dusk is the same as it was at my previous job. I fucking hate being groped by any man, but especially by the drunk and stupid kind. And bikers. Dusk is one of those places that gets frequented by bikers, especially since Dusk is under club protection from one of the local clubs. Again, bikers terrify me. Knowing they're there, even if it is to offer protection, scares the ever-loving shit out of me.

Storm continues trying to coerce me into working with her at Dusk. "But we have bouncers at the club. Hell, I basically never get groped and I walk around naked most of the time. It'll be fine. Maurice doesn't really care what you wear long as you have on your staff t-shirt and a smile. He looks out for all of his girls and he really is a nice guy. I've worked at a lot of worse places so I should know."

My expression is vacant as I stare at her.

She simply continues. "Yes, I know how you feel about bikers. But I promise you on my life and our friendship that you have nothing to worry about. The guys are great and if you would just get to know them, you would see it too."

Leaning back against the couch, I take a nice big swig of the tequila—straight from the bottle—and listen to the music filtering through my stereo. I think about it and the song rings true in more ways than one. Life has made a monster of me and this is what I have left. Looking toward Storm, I nod my head.

She jumps off the floor and grabs me, wrapping me up in a hug while jumping and squealing at the same time. After grabbing the bottle of tequila from my hand, she gulps down a huge mouthful before handing it back to me.

"You have made me so extremely happy. I can't believe we're gonna work together. This is gonna be so much fun. Now if I can get you to let me put some streaks of blue through your hair, my year would be made."

Glaring at her, I say nothing. For a minute, silence reigns and then we both burst out laughing.

****

With a hangover that cannot be beaten, we go into Dusk at three the following day. Training takes about half an hour. There isn't much to learn and there isn't a menu to memorize. Just as I am about to leave, Maurice walks up to me, tilts his head to the left, and smiles.

"Girl, are you sure you ain't in the market to be a dancer? Just askin' 'cuz you got an ass that a man could bounce a coin off."

Maurice's Cajun accent flows over me. For a large black man, he has a real soothing voice. He's an intimidating figure when you first meet him. Broad shoulders and a barrel chest with a clean-shaven head. He looks like he could snap me in two with a flick of his wrist but, within five minutes of meeting him, I realized he's a big old softy. Especially with his wife Celine.

I laugh and blush slightly at the weird compliment. "No thanks, Maurice. I'm fine keeping my clothes on."

"Well, if you ever change your mind, be sure to let me know. I'll give you a nice prime spot and you'll be raking in the cash, girl. I can promise you that."

Smiling at his back as he walks away, I'm grateful I agreed to this gig. This is a job I could definitely enjoy.

Time passes quickly and soon Dusk will be

opening for the evening. My first shift starts tomorrow as I still need some training on the cash register. After saying goodbye to Storm and Maurice, I head out for the evening.

Not having a car sucks and is definitely a priority, but at least I don't live too far from Dusk, so the walk isn't that bad. The only problem is I constantly feel like I'm being watched. Numerous times I look around, but there's never anyone there. Deciding to write it off as paranoia, I keep moving. Half an hour later, I crawl into bed, and not having to worry about anything, I drift off into a fitful sleep.

****

My time is filled with shifts and friends. I've been working at Dusk for almost a week now and have met most of the girls at the club. I'm really surprised by how well we get along. The only person I don't get along with is Cherry. It would seem that in her mind, she's the main attraction and expects everyone to fall in line with her wishes. She's an utter bitch toward me at every opportunity. Obviously, there will always be one or two people who want to rock the boat and make life difficult, but having decided that I love my new job, I choose to completely ignore her.

The tips are rolling in and I haven't had this much money since well, ever. My spirits are high and I even allowed Storm to put blue streaks into my hair this morning. Even though I doubted how it would look, I really am satisfied with the outcome. My hair looks great and everyone keeps paying me compliments. Standing at the service bar, I hear a loud squeal from one of the girls.

Turning, I see a large group of bikers walk through the front door and take a seat in one of the other girl's booths. Looking around, I search for Storm. I spot her and watch as she smiles at a large, redheaded biker before he leans down to kiss her cheek. Even from this distance, I swear I can hear her swoon.

Squinting my eyes, I'm able to recognize the Gypsy Bastards patch on his back, and though I fail to recognize the man wearing it, the familiar patch has me relaxing.

Over the past week, I've met some of the members of the Gypsy Bastards MC and true to Storm's word, they are great guys. Most of them have tried to hit on me but none have made me feel uncomfortable. The moment I tell them I'm not interested, they back off and leave me be, automatically starting to treat me like a sister. They are genuinely great guys.

Heading back to the bar, I wait on my order. After grabbing the drinks, I make to turn around when a large body presses mine up against the bar. Right away, panic threatens to overwhelm me but the voice in my ear instantly calms me.

"Gonna give me one of your special hugs tonight, sugar?"

"Damn it, Viking." I turn in his arms and push against his chest. "I could have dropped that whole order. Can't you announce yourself or something? You are way too quiet for a guy your size."

Throwing his head back, he pulls my face to his chest as a belly laugh pours from him. He hugs me to him tightly like I imagine my father would if he were still alive and I wrap my arms around his middle.

"I love scaring you, doll, that's why I do it."

"You're an ass."

The affection in my tone is unmistakable. How did I get caught up with bikers again? How can I care for someone like Viking as much as I do? I know what bikers are like and what they do for a living. As the thoughts circle in my brain, I can clearly remember how I ended up in this situation.

The day I met Viking, I almost died. Not literally, but I was scared out of my mind. He simply walked up to me and slung his arm around my shoulder.

"Hey, pretty girl. Why don't you relax a little and smile at an old man?"

The smile I pasted on must have been horrible because it made him laugh until tears poured down his face.

"Girlie, my name is Viking." Pausing for a breath, he smiled down at me. "You need to relax. Not one person in here is going to give you any shit and if they do, you call me."

Staring up at him with wide eyes, the only thought running through my mind was that I didn't do bikers. I didn't talk to bikers, I didn't hang out with bikers, and I definitely didn't trust bikers.

"I don't sleep around." The words popped from my mouth before I had the chance to stop them. Viking looked at me with an intensity I didn't understand.

"The last thing I want from you is sex. You remind me of my daughter. Let's you and me make a deal."

He paused for a moment, as though expecting an answer. Not knowing what he wanted from me, I nodded.

"When you see me, get me a drink and make some small talk. Smile a genuine smile for me, and I'll always have your back."

Staring up at him, I realized what he was doing. He could see how uncomfortable I was in my own skin and he was simply trying to be my friend. A genuine smile spread across my face.

Turning to collect the drink order now, I hear Viking chuckle again. The memory fills my heart to overflowing.

"You have a good shift, sugar." Giving me a slap on the ass that causes me to yelp, he strides away with a grin on his face. He has never made a move or tried to get me into bed, and I appreciate that more than he knows.

The club gets busy and the music pumps through the speakers. Time flies and by the time I realize it, Storm gets called to the stage. I don't have time to watch her show, but I do catch a glimpse of the biker she hugged earlier, and he looks like he might get on stage and carry her off.

Of all the men sitting at his table, I only know Viking and Sparrow. Sparrow spends a lot of time at Dusk helping Maurice with the books, but tonight is the first time I have actually seen him socializing. He is an extremely attractive man of Hispanic heritage. But he's also married with a kid, Gabe, so for the most part, the girls avoid him.

Turning away, I make my way back to the bar to collect another round of drinks and when I look up, I meet the stormy eyes of a giant man. Tall, at least six-two, if not taller, lean but not skinny, with blond hair that hangs down to brush his shoulders and eyes a gray that you only see on storm clouds. Basically, he's beautiful with a roughness to him that makes me tingle all over, and not in a bad way.

He's got black shitkickers with blue jeans encasing his muscular thighs, and a plain black t-shirt that molds to every muscle in his torso. He wears a cut and on his left breast is the enforcer tag, showing him to be one of the members of his club that would be the most prone to violence. His hands are calloused and a shiver runs up my spine as I imagine him using them on me. A strong jaw and a nose that has clearly been broken before add to his rugged handsomeness.

While staring at this insanely hot specimen of male perfection, I watch him look me over, twice, and then a frown appears on his face. He shakes his head as if to clear it and then looks at a Sparrow next to him, says something I can't quite make out, and strides out of the club. Assuming he didn't find the view as appealing as I did, I smile at the Sparrow and continue to work.

Three hours later, Dusk closes for the night. My feet ache but my smile never fades. Everyone is still cashing out but since I'm done, I decide to go outside for a smoke.

I stand against the wall a little way from the door and light the smoke, inhaling deeply. I don't usually smoke but always have a pack of menthols with me for when the craving hits. Kicking off my heels, I stand with my bare feet on the pavement, savoring the feel. Standing there in the pre-morning silence, I'm simply happy to be alive. I love my new job, my rent is paid in full, and tomorrow I can go get my daddy's 1967 Pontiac GTO from the mechanic.

The transmission conked out a while back and I never could afford to get it fixed. But that's all in the past and I will have my baby back. Walking everywhere I want to be will finally be a thing of the past.

The door to Dusk opens before Storm and the redheaded biker walk out, followed shortly by what seems to be at least ten other Gypsy Bastards members. Laughter fills the air as Storm talks a mile a minute, and for a moment, I simply watch them interact. Storm has a wide smile spread across her face, as do some of the guys. Jealousy envelops me and again I wish I were more like her. To be able to overcome my fears and interact normally with those around me would be a dream come true.

"Pretty girl!"

The sound of Viking's booming voice can be heard clear across the parking lot.

"Join us for the after-party?"

Already he has his arm slung—once again—around my shoulder as he leads me to where the motorcycles are parked.

"I can't party with you, old man." Slipping from beneath his arm, I can't help but smirk at him.

In an exaggerated gesture, he clutches at his chest. "You wound me, woman. My fragile ego can barely handle you not wanting to drink with me. But calling me old? That's just mean."

Laughter surrounds us as the guys watch our interaction.

"Aww, don't worry." Playfully, I pet his cheek. "Although you are old, you're still handsome. And me? Not drinking with you is a matter of survival. I most definitely cannot drink the way you are all about to."

The snort from behind Viking's back has me glaring around him at Storm. With a raised eyebrow, she defends herself.

"I can drink more than most men that show up at Dusk and you have drunk me under the table every single time."

"See?" Viking's voice is filled with victory. "Come on, pretty girl. Tomorrow is Sunday. No work. Ride with me?"

Shaking my head and laughing, I hook my arm through his as we make our way over to his motorcycle. After strapping on a helmet, I mount his bike and hold on tight. Tonight, I take back being me. Tonight, I start living my life by putting my fear behind me, and the first step to doing that is going to the clubhouse.

Chapter Four
Wolf

After walking through the kitchen, I take a seat on my back porch, just watching the sun set and enjoying a beer, I think back on how the day went exactly as I had it planned. I had enough time to finish the custom paint job on a 1977 Confederate Edition Harley Davidson for a customer at the shop and I can honestly say I'm looking forward to showing the end product to him tomorrow.

Sparrow's old lady, Luna, stopped by the shop for lunch with their four-year-old son Gage and some kick-ass pulled pork sandwiches for Sparrow and me. Gage is a carbon cut out of his daddy and follows him everywhere, trying to do everything he does. Some days I sit and watch Gage and I wonder if my little Rose would have looked more like Amber or myself.

Those are the hard days, days where I have to convince myself that life is worth living and remind myself to put one foot in front of the other. My club helps me through those days even though most don't even know it. I carry an immense gratefulness that I'll never be able to fully verbalize.

Deep in thought about bikes and kids and life in general, it takes a moment for me to realize my cell is ringing in the house. After lifting myself out of the deck chair, I make my way inside.

"What's up?" I answer without hesitation, seeing on the caller ID that the President of my club is calling.

"Wolf, how about a beer, brother?" Pope replies in that smooth Irish accent that seems to make the ladies lose their underwear and their inhibitions.

Laughing, I answer his question with another question. "Dusk?"

"Yeah, brother, where else would we be headed then?"

"Complete crew?"

"Absolutely, everyone could use one after this fucker of a couple of weeks," he replies solemnly.

"Great, I'll meet you all there in about an hour?"

"Good on you brother."

And that ends the call. Pope enjoys going to Dusk occasionally, but that would be purely to see Storm, although he denies it every chance he gets. Old man needs to own up to that shit and lock that woman down. Anyone with eyes can see how bad they got it for each other, and whether it's just chemistry or something more, no one knows. What I do know is that he always says he'll never lay a finger on her. Something about having his chance and blowing it. Whatever the fuck that means.

Heading into the house, I return the steak to the fridge. It will keep until tomorrow and tonight is for drinking. After making my way up the stairs of my three-bedroom house, I head directly to the shower. Standing under the spray, I lather up my hair, and after rinsing, I let the water cascade down my back and bring forth the memory I want.

The memory of my past life and love get me to where I want to be in mere moments. My cock is rock hard as I take it in hand. With a firm grip, I move from root to tip and back down again, using a rhythm I've grown accustomed to. A ripple runs across my abs as they contract from the pleasure. My thighs tense as I hold back for as long as I can. Squeezing harder and moving my hand faster, the pleasure soon overwhelms me. Sooner than I like, I feel the familiar tingling sensation move down the column of my spine and into my tightly drawn-up balls before exploding.

Watching my cum slip down the drain from yet

another self-help job, I wish I could get laid. God knows I've tried, again and again, but I just can't seem to make my dick work for anyone other than her. My cock won't get hard for any other woman except Amber and quite frankly, after five years, I'm starting to get pissed off. I really want to stop jerking off by myself, in the shower, to the same goddamned memory over and over.

Once I get out of the shower, I dry off, get dressed, and head over to Dusk. The drive over clears my head. Being on a motorcycle always does that for me. The open road and the fresh air always do wonders to improve my shitty mood. Parking in front of Dusk in the spot I always use, I can see the guys are already there and seem to be waiting on me. Moving closer to my brothers, we enter the club together.

The room is smoky and there's a smell I can't describe. It's neither sex nor desperation but rather a mixture of the two. Large black leather booths take up both sides of the room with a large stage in the center. In the back is a full-length mahogany bar tended by two men. There are some waitresses in heels and various stages of undress moving between the tables, and four bouncers mill around.

Someone on the far side of the bar makes a squealing sound and already I'm irritated at being here. The women all want a piece of one of us and no matter how many times Sparrow and I decline, there's always one dumb cunt who thinks she has the golden pussy that will get us to cave tonight. We have many single members in our club and even some married members that don't mind having a piece on the side. I just want to be left alone and I can't seem to get the message across to them.

I watch as Storm saunters from the front of the club to meet us, and she greets Pope with their customary cheek kiss. It bothers me more than it should, but I can see the looks they give each other and although I've lost my happiness and am destined to never find another, I want my brothers to find theirs.

We move over to a corner booth so everyone can sit and have their backs covered and I can watch the door. Force of habit, I guess, but we always get a corner booth facing the door no matter where we are. We order a round of beers and watch the girls dance and just shoot the shit. No club business, no politics, just guys being guys.

Shortly after arriving, Cherry sidles up to our table in a wave of perfume strong enough to burn my nostrils and make my eyes tear up. She leans in against my arm and presses her firm, plastic breasts against me. Glaring up at her, I wait for her to back up and give me some goddamned space.

"Hi Wolf," she says in what I think is supposed to be a seductive purr.

I don't reply, just nod and look over her shoulder, watching Viking talk to a girl I've never seen at Dusk before. Not that I find it surprising since I haven't been here in more than a month and Maurice always keeps the new talent flowing. As Viking makes his way to us, a flash of blue catches my eye. I try to follow it through the room but lose sight. Apparently, I've also lost all ability to follow a conversation as Cherry was yapping away. When I don't answer her, she huffs and stomps away.

The guys are all laughing, and I join in. I continue scanning the room for the flash of blue from earlier. As soon as I am able to fix my sights on it, I track the woman with my eyes. The blue streaks in her hair are what caught my attention. Trying to brush off my fascination with this woman, I return to my beer and the conversation between my brothers. The problem is my damn attention keeps going back to her. Knowing that Viking has a claim on her—I mean, anyone with eyes could see how she smiled at him earlier—I try to look away. Clearly, there's something going on between them. Curiosity wins out and I stare at her, not caring who sees me.

The woman attached to the streak of blue is beautiful. She's about five-two in the heels she's currently rocking, with black skinny jeans hugging a well-rounded ass. Her hair looks to be blonde but not the kind that comes out of a bottle and even from where I'm sitting, I can see she has nice perky breasts. Not too large but not so small.

After downing my beer, I make my way to the bar as I track her doing the same. I hear one of the guys behind me say something but I don't care and don't turn around for clarification. There's an overwhelming, irrational need burning in me to see her up close. Feeling someone follow me, I glance over my shoulder to see Sparrow with a frown on his face. Ignoring him, I continue on my way to the bar.

She has one foot lifted to the footrest beneath the bar and it makes those jeans even fucking tighter. Moving closer, I stand beside her but at least a foot away. As I order another beer from the bartender, I turn to examine her and find her eyes already on me. Starting my way from the bottom, I allow my gaze to leisurely caress its way up her form. From her painted toenails, to her flat stomach and full lips, I take my time enjoying the view. During my perusal of her, her body has turned fully toward me. Clearly, she wants me to be able to see her completely.

The second time I scan her body, I take in all the parts I missed the first time. Her peep-toe heels are blood red and I swear her ass is so plump and juicy all I can think of is taking a bite out of it. She has a toned, flat stomach and a name or a word is tattooed on her right wrist. The urge to grab her wrist and inspect the tattoo almost overwhelms me.

My gaze moves up further and I don't know how I missed it the first time, but this girl isn't wearing a bra. No bra in a titty bar and her goddamned nipples are hard as rocks. I'm half-surprised they don't poke a hole through the damn fitted t-shirt Maurice got her to wear.

Instantly, I have this insane, jealous urge to pick her up and carry her away. Lock her in my room at the clubhouse so no other man can see that firm ass or those pebbled nipples. With that thought comes a startling realization.

I'm hard.

For the first time in five years, I have a hard-on for something other than a fucking memory, and I feel like a bastard. How can I just push Amber aside for this woman I have never met? Jesus, I truly am a fuckup. Shaking my head to clear away the worst of the lust, I turn to Sparrow.

"Gotta get out of here, brother. These bitches are grating on my nerves."

He glances over my shoulder at something and smiles. He nods to me and moves back to the table where the guys are seated. Walking across the club floor, I weave between tables and half-naked women until I reach the door and leave. I don't look back. There's no purpose to turning and seeing. I can't have her, and that's final.

****

Four hours later, I'm lying alone in bed, awake, staring at the ceiling. Sleep is impossible. Every time I close my eyes, all I can see are red stilettos and blue-streaked hair. Feeling like a bastard, I decide to take matters into my own hands.

After slipping my boxers down my hips and over an already semi-painful erection, I wrap my hand around the length. Pre-cum beads at the tip with the memory of the woman from Dusk. Closing my eyes, I conjure her in my mind but not as I saw her in the club.

She's spread on my bed, wearing nothing but the red stilettos. Her milky skin on display for me. Her nipples are dusky pink and hard under my view. Opening her legs, I can see her perfect cunt, dripping wet for me.

The hand on my cock starts moving fast, my breathing getting rough simply from the thought of her.

Her hand moves over her breast, tweaking a nipple before caressing down her stomach to land between her thighs. A single finger moves between her wet folds as hooded eyes stare back at me. A moan escapes from her as she pushed that finger inside her cunt...

Cum splatters on my abs as I explode. Nothing more than the mere idea of this woman has me coming like a fucking fourteen-year-old boy. I know nothing of her, not her name or what her voice sounds like, but she still has the capacity to drive me fucking crazy. After moving from my bed to the bathroom, I clean myself up and return to my bed for another round of self-loathing.

The problem is I wanted to move on from Amber, wanted to be able to get my dick wet—and not in the shower—and now, now I feel like a punk for doing just that. Not to mention that I have a brother with a prior claim on her. Viking just might rip me apart if he knew I was thinking about his new piece of ass.

A ping from my cell phone alerts me to a text message. Instead of leaving it for tomorrow like I usually would, I grab it and open the message.

The picture Sparrow sent me has me out of bed

and moving to get dressed. Knowing this is a colossal mistake and nothing good can come from it, I hop on my bike and head over to the clubhouse.

At my clubhouse, in my favorite chair, sits a woman wearing red stilettos with blue streaks in her hair, drinking my favorite fucking bourbon.

Chapter Five
Hadley

Walking into the Gypsy Bastard clubhouse is a terrifying experience for me. Having grown up and spent most of my time around the Iron Disciples has definitely shaped some preconceived notions in my mind.

Expecting a dirty, dingy place has my jaw falling slack when I walk in. The Gypsy Bastards clubhouse is extraordinary by biker standards. From the outside, it looks like an old warehouse, the only sign of inhabitants the bikes standing outside. There are large, double sliding doors with red paint that is peeling in places and a bare concrete slab out front that the guys use for parking. A door to the side of the building painted in the same faded and peeling red is where we enter.

The warehouse has a large open floor plan with what I'm assuming was previously used as a board room and a downstairs office. They have a humungous bar built against one wall with a door behind it that I assume leads to either a kitchen or some type of storage. The bar is made of wood that has been stained to a dark, rich color with a couple of leather stools placed in front of it.

The lighting is bright but not so much that it breaks the atmosphere or hurts my eyes upon entry. Rock music plays loudly in the background.

Against the wall on the opposite side of the bar are a ton of framed photos. My feet carry me forward until I can make out some of the people in them. Kids, women, group photos, prospects, and what seem to be family gatherings, are all over the wall. This is definitely not what I was expecting.

"Got you a beer, pretty girl."

Viking interrupts my ogling. Turning to take the

beer from him, I can see a thirty-something, bleached-blonde behind the bar staring daggers at me.

"First time in a clubhouse?" Viking queries.

"No." The temptation to lie almost overtakes me but I'm putting down roots and decide to lie as little as possible from this moment forth. "This is probably just the nicest and cleanest."

A belly laugh escapes Viking as he grabs my hand and pulls me toward the bar. "Got to introduce you to everyone."

From that moment, my night turns into a whirlwind of names and faces, accompanied by many shots. Viking pulls me from one person to the next, introducing me like a proud father showing everyone his new baby, and I find it endearing.

Meeting Pope is interesting. He speaks to me and asks all the questions one would expect of a club president but his eyes never stray from Storm for longer than a moment. His Irish accent flows over me and calms the last of my nerves.

Mad Dog is up next and although he is punching shots of tequila like there's no tomorrow, you can instantly see the military in him. Buzz-cut hair, bright brown eyes, and an impeccable posture. For a while, we get lost in conversation regarding his tattoos. Some he tells me the meaning about and some he simply smiles about.

"So you're the tattoo artist Storm has been hiding? Been trying to get your number but she wasn't giving it up."

"Do you need work done?" Already my mind is running a mile a minute with ideas. Adding on to his existing ink is going to be a dream job.

"We all do. Let me know when you're available and we can get together."

With a promise to call him and his number saved in my phone, I'm pulled away by Viking again.

He proceeds to show me around the entire clubhouse. From the bedrooms to the bathrooms and even the garage they use for any repairs a member might need, all the while introducing me to members, prospects, and even a couple of the club girls. By the time we make it back to the bar, I just want to rest my aching feet. There's a pretty decent amount of alcohol swimming through my veins but that doesn't stop me from drinking.

Lastly, Viking introduces me to the blonde behind the bar, saying her name is Jessie.

"What will you be having?" she questions in an unfriendly tone.

"Bourbon," I sass back at her. "But just give me the bottle and save us both the hassle."

The alcohol makes it easier to speak my mind, to do what I want. Jessie is being a fucking bitch and after all the hassle I get from Cherry at work, I've reached my limit. No more being friendly in the face of people who are blatantly rude to me. Viking laughs loudly at our exchange and leans over to whisper in my ear. "She's club ass. Probably just worried you're here to fill her position."

Scrunching my nose at him, I take the bottle from the bar where Jessie sat it down—a little too hard if I might add—and move away. Falling down into a green recliner, I lift the bottle to my lips and take a swig while watching some of the guys play pool.

"*Chica*," Sparrow calls to me as he leisurely strolls over toward me. "You're sitting in my brother's chair and he's very territorial about that ugly chair."

"*Gorriõn*, I don't see anyone sitting here." Calling him *sparrow* in Spanish catches him off guard if the size of his eyes is anything to go by.

"She speaks Spanish."

"Only enough to get myself in trouble. Either way, the rule stands, move your feet and you lose your seat."

Sparrow laughs, snapping a picture of me with his cell phone before making his way over to the pool table.

****

The guys come and go. Some just talking shit, some drinking with me, and at least a couple try to charm their way into my pants. But it's all in good fun. Very aware of the fact that I'm more than a little tipsy, I make my way through the bar, searching for Storm. A familiar song starts to play through the speakers, and Storm moves toward me. She smiles at me and before anyone is aware of what's going on or can attempt to stop us, we're up on the bar dancing. I'm sure for some it would seem like a childish thing to do, but it's always been our thing. Being in the middle of an MC clubhouse simply makes it more acceptable than doing it at a local bar.

Dancing and laughing and shaking our asses on top of the bar to the guys' hoots and hollers has me smiling so hard my face starts to hurt. As the song comes to an end and we're about to climb off the bar, I slip on a wet spot and go crashing toward the floor.

Chapter Six
Wolf

As soon as I shut down my ride and the rumbling from the pipes ceases, I can clearly hear the guys hooting and hollering inside the clubhouse. Making my way around to the side door, I decide that Storm and her friend—whom I now refer to as Blue—must have already taken off. There's no way in hell that Pope would allow the guys a strip show, assuming that's what the ruckus is about, if Storm was still in the clubhouse.

As I walk into the clubhouse, all the air is ripped from my lungs. Again, irrational anger courses through my veins like fire, but this time it's followed by a severe case of jealousy. Up on the bar, in the middle of my clubhouse, are Storm and Blue dancing. At their feet, smiling like the bunch of idiots they are, are all my brothers, which explains all the noise they have been making. Both girls are clearly enjoying themselves and the smile spread across Blue's face is enough to cause my chest to ache. That smile only makes her more beautiful.

For a moment, I simply watch them enjoy themselves before making my way closer to where all the other guys are standing. Watching Blue dance has my semi-hard cock throbbing to life behind the zipper of my jeans. Her hips shift from side to side before doing a roll I have only seen women do in music videos. Her braless breasts jiggle and softly sway as she moves to the rhythm of the music. Looking at the men around me, I can see their thoughts clearly plastered on their faces, and although I want to gouge their eyes out, I have no claim on the woman who's driving me crazy.

Turning back to her, I continue to watch her as

she mesmerizes and entices me with her body. From the corner of my eye, I see Jessie with a glass of what I am assuming is water, which she proceeds to pour on the bar top near the girls' feet. Before a word of warning can leave my mouth, Blue steps back, her stiletto slips, and she goes tumbling to the ground. Fortunately, I am standing against the bar and catch her easily, cradling her to my chest.

Her eyes pop open and she stares at me for a minute. Her gaze is like a caress running over my face, but when she looks into my eyes, I feel bared to her. Like she's looking directly into my soul, seeing every sin and fear that I usually hide from the outside world. Feeling completely exposed, I blink slowly as I lower her to her feet, keeping her steady with my hold on her hips. Her body is plastered against mine and I feel her hard nipples through both our shirts.

Her hand drifts to my cheek and I close my eyes at the contact.

"Gracias, chico bonito."

Shock fills me as she moves past me, not having expected her to speak Spanish. From behind me, Sparrow laughs loudly. Turning toward him, I raise a brow as I wait for clarification.

Sparrow struggles to get the words out through the laughter. "She called you a pretty boy."

My jaw almost hits the floor as I watch her saunter away. This woman is under my skin and she thinks I'm a fucking boy? Striding toward her, I watch her stumble over her own feet before she veers off to the left. She's clearly drunk off her ass. A protectiveness I feel for very few people in my life overtakes the need to throttle her pretty little neck.

Scooping her up in my arms, once again cradling her body to my chest, I make my way up the stairs. Hazel eyes stare up at me.

"Where are you taking me?" Her words are slightly slurred.

"To bed. You are clearly drunk."

"Well, aren't you presumptuous?" She struggles in my arms before I let her down in front of my room at the club.

Once again, my hands drift to her hips and although I continue to tell myself it's only to help her stay upright, I know it is a lie. My hands mold to her figure and even through her clothes I can feel the heat of her skin. I wonder if I run my hands to cup her ass or breasts if they would fit my hands just as perfectly. She intoxicates me like no alcohol or drug ever has and I have to keep my wits or I'll be completely lost in her.

"Presumptuous?" I question while holding her in place.

Her gaze travels the length of my body at a luxurious pace and again it feels like a touch.

"Assuming I would sleep with you because I'm drunk and you saved me."

Although I have imagined fucking her in the past few hours since I first saw her, I would never take advantage of a woman, drunk or not. I prefer a woman to be awake and aware when I fuck her. Thrusting her against the closed door, I press my body flush with hers. She takes a sharp breath and before my eyes, I can see the truth. Her pupils are dilated and her breathing is shallow. Slowly, I bump my erection against her belly, pulling a moan from her.

Stifling a groan, I lean down and whisper in her ear. "I promise you, Blue, the last thing I want to do tonight is fuck your drunk ass."

Pushing away, I turn and leave. It may be one of the hardest things I've ever had to do. If I don't walk away from her now, I will fuck her against the door, not caring whether she is drunk or claimed by Viking or if anyone could see us. For the second time in mere hours, I don't look back as I leave. When I get downstairs, I move straight toward Beast.

"Hey, brother, is Justice still looking to become a prospect?"

"Yeah, only thing that kid wants. Turned eighteen last week so I was going to bring it up at the next church meeting."

"Don't even worry. He's been hanging around here the last couple of years. Call his ass and tell him to be here at eight tomorrow morning. He's gonna be in charge of the bar and I will make sure to get him a prospect cut."

Beast nods but doesn't ask any questions. He knows me well enough that once I've made up my mind, there's very little that can change it.

Moving behind the bar, I nod at Pope. From below the bar, I remove the handbag that Jessie's always carrying with her and toss it on the counter in front of her. Her head snaps in my direction.

"Get out." The command in my voice is clear and can be heard above the music currently playing.

"Wolf?" Jessie has a look of confusion on her face that only serves to piss me off all the more.

"Get out, Jessie, and don't come back. You are no longer welcome at the Gypsy Bastards clubhouse or any of our other businesses."

Her eyes are large and I can see she wants to open up the waterworks.

"Is this about that blonde bitch?"

"If I hadn't caught her, she could have been seriously hurt. You did that shit on purpose. You would have caused more problems than your ass has ever been worth. Get your shit and get out."

In the blink of an eye, she's on me and trying to claw my eyes out. Beast pulls her off me and throws her over his shoulder before carrying her out the side door. All the way, she screams and curses about getting revenge and not being treated like a piece of trash. When Beast returns, he closes and locks the door. For a few moments, we can still hear Jessie screaming outside and pounding on the door before Mad Dog turns the volume up on the music.

Pope looks toward me before he lifts his drink in my direction. "Good riddance to bad rubbish." And everyone bursts out laughing.

Scanning my surroundings, I look for Viking. The conversation we have to have might not be something to look forward to but I'm loyal to my brothers. Having these thoughts and feelings about a brother's woman, even if she is just a casual piece of ass, isn't something I enjoy.

As I make my way to where he's standing, I steady myself for what could be an oncoming battle. What I don't expect are the words he tosses my way before heading upstairs.

"I have no claim on that girl and from what I know, she's unattached. But I love her and I will hurt you if you hurt her. Got it?"

Chapter Seven
Hadley

Waking slowly, I take a deep breath and gauge the severity of my hangover. All in all, I should survive as soon as I pee and brush my teeth. I lift my head and take in my surroundings. Beige walls, dark wood dresser, the double bed I am currently sitting on, and a bedside table with a lamp. In the corner is a lone chair made from iron with a wooden seat. The bedding on the bed is dark blue and the lampshade is black. The room is devoid of any personal items and there's no way of identifying whose room I'm in.

I make my way from the bed, head into the bathroom, and search for a spare toothbrush. When I find one, I say a little prayer of thanks it's still closed in its original wrapper. Deciding I need a shower, I rummage through the chest of drawers until I find a black t-shirt with the club logo on it. It will have to do until I can get home.

In the shower, I wrack my mind for details about the previous night. Talking, drinking, meeting new people, dancing, falling, and eyes the color of a storm. Mortification moves through me when I remember the conversation we had in the hallway. Alcohol has always had a way of removing the filter between my mind and my mouth.

Finishing up in the shower, I decide to find my mystery man and apologize for my behavior. Dressed in my jeans from last night, I put on the Gypsy Bastards t-shirt and tie it in a knot at my waist and secure my wet hair in a messy bun atop my head. With my heels in my hand, I make my way downstairs where I spot Sparrow sitting alone at the bar.

"Morning, *chica*." Sparrow smiles at me when he sees me approaching. "How's the hangover?"

"Not as bad as you would expect, but I would love a Bloody Mary."

The man behind the bar smiles at me and gets to work. From my vantage point, I can freely enjoy his good looks. Tall and athletic with dark skin and dreadlocks that hang way past his shoulders. Although I can tell he's still young, he exudes confidence and it only serves to make him more attractive.

"The shirt suits you," Sparrow comments from beside me.

A blush spreads across my cheeks, and I know I've been caught ogling the bartender. Dreadlock man places my drink in front of me and I take a sip before replying.

"I have no idea whose room that was but I owe them a toothbrush and will get the shirt back as soon as possible."

"No worries, girl. Wolf won't mind."

The snort that follows from behind the bar has me thinking Wolf would definitely mind. Before I can question who Wolf is—because I'm sure I didn't meet him last night—the side door opens and a woman with a little boy who is the exact copy of his daddy enters. The little boy breaks away from his mother before running toward me and flinging himself into my arms.

"Hadley!" he squeals loudly.

"Hey, Gage," I say, hugging him tightly. "How are you doing, *mi piqueno amigo*?"

"What does that mean?" Gage looks at me with his large brown eyes, waiting for my answer.

"It means *my little friend*."

Gage smiles like I just gifted him the moon before squirming to get down. Running toward his mother and father, I watch them. His mother is a tiny woman, maybe five feet tall with long, luscious, chocolate-brown hair, large, almond-shaped eyes, and clear, tan skin.

"We're fucked, Niko. I have to go into the hospital as three of the girls called in sick today. You're leaving on a run in an hour with the guys and the damn babysitter is drunk. What are we going to do with Gage?"

His wife is clearly stressed out and upset. Before I can reconsider, I open my mouth and words come pouring out. "I can watch him."

Both of their gazes land on me.

"I know you're not club ass because I would kill my husband for bringing my son near any of those whores. So who are you?"

"Um, my name is Hadley." I nervously wave at her before I realize what I'm doing. "I'm a waitress at Dusk and most definitely not a club whore. And for the record, I would help you kick Sparrow's ass if he brought Gage near those nasty bitches."

Laughter tinkles from her. "I'm Luna. His wife." She nods her head in Sparrow's direction. "And from this first meeting, I have a feeling we'll definitely become great friends."

"Can I stay with Hadley, Momma?"

"Well, that depends. What does your dad think?" Luna winks at me before turning to Sparrow.

"I don't mind, but Justice will be with you at all times." Sparrow looks me directly in the eye as he motions to the dreadlock man before continuing. "Agreed?"

"Agreed."

"Great. Please let Sparrow know if you need anything before he leaves." Luna is already making her way to the door. "Sparrow is a great judge of character and if he says it's okay then so do I. Get my number from him in case you need anything, although I doubt I would be able to answer. I'm so late. Love you both."

With two air-blown kisses, Luna is out the door and on her way. Gage runs toward the pool table and starts playing with the balls lying there.

"Thanks, *chica*. You're a complete lifesaver. "

"No worries." I smile at Sparrow. "I love kids and Gage is great. I think we'll have a great time today."

"Any plans?"

"Thought of maybe taking him to the aquarium. It's always a fun place and should keep us busy for most of the day."

"Sounds like a great idea. You're here with your truck, Justice?" Sparrow turns away from me to talk to Justice, who only nods at him.

"Great." Sparrow motions to the empty clubhouse. "There won't be anyone around today so you guys can leave whenever you're ready."

I look at Justice for confirmation again, he only nods.

"Gage, let's do this little buddy."

Gage runs over and jumps into my arms again. Sparrow shoves a bundle of cash into my hand, kisses his son goodbye, and we're off. After getting into Justice's truck, we make our way out just as some of the guys are arriving. Gage waves at them from his spot on the back seat as we head out for our day of adventure.

****

Wolf

After a restless night with little to no sleep, I haul my ass out of bed, shower, get dressed, and hop on my bike to make my way to the clubhouse. We have a run today. Nothing too complicated, just drive two hours away and do a gun drop for the cartel. New day, during daylight hours, and at a new location. We're hoping to avoid the same fuckup as last time.

Halfway to the clubhouse, I fall in behind some of the other guys as we make our way through town. The rumbling of motorcycles can be heard from far away. As we pass through a residential area, the kids outside smile and wave at us as we pass. The Gypsy Bastards are well-loved. We do all we can to keep unsavory characters out of town, keep the drugs away from the schools, and even do a charity run every now and then.

Reaching the clubhouse, I arrive just in time to witness Blue climbing into Justice's truck, wearing one of my shirts. Anger floods me. Where the hell is she going? And why is Justice the one taking her?

The plan was to find her once I got to the clubhouse and apologize for being such a rude asshole last night. But she has to be here for me to accomplish any of that. Sparrow comes walking out of the clubhouse to greet us all. While the guys get the shipment situated I pull him aside to find out what the fuck is going on. Instantly, he lifts his hands in surrender.

"*Mi hermano*, I have seen the way that you watch that girl, even after just one night. Since Amber died, you've been a shadow of the man I once knew, but I see it coming back. Anger, lust, and so many other emotions, and they all seem tied in her." He shakes his head at me. "Don't fuck this up, man. Your girl's watching Gage today and Justice is watching them both. That's what we have prospects for."

For several moments, I stare at him before walking away. He chuckles behind me and I almost turn around and beat the fuck out of him. But I don't, I keep moving to my bike. Time to get this show on the road.

The drive seems to take forever. The road feels never-ending and with it my thoughts have the chance to run wild. *Blue.* The woman who walked into my life and turned it upside down without even knowing it. Perhaps Sparrow is right. Maybe she can breathe life back into me. What I need to do now is figure out how to get her to forgive me for my shitty behavior last night and start spending some time with me.

The drop goes off without a hitch. The cartel is happy and in return that makes us very happy. Driving back to Gypsy Falls, I don't have anything but one thought on my mind. Finding my girl and have a conversation with her. At least to start with.

Making our way to the aquarium as we enter town, I lay my plan out in my mind. Everything I want to say is already mapped out in my mind. For the first time in five years, I'm looking forward to the future. I want to get to know this woman and perhaps she'll be able to fill this gaping hole in my heart and soul.

Chapter Eight
Hadley

Before we head to the aquarium, we stop at my apartment so I can get my sneakers. There's no way I would be able to keep up with a kid while wearing stilettos. Arriving at the aquarium, Gage turns into a mini tornado of excitement. We are constantly moving from spot to spot and looking at the same thing three and four times, but he's so happy. The day speeds by in a blur of dolphins, penguins, and other sea life. After a few hours, we find a table in the food court and sit down for lunch. The food court is outside, allowing us to spend some time in the afternoon sun and listen to the noises around us.

During lunch, we all talk to one another. Justice tells me about becoming a prospect for the club, about his brother who I now know is Beast, and his sister Grace. Gage tells me about his friend Liam whose father is Luger—another club member. He tells me about school and the puppy he recently got for his birthday.

My stories are less personal. Mostly, I talk about tattoos and my dad's car but we still manage to have more fun together than I've had in years. Sitting beside Justice with Gage across from us, I can easily see how some would assume we are a family. Laughing and joking, we're oblivious to anything happening around us.

Gage's little face lights up before he takes off running. Turning, I see him jump into his father's waiting arms before he starts talking animatedly about our day. Beside Sparrow is the man from last night, and he's glaring at Justice.

"Gotta go, Hadley. But I'll probably see you around." He hugs me and kisses my cheek before taking off.

Sparrow, Gage, and my mystery man join me at the table.

"Thank you again for doing this for us. Gage seems to have enjoyed his time with you." Sparrow smiles at his son and the look of love in his eyes is clear for anyone to see. Feeling the tears gather in my eyes, I look away. Seeing Sparrow with Gage makes me miss my father more than I thought was possible.

"It really was my pleasure. If at any time you need help and I'm not working, I would gladly do it again."

"You're a saint, *chica. Estoy agradicido.*"

"No need to be grateful. I enjoyed it just as much as he did." Leaning over, Gage and I fist bump each other while smiling like loons. I reach into my jean pocket, remove the bundle of cash he handed me earlier, and put it on the table in front of him.

"Here's your money back, too. We didn't need it."

Sparrow shakes his head but takes the cash and puts it into his pocket. "Time to go, Gage. Gotta head home and see your momma. Say goodbye to Hadley and Wolf."

Gage scrambles from his father's lap and hugs me close. My gaze follows the man I now know to be Wolf as his gaze bores into me.

"*Gracias*, Hadley." Gage presses a kiss to my cheek and at that moment, I see a look of softness and longing move over Wolf's face.

"Of course, Gage."

He grabs his father's hand as he waves at Wolf before they make their way out of the aquarium.

"I just want to apologize for last night. Alcohol tends to remove my filter and I end up saying a lot of stupid shit." Apologizing isn't one of my strong suits and all through my apology, I stare directly at my intertwined fingers. Slowly, I lift my gaze toward him to gauge his reaction.

"My shirt looks good on you." He nods toward my chest.

"I'll get it back to you."

"Don't worry about it. Let's get you home."

Wolf rises from the table before moving toward the entrance. When we reach the parking lot, I see him move toward the most beautiful 1958 Harley Davidson Duo-glide I've ever seen. Matte black with chrome finishing and custom leather work. Wolf clears his throat and I look back toward him. He has a quizzical expression on his face and I wait for him to say something.

"Seems like you might be in love there, Blue." He smirks at me.

Running my hand along the leather seat, I burst out laughing. "You may be right."

He hands me a helmet as he straddles the Harley and I hop on behind him. We make our way through town toward my apartment. The fact that he knows where to go without asking me doesn't surprise me at all. The moment you get involved with a club, they tend to know everything about you, and that includes your address. The wind whips through my hair and I remember why I have always loved riding on a motorcycle.

As we pull up outside my apartment, I wish the ride had lasted longer. After unclasping my hands from around his waist, I remove the helmet and dismount.

"Thank you for the ride, Wolf. I'll have your shirt cleaned and get it back to you soon."

He stares at me like he has something to say, but

simply nods.

Walking away from him, I wish he would call me back or say something. There's definitely something there. There's a mutual attraction between us. The hard-on I just saw pressing against the front of his jeans is all the evidence I need. But he says nothing as I make my way up the stairs to my apartment.

Chapter Nine
Wolf

We move through the aquarium and make our way to the outside seating area where Justice let us know they are currently having lunch. The moment we step outside, rage fills my veins and my vision has a tinge of red to it. Besides the woman I want to claim for myself sits Justice, the new prospect I just brought into the damn club. The sitting part isn't what bothers me, it's the picture they are presenting to the world. Sitting there, they look like a couple taking their kid out for the day. Before I can lose my shit, Gage spots us and comes running over.

"Brother, it isn't what it looks like and you know it." Sparrow diverts my attention momentarily.

Gage slams into his father and starts talking a mile a minute while gesturing with his little hands. He looks so happy that I can't look away and smile at him while listening to his story about the dolphins.

When my gaze drifts back to the table Blue is sitting alone. Justice must have seen the look on my face and left in a hurry. Joining her at the table, I finally find out her name. *Hadley.* Listening to her and Sparrow speak, I wonder how I missed this woman, when clearly Sparrow and some of the other guys already know her. Gage climbs onto her lap and thanks her for the day. The way she looks at him warms my heart and I can't help but stare. This woman has the capacity to either break me or fix me.

Sparrow takes off with a greeting as Gage waves at me, and suddenly we are alone. Watching her closely, I see her wringing her hands together. The apology on the tip of my tongue never makes it out as she apologizes first. Her eyes don't meet mine as she speaks, but after a moment, she looks up at me.

"My shirt looks good on you."

It may actually be the dumbest thing I have ever said to a woman but it simply slipped out. But I don't care that I didn't intend to say it because it's true. Watching her blush over my half-assed compliment, I wonder if the same flush would steal over her as she orgasms. Deep in thought, I almost miss her telling me that she'll return it but tell her not to worry. Moving away from the table, we make our way back outside. I know I'm her ride home since I'm the one who basically ran Justice off. Proceeding toward my bike, I expect her to shit a brick about having to ride on a motorcycle, but she surprises me yet again. Walking around my bike slowly, she has her hand less than an inch away but never touches it. Her breathing accelerates and her pupils dilate, while her nipples tighten and a visible shiver works its way through her.

Watching her react to my bike that way, I can't wait to get her on the back.

"Looks like you might be in love there, Blue."

She doesn't answer right away, just runs her hand lightly across the custom leather seat. Does she even know what she's doing? How her body is reacting? Laughing, she looks up at me. "You may be right, Wolf."

Handing her a helmet as I straddle the Harley, she mounts the bike and clasps her hands in front of my stomach. For the first time ever, I hate my nickname. The need to hear her call me by my first name—Brandon—burns through me. The fact that she's pressed up against my back nearly does me in. She isn't stiff behind me or tense around corners, but instead, I can feel her relaxed posture behind me. She rides like she's done this before and I can't help but wonder whose bike she's been on.

Irrational jealousy crashes through me again. This woman is driving me insane and I don't even think she's aware of it.

The ride is over too soon as we pull up outside of her apartment building. She removes the helmet and dismounts like a pro. She thanks me for the ride and promises to return my shirt soon, but I don't say a word to her. As I watch her walk toward her apartment, a million thoughts run through my mind, but I don't say any of them to her. For ten full minutes, I simply sit on my Harley and stare at her apartment building. Realizing that I have to do something before I lose my opportunity, I dismount my bike and make my way up to her apartment door.

Taking a deep breath, I knock on her door. Inside her apartment, I can hear her moving around before she opens the door. All the air in my lunges leaves me in a whoosh. In front of me, Hadley stands with her hair piled on her head in a messy bun, wearing nothing but my t-shirt.

Chapter Ten
Hadley

Moving on from the disappointment of Wolf not stopping me, I get comfortable. I get out of my jeans and sneakers, loosen the knot in Wolf's t-shirt, and bundle my hair on my head in a messy bun. My hangover has completely left me and I decide to have a glass of wine and relax. A knock at my door has me putting down the glass and moving toward it. Storm sent a message earlier, saying she would be stopping by later to check on me. I don't check the peephole but fling the door open, expecting to find her on the other side. Instead, Wolf stands there staring at me. His gaze scans me from top to toe before a mask of rage covers his face. He propels me back into the apartment, shutting the door behind him with the heel of his boot before he crowds me against the wall.

"Do you always answer the door half fucking naked?"

His voice is a low growl that causes goosebumps to pop up along my arms. "Huh?"

I know what he's asking, but having him this close to me has fried my brain.

"Or were you expecting someone else?" He stares deep into my eyes as he waits for an answer.

"Who do you think I would be expecting?" Goading him probably isn't the best idea, but at this moment, it's all I have.

"Justice? Or perhaps whoever taught you how to ride on a bike?"

A burst of laughter leaves me. When it comes to this man, I rarely react the way I'm supposed to.

"Justice? Sure, he's cute and all, but he just

turned eighteen. That wouldn't work for me. As for the riding, he won't be coming around again."

"So, you simply walk around half-naked and open the door without even checking first?"

Staring up at him, I have no answer. He steps closer and stands against me. His erection presses into my stomach and a sound I don't even recognize leaves me. I sound wanton and needy.

Before I can comprehend what's happening, Wolf crashes his mouth down on mine. His kiss isn't soft. He runs his tongue along the seam of my lips before nipping at my bottom lip, prompting me to gasp. The moment my mouth opens, his tongue invades inside. His kiss overwhelms and dominates me, triggering my body to melt into him.

His hands glide down my back to grip my ass as he lifts me into the air. Wrapping my legs around him, I pull him closer to me. He grinds his considerable hard-on against my pussy and I moan out loud again. Not having had sex in over three years has clearly turned me into a wanton slut. The feel of his hands, lips, and erection drives me to the brink of insanity. With his body pressing me firmly against the wall, his hands are free to roam over my body.

His left hand slips beneath the hem of my t-shirt and works its way up to my breast. Then he holds my breast before giving it a slight squeeze. The roughness of his hand adds to the sensations he's creating. Taking my nipple between two of his fingers, he pinches it while grinding his erection against my center. My orgasm takes me by surprise and I whimper into his mouth. Never have I come so quickly for a man, especially with him barely having touched me. Wolf presses his face into my neck, panting heavily while I come down from my high.

"Shit." He draws in another deep breath. "I didn't

mean to do that. I only want to talk to you."

Nodding is the only reply I have for him. All capacity to form words and sentences has fled me. Slowly, he lowers me to my feet, but he doesn't let go. Instead, he tilts my head back and kisses me again. This kiss is soft and exploratory and unrushed. My hands move of their own volition, around his neck and twisting into his hair as he slowly continues to seduce my mouth.

"I'm going to leave before this goes any further, but I want to get to know you. I want to spend time with you. Go out with me tomorrow?"

"I can't." My reply has a scowl instantly appearing on his face. Touching my lips to his, I explain, "I'm on shift tomorrow."

"Fuck that. I'll sort that out as long as you give me a chance."

He looks so hopeful as he waits for me to answer. After I nod my agreement, he kisses me before he pulls away.

"I'll pick you up at six. You should wear something comfortable."

He grabs my phone and programs his number in it before calling himself. He lightly kisses my forehead before returning to his motorcycle, leaving me behind wanting more.

****

Wolf called at eight this morning to let me know that he got someone to cover my shift at Dusk tonight but couldn't get someone to cover my morning shift. My compromise was to simply have him pick me up from Dusk after my shift. So here I am, getting ready in the back room for my first date in at least two years. Storms stands in the entryway, smiling like a proud momma.

"Stop smiling at me like that. You're making me nervous."

"I'm just happy." The smile never leaves her face. "Both of you deserve to be happy, with someone who will treat you right."

"Can we please get past the first date before you start planning the wedding?" I sass at her.

"Yeah, yeah." Storm rolls her eyes. "Are you done yet? He's waiting on you."

Standing in front of the mirror, I check myself over one last time. I didn't do much. Black skinny jeans, black knee-high boots with a flat heel, a fitted purple t-shirt, and a black leather jacket. My hair is tied back into a high ponytail, and as usual, I don't have on a ton of makeup.

I head toward the bar where Wolf waits for me. Cherry stands beside him in nothing but a set of soft pink lingerie. She's clearly interested in him and self-doubt starts to creep in. Cherry is exactly the type of woman that will always be around Wolf and the Gypsy Bastards. The way she looks and carries herself are suddenly intimidating to me.

Wolf lifts his head and his gaze lands on me. All my insecurities flee. He moves away from the bar without giving Cherry a second glance and makes his way toward me. His palms cup my cheeks and he kisses me like he's starving for it. After moments of letting him kiss me and kissing him back, he rests his forehead against mine and takes a deep breath. "Been waiting to do that all day. You look beautiful."

"Thanks." My reply comes out as a whisper.

"Let's get out of here." Wolf grabs my hand as he leads the way outside. On the way out, I can't help but notice the rage painted across Cherry's face.

****

We drive out to a secluded spot by the lake. Wolf has packed some food into his saddlebags and lays out a small blanket for us to have a picnic. The sunset in the background paints the sky in hues of purple, red, orange, and yellow.

"So tell me who taught you to ride a bike. I know you said they wouldn't be coming around anymore, but I still want to know who he is."

Wolf is lying across the blanket with my head resting on his stomach. Usually, I don't delve into my past but I like him and I want him to get to know me. Besides, this isn't a huge thing to tell someone.

"My dad taught me, and then when my brother was old enough, I would ride with him."

"That's cool. Do they live far from here or did they stop riding?"

"No. My dad used to be the vice president for the Iron Disciples before he passed and my brother barely got his full patch before he passed." Tears sting my eyes like they always do when I talk about my family.

Wolf pulls me up his chest and holds me close to him. "Shit. I didn't mean to upset you. Do you want to talk about it?"

"No, I really don't. Maybe one day but not tonight. I really don't want to ruin the mood." I have swallowed back my tears and want to forget we even had this conversation.

Leaning up on my elbows, I support my upper body weight and press my lips to his. He rolls us so I am beneath him as he kisses me back. He's cradled between my legs and I can feel his erection pressed against my thigh. His hand moves from the breast he's currently fondling, down over my belly to the waistband of my jeans. He pops the button and his hand finds its way into my underwear. One finger moves across my clit and glides into my wetness. I arch my back on a moan.

"Fuck," he growls in my ear. "You're so fucking

wet."

"Wolf, that feels so good." The words come out on a whisper.

"No. When we're alone, you call me Brandon. I need to hear you say my name."

After that, everything is a blur. My jacket and shirt are discarded and my breasts are bared to the cool night air. My nipples contract to the point of almost being painful. My arousal has spiked, making me think that I might burst into flames from it.

"You need to start wearing a bra," he mumbles before taking a nipple into his mouth, biting it, and then laving it with his tongue.

"I can't have my guys staring at your tits and seeing your nipples harden through your shirt. I might hurt one of them if I catch them."

Forcing him away from me, I pull his shirt over his head, wanting to feel his skin against mine. I reach down and undo his belt to slip my hand into his jeans. Brandon isn't wearing any underwear, and I circle my hand around his erection the moment he penetrates me with two long, calloused fingers.

"So hot, so wet, so tight."

Brandon plunges his fingers deeper into me and ups the tempo. My hand grips his erection tighter as I stroke him from root to tip, causing him to growl in my ear.

"Please, Brandon," I beg without shame.

"Fuck, Hadley, you can't beg me like that. Saying my name while looking so beautiful in the fading sunlight. It's enough to make any man lose his control."

He stares down at me with hunger written across his face. When I move my hand around his cock, his eyes fall closed and a look of bliss passes over his face.

"Maybe I want you to lose control."

Before he can answer me, his cell phone rings beside my head. "Fuck, it's Pope. I have to take this."

I smirk up at him. "It's fine. Club business. I understand."

Pulling his fingers from me, he moves to answer his phone. He stands and runs his fingers through his hair in frustration. Watching him closely, I tune out the conversation and put my shirt back on. I don't need to be a mind reader to know our date is about to be cut short. While he's shirtless, I'm able to better appreciate him. Sculpted chest and toned stomach. Slight trail of hair leading into his unbuttoned jeans, teasing at what's behind them. His impressive bulge is still visible.

"Fuck." Wolf pushes the phone into his pocket before extending a hand toward me. Taking it, he lifts me to my feet and pulls me into his body.

"I'm so sorry but I have to head to the clubhouse. There's some sort of problem."

"Club business," I repeat. "Don't worry. Just drop me off at home?"

"I'll be around later if I can. Like I said earlier, I want to get to know you."

He takes my chin in his grasp and tilts my head toward him, making sure that I'm looking at him.

"I definitely want to see more of you." And then he kisses me again.

Chapter Eleven
Wolf

After dropping Hadley off at her apartment, I head straight to the clubhouse. The last thing I want to do is leave her at home alone, but I have a duty to my club. Driving down the road, I can't shake the image of Hadley spread beneath me in the sunset. That woman has the capacity to bring me to my knees and she isn't even aware of it. All I want to do is turn around and head back to Hadley's apartment, finish what we started.

Pulling into my spot outside the clubhouse, I see that only Pope's and Sparrow's bikes are here. I find it strange that only the two of them would be here if there was actually a problem, and I move into the bar. Pope is seated in front of the bar with Sparrow standing behind it, acting as bartender.

"What's so damn important?" I grunt as I pull out a chair.

"Sorry to pull you away from your date, brother, but we have problems." Pope works his hand down his face in irritation.

Staring at him, I wait for him to elaborate.

"The fucking Mongrels are trying to move in on our turf."

"Jesus, what the fuck did they do now?"

"Well, they burned Mary's Rib Shack to the ground, beat and threatened two of the girls from Dusk, and about an hour ago, they sent this." Pope hands his phone to me.

Rage courses through me. The picture was taken when Hadley was straddling my waist to kiss me. Knowing that someone was there watching us makes my stomach turn. Pushing my chair back abruptly, I make my way to the door. Hadley is alone at home and these fuckers could get to her.

"Justice is watching her, *hermano*. We knew you wouldn't want her alone after that photo."

Sparrow is trying to reassure me, but at the mention of Justice's name, I want to lose my shit. Barely holding it together, I make my way back to the bar and take a seat.

"So do we have a solution for this situation?" My gaze moves from Pope to Sparrow and back again. Pope rests his elbows on the bar before answering my question.

"It's time to take them the fuck out, *no* church, *no* vote, just getting shit done. The rest of the guys will be back on Friday. By then, the three of us should be able to gather all the intel we need. We can end them this weekend as soon as we have the numbers."

Sparrow and I nod in unison as we agree to his plan. Rising, I make my way to the door. "See you fuckers tomorrow."

****

Before I head over to Hadley's place, I stop at home and change out my bike for my truck. She's probably asleep already and I don't want to wake her, so I'll stay in my truck, keeping watch. The need to get Justice as far away from her as possible is at the front of my mind.

Pulling up outside her building, I see Justice sitting on his bike, fiddling with his phone.

"Justice. You can hightail back to the clubhouse. I've got this." I'm sitting in my truck with the window rolled down.

"Sure, Wolf. Just so you know, your girl was down here about ten minutes ago, asking if I wanted to come inside. Told her I'd be fine but she wasn't happy."

"Thanks, I'll sort that out."

Justice drives off and I lock my truck before making my way up to her apartment. Knocking on her door, I wait until she opens it. Standing before me in nothing but a black tank top—again without a bra—and lime-green sleep shorts, she looks more exquisite than I remember. The kicker is we haven't even been apart for more than a couple of hours. She opens the door wider to let me in before moving toward the kitchen.

"Coffee?" she asks over her shoulder.

It takes me a moment to answer her because my gaze is glued to her ass as she walks away.

"Sure." Following her into the kitchen, I move in behind her and fix my left hand to her hip. My other hand pushes her hair off her shoulder and I place a kiss to the side of her neck.

"We need to have a talk." She needs to know what's going on. It's her life and her safety, but I can't tell her. It's club business. Even though I can't tell her, I do have something on my mind that we need to clear up. Turning her to face me, I watch her expression closely.

She smiles. "Sure."

"Okay. If we are going to do this, you and me, you need to know one very important thing. No other guys. Especially not in your apartment. Even if they are my brothers."

Watching her, I see every emotion as it flits across her face at my announcement. Shock, surprise, and finally anger. She steps away from me and places her hands on her hips. She looks me straight in the eye and I know I'm about to be handed my ass.

"Don't come into my home and presume you have any say about what I do or who I associate with." Her eyes are full of fire.

"Hadley, don't be fucking difficult about this.

This is the only thing I will never bend on."

"I think you should leave. One date and some heavy petting doesn't give you the right to tell me what to do or who I can be friends with."

She steps past me and opens the door. Standing outside, I turn around to say something, but she slams the door in my face. Moments later, I listen as the lock clicks into place.

I sit in my truck and stare up at Hadley's apartment door. There was a moment when I contemplated leaving. I don't need this fucking complication in my life. Let her do whoever and whatever she wants. Even as I start the truck, I know I'm lying to myself. I'm not going anywhere.

****

The sound of someone knocking on my window wakes me. Rubbing the sleep from my eyes, I find Hadley watching me. I roll down the window, prepared to apologize, but she speaks before I can.

"Go home, Wolf. I'm done with you."

Turning on her heel, she walks away from me, making her way around the corner and down the street. After I start my truck, I follow her.

"Get in the truck, Hadley."

My temper is getting the best of me. Last night, I had the worst sleep in probably the last three years, and she's pressing all my buttons. She can't be walking around alone, especially not with the shit going down at the moment.

"Fuck off, Wolf." She doesn't look at me, simply keeps on walking. The fact that she has reverted back to calling me Wolf irritates the shit out of me.

"Just get in. I'll drop you off at Dusk and you don't have to see me again. You don't even have to talk to me."

Stopping, she turns to look at me with skeptical eyes.

"It's not safe, Blue."

A look passes over her face that can only be described as sadness before she raises an eyebrow at me.

"You know I can't tell you any club business, but please, just trust me. I only want to keep you safe."

Taking a deep breath, she moves toward the truck and gets in. The entire ride to Dusk, she doesn't even look at me. When we come to a stop, she opens the door and gets out.

"Hadley…"

"Thanks for the ride, Wolf."

And then she's gone.

****

How the fuck did my life come to this? For three days, I sleep in my fucking truck. My back is killing me but I can't leave her to fend for herself. Every morning, I drive her to work, neither of us saying a word. During the day, I help Pope and Sparrow collect all the intel we need on the Mongrels MC. How many members there are, where they hang out, their clubhouse, families, and friends. We know more about that club than most of the fucking members probably do.

After Hadley's shift ends, I head back to Dusk and pick her up again. Still, we don't speak and still, she won't look at me. Her smell has become part of the interior of my truck. Every minute I spend in my fucking truck, I spend it with the smell of her in my nostrils.

Everything is fucked, but I decide that today is the day that we're going to talk this shit out. And if it can't be fixed, I'm going to get one of the other guys to watch her until this shit with the Mongrels is sorted out. I can't keep being this close to her and knowing that I can't have her.

Chapter Twelve
Hadley

The last three days have been hell. Knowing that Wolf—because I can't call him Brandon anymore—is sleeping in his truck is driving me insane. All I want to do is go down there and drag him to my bed. But I don't and I won't. After our fight on Monday and crying myself to sleep after he left, I can't go back. Hardening myself to him and doing my best to ignore him is all that I have at the moment. Many times, I've thought about explaining to him why his controlling behavior set me off the way it did. The way I grew up and being cut off from everyone isn't something I want to go through again.

Lying in bed, staring at the ceiling, I contemplate calling in sick to work just so I don't have to see him today. Just as I grab my phone from the bedside table, a text comes through. Seems I don't have to go into work after all. It's a text saying the girl I'm supposed to cover is feeling better and back on shift.

Pulling my robe over Wolf's shirt—because I now sleep in it—I make my way outside. He's standing beside his truck, waiting on me, looking better than anyone should after sleeping in their truck.

"What's wrong?" Wolf strides toward me with concern covering his face. Immediately, I fall back a step.

"Nothing." Holding my hand up, I stop him from getting any closer. "The girl who was out is back so I don't have to work today. You can leave."

Turning around, I haul ass away from him.

"Blue." He waits for me to turn around before he continues.

"My shirt still looks good on you." He smiles at

me but it doesn't reach his eyes.

Looking down, I see that the front of my robe has parted slightly, showing that I am indeed wearing his shirt. I pull the sides together, turn away, and head back to my apartment. After I crawl back into my bed, I turn off the alarm and go back to sleep.

An hour later, my phone rings for the third fucking time and I finally answer it.

"What?"

"Where are you, girlie? Your shift started twenty minutes ago," Maurice queries from the other side.

"Someone sent me a message saying I didn't have to come in today." Rubbing the sleep from my eyes, I sit upright in bed.

"Goddammit. Okay. I'll sort this shit out but I need you to come in. Please?"

"Sure, give me thirty minutes and I'll be there."

After jumping out of bed, I fly through the shower in record time.

Making my way out of the apartment, I have my heels in my hand because I can walk faster in my flats. As I walk down the street, I consider calling Wolf and letting him know what's going on but decide against it. There isn't a chance in hell that I want him thinking that I need him, that I'm dependant on him.

I walk past an alley, and a hand shoots out and grips my arm, pulling me into the darkness. Before I can scream or try to defend myself, a fist connects with my face.

****

Upon waking, I realize I'm most definitely not where I should be. My hands are bound behind my back while I'm sitting upright in a chair. It takes me a moment to pry my eyelids apart although the action does me no good at all.

Darkness surrounds me. Turning my head to either side, I try to identify a source of light but find none. I'm sitting in the chair, and I inhale the moldy scent around me. The smell triggers a memory and immediately I know I'm in some sort of cellar or underground room. The smell reminds me of the cellar at my grandmother's house from when I was younger.

My shoulders throb from the position they have been holding me in for only God knows how long. I have pins and needles from my elbows to my fingertips. Panic slowly starts to settle in.

Where am I?

What happened?

How the hell do I get out of here?

As these questions run through my mind, I have a flashback of a fist sailing through the air and connecting with my face. A large snake tattoo was prominent on that arm and realization dawns on me. I've been kidnapped. My blood runs cold and the icy hand of fear takes hold of me. My throat feels constricted and I have trouble breathing as my body betrays me. The first panic attack in five years consumes me and darkness envelopes me.

****

When I wake for the second time, it's because of a noise. Stairs creak somewhere close by. A key rattles in the lock before the door swings open on creaking hinges. The light filtering in from the hallway blinds me momentarily but it's nothing compared to the glare of the overhead light my captor flips on.

Scanning the room as quickly as possible, I try to find an escape route. I quickly return my gaze to my captor, cataloging the room in my mind. Four bare, dirty walls with paint peeling in places, the ceiling sagging in the back-right corner, and no other doors. No windows. Besides myself, the chair which I occupy firmly in the middle of the room is the only item, except for the bare bulb swinging above my head. There's no other exit than the one directly in front of me, and in that doorway stands no other than Viper himself.

"Morning, sleeping beauty," he drawls. "Did you have a good nap?"

Refusing to answer, I ignore him. Fear claws its way up my throat, and if I open my mouth and say one word, I'll choke on it.

"Are you going to answer me, bitch?" He glares at me and the pure hatred that shows in his muddy brown eyes is enough for me to recoil as if I've been slapped in the face.

A sound erupts from deep in his chest. The sound grates on my already frayed nerves. Watching as his belly jiggles, I realize he's laughing at me. This man— no, this monster—is taking pleasure in what he's doing to me. He's an asshole for enjoying this and anything I do, any movement, anything I say will just further motivate his crazy ass.

This man with his dead eyes, ugly tattoos, and beer belly is going to break me. Of that, I'm certain, but I won't give him the satisfaction of seeing it happen. I have lived through worse.

He stalks over to where I'm sitting and stares at me. Averting my gaze from his, I can try to hide the unadulterated fear that I know is shining bright in my eyes. He wraps my ponytail around his fist and yanks my head back. There's nothing I can do but allow him to look me straight in the eye. There's no way he can't see the fear or the unshed tears. A smirk forms on his lips.

"You are one tough bitch to get alone. Do you know that?" He tilts his head to the side and curiously watches me for any reaction.

"First, Storm comes to your rescue at the diner,

then all those damn muscle-bound bouncers at the titty bar." He exhales loudly. "Wolf doesn't leave your apartment after you go inside. Can't start a war with them even though I could kill any one of them with my hands tied behind my back. I watched, and I waited. I waited, and I watched, and I saw something real interesting. Want to know what I saw?"

He has a manic look in his eyes that I know all too well. He's tweaked out of his goddamn mind and that realization only fuels the fear clawing at my throat. Still, I don't answer him.

He tugs sharply on my hair and smiles. "I saw Wolf. I saw that damn enforcer track your every move. And then I knew, I knew I had to take you. I couldn't just grab you and have my fun in the alley for what you did in the diner. No, I had to have you here, in my clubhouse where I could take my time. Do you want to know what I am going to do to you?"

He laughs a grating, maniacal laugh again and I know the question is rhetorical.

"I'm going to break you. I'm going to take my time and fuck every hole you have until I'm tired of you and then I'm going to walk your ass upstairs and give you to the rest of my club as a party favor."

He releases my hair and takes a step back, studying me. All the blood drains from my face and I start to shake uncontrollably. Wolf is going to be so pissed off when he finds out. If I had only called him, none of this would have happened. If only I had listened, I wouldn't be in this fucking mess.

"When we're done, we're going to drop you off at the Iron Disciples clubhouse. King has a nice reward out for you. Bruised and broken, I can blame it all on the Gypsy Bastards. The Iron Disciples will ride in and exterminate those fuckers and they won't even know what hit them. Like lambs to the slaughter."

He looks intently into my eyes, showing me the truth of all that he has just spoken. Understanding dawns on me. Thus far, I have feared for my life, but I keep forgetting there are worse things than death. Death would be welcomed above what he has planned for me.

"But, if you are a good little whore, I'll let you live after the Gypsy Bastards are dead. I'll bring you back to the club and you can continue to service us. Earn your keep, in a manner of speaking."

He walks over to me and grabs my shirt in his right fist. With a tug, he rips it down the center of my torso, exposing my bare breasts to his eyes. My nipples shrivel in the chill of the room as he watches. He releases the shirt to leave it hanging around my middle with the sleeves still hanging on my shoulders. Wolf's words about wearing a fucking bra plays in the back of my mind and for the second time today, I regret not listening to him. He grabs his crotch and adjusts his cock in his jeans. After lifting his hand to my neck, he runs it down the front of my chest to my right breast. Willing myself to sit still, I can't stop the flinch as soon as he touches my breast.

Goosebumps break out on my skin and an involuntary shudder of revulsion works its way through my body. The slap catches me off guard as my head snaps in the opposite direction.

"You fucking whore!" He rages at me." You can let the goddamn Gypsy Bastards put their hands on you, but I disgust you?"

His chest is heaving with the anger he directs at me. The second slap splits my lip open and is just as jarring as the first. He takes my left nipple between his thumb and forefinger and twists it. A scream rips free from my lungs and at that moment, I know I'm not strong enough not to beg.

"Please," I whisper hoarsely. "Please don't do this."

He throws his head back and roars in laughter. "You don't have a choice. I'm going to take what I want."

In the wake of that declaration comes another fist straight to my face. It hurts like a bitch but for some reason, I remain conscious this time. My right eye is completely swollen shut but I watch him through the left. After unbuckling his belt, he unbuttons his jeans and slides his zipper down. With a clarity I didn't think I possessed at this moment, I realize this room is where I will die. Alone with this maniac, I will breathe my last breath and there is no one to save me.

As he pulls out his cock, he starts working his hand over his prick in short, quick movements. The realization that I am going to die is quickly replaced by another. Before death comes for me, I'll be raped and beaten beyond recognition. His breathing speeds up and then a groan escapes from him as his cum splatters all over my torn shit and exposed breasts.

"Kaiya," he bellows into the hall outside while tucking himself back into his pants.

A young woman who couldn't be any older than eighteen scurries into the room. Her head is bent forward and her eyes are downcast.

"Bring a mattress in here from next door and a bucket with water. Get this whore out of the chair and cleaned up. I'm going for a drink with the boys and when I get back, I want full access to my new toy."

The girl nods her head but says nothing. Viper reaches into his back pocket and produces a syringe which he effortlessly sticks into the left side of my neck. Squirming, I try to get away, but whatever the syringe is filled with is already saturating my veins. My limbs go weak and a feeling of floating envelopes me. The last thought that crosses my mind is that I'm beyond fucked.

Chapter Thirteen
Wolf

Hadley is smiling at me and beckoning me closer. As I move toward her, my cell phone starts ringing and I try to ignore it.

The dream fades as the incessant ringing finally wakes me. My cell phone is ringing next to my bed. Caller ID confirms that it's a club call and can't be ignored.

"Sparrow," I answer while trying to get my bearings.

"You need to get here. Now."

He doesn't say anything else before hanging up and I know that something is seriously fucked. Instantly, I am fully awake and moving around. Jumping into the shower, I make sure to hurry.

Dressed in a black t-shirt, shitkickers, and blue jeans, I grab my jacket and colors and lock the house on the way out. I jump on my Harley and make my way to the clubhouse. Proceeding through town, I weave between the morning traffic. As I pull in through the gates at the clubhouse, I see that nearly every members' bike is already parked in the lot. The clubhouse sits on the outskirts of town in what used to be an abandoned furniture factory. Double stories with a large set of double doors in the front and single side door. Easily defendable.

After striding inside to the bar, I grab a beer and head to church. Entering the conference room, I see that except for the ranking members and oldest patched members, it's standing room only. There's a somber mood in the room. Taking my seat two chairs down from our president on the right side of the table, I look up to judge his mood, but my gaze falls to Storm sitting in the corner. First, shock flows through me and then apprehension. A weight settles in the center of my chest when her eyes meet mine and I know this has something to do with Hadley.

She's crying. This is what shocks me the most. She's sitting on an old, worn-out brown recliner, her legs pulled up underneath her, and tears stream down her face. In all the years I've known Storm, I have never, and I mean never, seen her at less than one hundred percent. She's always ready to go, full makeup, sexy clothes, and those damn heels she always wears. But not today, no, today she's wearing gray leggings with flip-flops and a shirt that seems to be a hundred times too big with the Gypsy Bastards logo on the front. I know from experience that the back either reads *support* or *crew*, depending whose shirt it is.

I have a feeling her shirt is marked *crew*.

She isn't wearing any makeup and her eyes are puffy and red-rimmed. Seeing her like this freaks me the fuck out. Pushing my chair back, I move to go to her, but a stern look from Pope halts me and I take my seat again. He bangs his fist on the table to silence all those gathered. One by one, all eyes turn to him.

"All right." He draws in a deep breath. "We have a problem. You all know Hadley from either down at Dusk, here at the clubhouse, seeing her with Wolf, or even as a babysitter."

His gaze drifts over to me and then to Sparrow. The guys all murmur in agreement. It feels like a vise is on my chest, and it and squeezes tighter with every word he speaks.

"Hadley was taken this morning."

A roar erupts from the men around me, but I watch Pope. If I dare to move or speak, I will be on him.

How long has she been missing? It's six in the goddamned evening. How long have they known about this, and why am I only finding out now?

Pope looks me straight in the eye as he fills us in.

"There was confusion at Dusk as to when she should be working, but Maurice called and asked her to come in. She never made it. No one notified us because … I don't fucking know why, but Storm was worried when she got to work. She went over to Hadley's and the place was locked up tight. No signs of a struggle or anything so there are still some blanks for us to fill in."

Gripping the wooden edge of the table tightly, I hear it crack as I try to keep my cool. I spoke to her less than twelve hours ago. Scenarios run through my mind and the longer I sit and wonder where she could be, the more worked up I get.

Someone speaks and then silence falls. Looking up, I see everyone looking at me.

"What?" My voice doesn't sound like my own. It sounds far away and strained. Is that really my voice?

"What do you want to do?" Viking looks at me. As their enforcer, it's my job to make the decisions on things like this

"We all know you were getting close." His voice is softer now and there's worry written all across his face.

"I want to know where the fuck she is. Is she missing or did she just leave?" My gaze zeroes in on Storm.

She shakes her head vehemently as she continues to cry. "She wouldn't just leave, Wolf. Something happened to her. All her stuff is still at the apartment and her dad's car is still in the shop. If I know one thing about her, it's that she would never leave that car. Something happened."

Nodding, I take a deep breath before continuing. My emotions are all over the place. She's supposed to be my second chance at life. What if something happens to her? But I can't let those thoughts or my emotions control me, I need to be in charge.

"Okay. Then we do this like we always would. Beast, take Justice with you and check any security footage you can find between her building and Dusk. If she was headed to work, one of them would have caught her."

Beast and Justice nod at me and move to get going.

"Sparrow, check her phone log. See if there's anything weird. Maybe we'll get lucky and it's still on and we can track her through that."

Sparrow nods and moves to get his laptop before sitting down again. Looking at Pope, I wait for his input.

"The rest of you need to be ready to move. If something did happen to her, I want to be able to sort this out immediately." His gaze travels from member to member as each nods in acceptance. "Hadley is a good woman and we need to find out what the fuck is going on."

Storm rises from her spot to stand behind Pope and leans down to whisper something in his ear. For a moment, we all watch and wait. A red flush steals over Pope and his eyes narrow to slits before he rounds on her.

"Jesus Christ, Storm. How can you only be telling me about this now? It's a bit fucking late, yeah?" he snaps at her.

Storm's eyes widen before her hands go to her hips. The fire in her eyes is clear for anyone to see.

"Fuck," Viking says below his breath.

"It's a little hard to tell you anything with you

keeping me at arm's length." Storm squares her shoulders and faces the president of my club head-on with no fear. At that moment, I respect her more than most other women I have ever met.

"You decided to keep me separate from you and your club and your life so don't you dare yell at me because you don't know the most basic shit about me anymore." Storm turns to look at us and catches us all staring.

"Hadley and I had an altercation with Viper and the Mongrels a couple weeks back at Mary's Rib Shack. He threatened to get back at us both." Her eyes zero in on me. "Could this be them?"

Swallowing the lump in my throat, I nod at her. "Yeah. We've been having some problems with their dumbasses too."

Pope sighs loudly. "At least if it's them, we have all the intel we need to get her back. Let's wait and see what Beast and Justice get and then we can proceed."

The guys file out of the room after that, each moving in their own direction. Many of them are unhappy with having to wait to find out if it was even the Mongrels that took her. Some of the men are so fed up with this shit that they simply want it done. Pope eyes me carefully before approaching me.

"Wolf?"

"Don't, *brother*. How long have you known? How long haven't I been told?" My gaze shifts from him to Sparrow. "That's someone I care for and none of you had the courtesy to notify me the moment you knew?"

My roar rings through the clubhouse and I watch Storm flinch back. Without listening to a word any of them say, I leave and head to my room.

Two hours later, a knock comes on my bedroom door. Flinging the door back, I expect to see Pope or

Sparrow but find Justice there.

"We found her on a camera." He doesn't wait for me or explain further. He turns around and moves down the stairs. When I reach the bottom, Pope is already in his alpha mode, planning our next steps. His eyes find mine.

"Viper took her. We have all the info and we are going to hit them and get her back. How do you want to handle this?"

Looking from man to man, I see that they're ready for this. For months, this has been brewing and them taking someone we all care about is just the straw that broke the camel's back. Nodding, I lean in and start explaining my plan.

Chapter Fourteen
Hadley

Waking to the same darkness as the previous time, the only differences I pick up are the mattress I am lying on that smells of piss and that my hands are no longer bound behind my back. My mouth feels like it has cotton wool in it and my limbs are stiff and sore. Lying still on the mattress, I start a mental inventory of my body. Everything aches and pains from my little toe to the top of my head.

Besides the aches and pains, I'm relieved to find that I'm still wearing my jeans and have no soreness between my thighs. I'm still wearing the remains of my tattered shirt but at least I don't feel like I was violated while under the influence of whatever drug he shot into my veins.

Sitting up, I look around. The room is still as dark as the previous time I woke. I remember the room clearly, not that there's much to remember. Moving off the mattress, I go to the far corner to get away from the stench that's making me constantly gag. A cough from the opposite end of the room startles me.

"Who's there?"

Turning around, I face the side of the room the sound came from. Fear courses through my veins as I know I can't defend myself if I can't see what I'm fighting.

"It's me, Kaiya. Didn't mean to frighten you. Thought you were still asleep."

As she talks to me, I have to listen carefully. Her voice is quiet and there's a wheezing sound in her chest with every word that is forced from her.

"Why are you in here? You were helping Viper

earlier."

I sound like a complete and utter bitch, but I simply don't give a shit. This woman was charged with taking care of me until he got back from drinking with the boys and that fact puts her at the bottom of my trust totem.

"Help?" she asks and then bursts out laughing. She chokes off mid-laugh to cough loudly and I can hear that she is in pain.

"I haven't helped that man one goddamned day in my entire life. I'm his little sister and I haven't been out of this clubhouse since I was twelve. This is my hell and because I tried to help your ass, it has become significantly worse."

"I didn't ask for your help." Again, with the bitch in me coming to the forefront.

"Okay. So next time my brother comes in here with the purpose of raping you, tweaked out of his mind and so drunk he can't remember his own name, I'll simply mind my own motherfucking business. Thanks for the heads up."

Shock radiates through me. Besides Storm, no one has ever put themselves in harm to protect me. It's a strange feeling knowing that a stranger cares for me more than most of the other people in my life.

"I'm sorry. I didn't mean to be a bitch but I'm freaking the fuck out and all I knew was what I heard him tell you."

Kaiya doesn't answer me and we both fall into silence. As I sit on the floor, I relive my few short years on earth. There's so little I have done in my life and there's still so much I want to accomplish. My memories are more bad than good and I was looking forward to creating new memories with the people I am slowly letting into my life. This is the room I'll die in and no one will mourn me accept Storm and maybe some of the guys.

For what feels like forever, I sit on the floor and feel sorry for myself. Hearing footsteps on the outside of the door, I know someone's on their way. Sitting deathly still, I wait as my death approaches. The door swings inward on a creak so loud and shrill that my ears feel like they might start bleeding.

The strangest thought flits through my mind. Why don't they just oil the damn hinges? At that moment, I burst out laughing, and even to my own ears it's a crazy sound. The overhead light flares to life and blinds me for a minute. As my sight returns, I hear Kaiya scramble further into the corner of the room. Looking up from my spot on the floor, I can see Viper leaning against the door jamb.

"What you laughing at, bitch?" he snarls in my direction.

I take him in from his scuffed-up boots to the top of his head. The man is a fucking mess. His boots are covered in what I assume to be puke, his jeans are torn and ill-fitting. His white shirt has sweat stains under his armpits and a huge mustard stain down the middle, and his beard is scraggly and thin. Tilting my head to the side, I make a split-second decision. If I'm going to die … I'm going down swinging.

As I slowly lift myself from the floor, using the wall for support and covering my breasts with my other arm, another man enters. He doesn't look at me and simply walks straight to Kaiya, then he lifts her from the floor using her hair.

"Leave her alone," I yell at the new man.

He has dark hair, but I never see his face as he doesn't turn to acknowledge my existence.

"I'm so sorry. I tried to help." Kaiya looks me

right in the eyes as tears stream down her face. The look in her eyes frightens me. It's one I know well from looking at it for years in the mirror—defeat. It's acceptance. She has accepted the fact that no one's coming for us and that this will be the end. The door closes behind her and the man. Looking to Viper, I see that he's licking his lips and staring at my barely covered breasts.

When I have my feet planted firmly beneath me, I tilt my head slightly to the right and smile maniacally at him.

"Are you stupid? You dumb fucking whore," he sneers at me. "You think this is a game or a joke?"

"The only joke here is you, asshole. You with your tiny prick. Needing to tie women up and intimidate them so you feel like you actually got some sack? I've seen bigger cocks on cockroaches." I cackle at him.

Antagonizing the guy who kidnapped me can't be a good idea. My mind must've finally snapped from all the stress. His face goes beet red and then purple and I wonder if he'll simply have an aneurysm and I can just walk out. My luck isn't that good. Before I can prepare, he's on me, pushing me against the wall and wrapping his hand around my throat. My feet leave the floor as my head smashes against the wall behind me and my brain rattles around in my skull. Black spots appear in front of my eyes and I will myself to stay conscious. I need to stay awake, I need to be present for the last fight of my life. I would rather die standing on my own two feet than live another day on my damn knees.

"I'll kill you, you cunt," he roars in my face.

An immense calm overtakes me as I smile. He seems confused by the smile and my feet touch the concrete floor again. Leaning my upper body forward, I look directly into his eyes. "So you've said, asshole."

He looks at me for a moment before he regains his control. Right then, I choose to start fighting. Lifting my knee to his groin, I attempt to shove his balls back into his body. His hold on my neck slips and I can adjust my stance just enough to bring my knee into his nose as he doubles over, holding his crown jewels. Feeling the bone crack, I have never been so damn grateful for self-defense classes in my entire life.

Slipping past him, I make it halfway to the door before I hear it. A boom rings through the room and a blinding, scorching pain runs through my left side. Propelling headfirst into the wall beside the door, I hit my head yet again.

Turning over, I sit with my back against the wall and stare at Viper. He's holding a gun in his hand, pointed straight at me. The motherfucker actually shot me. I press my hand to my side in a futile attempt to stop the pain or the bleeding, or both. The moment he snaps is written clearly across his face. He doesn't say a word, he simply limps over to me and cracks me in the side of my head with the butt of his gun.

Toppling over to my left side, I shriek in pain. The fact that I landed on my bullet wound is probably the only reason I'm still conscious. That won't last long. He starts kicking me, landing the blows anywhere and everywhere he can. Feeling my ribs give way, I try to cover myself and make myself as small a target as possible. He kicks my stomach repeatedly until I throw up whatever was still in my stomach. At some point during all this, my bladder decides to relieve itself and this only seems to anger him further.

"Dirty fucking whore."

He rages at me and kicks me in the left side of my head. Just as I finally pass out, I hear gunshots. At least it didn't hurt when he shot me this time.

Chapter Fifteen
Wolf

We have formulated a plan and the strategy is sound. We'll separate into three teams. One team will hit the club bar, one team will hit Viper's residence, and the third team will hit their compound. Team one and team three are composed of ten men each with eight men on team two. I will be the lead on the team taking their compound. My gut tells me that's where she is.

Fear crawls under my skin and makes my stomach churn. It's a strange feeling and I haven't felt this way since Amber went into labor early. But this is somehow a different type of fear. Fear for her safety. Fear for the unknown. Fear of losing her before I even had her. But the worst part? Fearing that I am going to the wrong place, that I won't find her there.

Getting on my bike, I wait for the rest of the guys. Restlessness fills me and it feels like my skin is too tight. I check my weapons to make sure they are loaded and that I have enough extra clips. Under my black t-shirt, I'm wearing a bulletproof vest—just in case. Along with my two 9mm Berettas, there's also a twelve-gauge shotgun strapped to my back.

As soon as all my guys are together, we start up and head to the Mongrels MC compound. We wind through the hills on the outskirts of town until we are about half a mile away. We stop our bikes off to the side of the road so as not to be seen or heard. Moving through the trees and the underbrush toward their compound, we do our best to go undetected, staying quiet and moving in the shadows.

As we reach their perimeter fence, I realize how dumb these assholes really are. There is one guard sitting next to the gate with an empty bourbon bottle beside him. He's slouched over and loudly snoring. Giving Sparrow the signal, I watch as he approaches the guard from behind and snaps his neck with the flick of his wrist. The gate is quickly pushed open by one of the other guys and then we are approaching across the gravel driveway. There are no CCTV cameras on the outside of the building so there's definitely not anyone in there monitoring us.

The outside of the building is decrepit and there's rubbish lying everywhere. From food cartons to beer bottles, condoms, crack pipes, clothes, baby diapers, and shit I would rather not inspect. The building itself seems to have been a farmhouse a million years ago. The porch stairs look like people have fallen through a couple of times and the railing along the front has been broken. It hangs at a weird angle from the post that it's barely still attached to. The house itself has faded from the original color to a dirty gray, most of the windows are broken, and the screen door is hanging on by a thread.

Skipping the stairs, I pull myself onto the porch where the railing is broken. I lead my team to the door and silently gesture for us to split up. Four guys are to cover the yard with the rest of us splitting up between the front and the back entrances. Giving the other team to the count of ten to get to the back door, I gently and casually open the front door and peer in. Calmly, I move forward into the house.

The carpet beneath my feet is threadbare and there are stains all over the place. The smell that hits the second I enter is enough to keep me from trying not to gag. Looking left, I see a kitchen. Dishes are piled up in the basin and there are cockroaches running everywhere. Molding food sits on the table and upon closer inspection, I see maggots crawling around on a plate.

Exiting the room, I move deeper into the house. I don't look back to see where my men are. They're behind me, I know that as well as I know my own name. I will give my life for any of these men just as any of them would give their life for me.

The further into the house, the harder the music becomes. At the end of the hall, the house opens to a large room I'm assuming was once the dining room and living room but is now a mess. They have ripped out the wall that used to separate the two rooms and use it as a get-together room. There are bottles lying around everywhere, all the furniture is tattered or broken, and there's no one in sight.

As I turn to my left, I freeze. Held down over the top of what appears to have once been is kitchen table is a young woman. She's probably no older than seventeen or eighteen and has a shock of red hair and a shiner the size of an apple. She's buck-naked and even from this distance, I can see the bruises and scars all over her body.

Tears stream down her dirt-stained face as the scrawny, dirty man behind her continues pumping his hips. He's so out of it his head is thrown back and his eyes are closed. She looks me straight in the eyes and a sob racks her body.

"Take it, you whore," the guy behind her slurs and wraps a hand around her throat. Her eyes bug out and I put my finger to my lips, showing her to be quiet. She stares straight at me and I see that she understands the gesture.

"Don't make me hurt you, Kaiya. I don't want to, but I will," the man says again.

The urge to shoot him right between the eyes almost overwhelms me, but that will alert whoever else is in the building that we're here. Out of the corner of my eye, I see Mad Dog approach the man holding Kaiya down.

Mad Dog doesn't cower or slink toward the man. He doesn't draw his gun or have any form of weapon in either of his hands. He walks up behind the man, takes him in a headlock, whispers something in the man's ear, and simply snaps his neck. It all happens so fast. If I didn't see it with my own eyes, I wouldn't believe it.

Kaiya slides from the table and crawls underneath it, pulling her knees up to her chest and sobbing quietly. Mad Dog removes his cut and then his shirt. He puts the cut back on and then crawls beneath the table. He holds his hands up, palms out to show he isn't a threat while Kaiya tries to scurry further away from him. He talks to her softly in calming tones to convince her to take the shirt from him and cover herself.

My heart breaks a little at the confusion on her face. Just as she gingerly reaches out to take the shirt from him, a gunshot rips through the house. The scream that follows chills me to the bone and I want to run straight in that direction.

At the sound of it, Kaiya looks over at me.

"He has her in the basement. Middle room. Hurry please, he's going to hurt her bad. Please, please help her." She hiccups through her tears and even though her voice is soft, I hear every word.

"Kaiya, are there any other people in the house?" I look her in the eyes as I ask her the question.

"Only my brother Sam." I must look confused, so she adds, "Viper."

Momentum propels me to the stairs on the far end of the room. I know that Sparrow will follow me as we move down the stairs, but there are also two of my other brothers with us. Quietly, we move down the corridor until we reach the second door of the three. Peering into the room, I get to see the kick that he delivers to

Hadley's head before I storm at him.

I don't think, I simply react without thinking of my own safety or that of my men. In the distance, I hear gunfire erupting, but all I can think of is the kick that Viper delivered. Relentlessly and mercilessly, I continue to punch him.

Arms come around my upper body, pinning my arms. I struggle against the hold even though I know it's no use. Beast is one of our newest members and huge. He used to play college football until an injury took him out.

"Boss," he says in my ear.

"We got to go, boss. Other members of this godforsaken club have shown up and shooting has started outside. The girl needs to get to a hospital. Come on, boss."

I shake off his hold—knowing that it's only because he allowed it—and turn to look at him. "Take him with us. I want him put in the shed so that I can sort out this mess."

Beast nods, lifts Viper's prone body, and hefts him over his shoulder. Turning around, I look to where Hadley's lifeless body lay and my blood reaches boiling point. I take a deep breath and struggle to clear the red haze clouding my vision. Sparrow is hunched down, leaning over her and feeling for a pulse. An irrational urge to rip his arm from his body rolls through me. No one should touch her but me. Walking up behind him, I lay my hand on his shoulder, knowing that I'm using too much force.

"Step away, brother, I've got this," I say to him.

He looks up at me and nods before moving away. He tries to school his features but I still see the shock on his face.

"Make the call," I instruct. "Get the van here. Both the girls need to see a doctor and we have a prisoner to transport."

Putting his phone to his ear, he rises. The gunfire outside has stopped and I'm praying everyone is okay. Leaning down, I inspect her. I'm terrified to move her and cause further injuries, but I can't bring a doctor here or call an ambulance. The only solution is to load her in the van.

Turning her slightly to the side, I can feel the blood drain from my face. There's blood, a lot of it, all from the left side of her body. Her entire face is black and blue and her hair is also stained with blood. Her shirt is torn down the front and her breasts are out for the world to see. They too are bruised and if I'm not mistaken, covered in dried cum.

She's pale, and when I feel for a pulse, it's so weak I almost miss it. Standing, I remove my cut to cover her breasts and keep them from the sight of my brothers. I don't need to lose my shit right now because one of them looks at her funny. Lifting her into my arms, I cradle her against my chest. She mewls in pain as she slightly opens the eye that isn't swollen shut and looks up at me. She lifts her hand and touches the side of my face.

"Brandon," she croaks before passing out again.

Chapter Sixteen
Wolf

By the time I reach the front door, all the guys are gathered and waiting. Pope pulls up the drive and parks the van, looking us all over.

"Everybody whole?" he questions no one in particular.

"Yeah, pres," Sparrow answers me from behind.

"Luger got clipped in the shoulder but we're whole. Both girls need medical attention and Viper got away. Three of the guys are out combing the surrounding woods."

Pope nods his head and moves to open the back doors. Mad Dog and I both get in the back each, holding a woman to our chests. Luger has his t-shirt pressed to his left shoulder where the bullet hit him.

"I'm sorry, boss. The fucker snuck up on me, but I'll find Viper and bring him back to you," Beast says as he gets in beside me.

He sounds disappointed in himself and even though I have pure rage running through my veins, I know it's not his fault. "Don't sweat it, man. We'll find him. I know it wasn't your fault."

He looks up at me and studies me closely before nodding his head and looking back to the floor of the van. As I glance past Beast, I see two members of the Mongrels MC lying dead on the grass. A perverse satisfaction weaves through me. Pope delegates the brothers who came with him to drive our bikes back to the compound and gets behind the steering wheel.

"Where to, Wolf?" he asks over his shoulder as he starts down the driveway.

"Is Doc at the clubhouse? I don't want to take her

to the hospital," I say after thinking it through quickly. "Too many questions and we have none of the answers."

"Yeah, Doc's waiting on us." He puts his foot down on the gas and drives like a bat out of hell.

"Is, is she going to be okay?" a small voice questions from in front of me.

"I don't know, Kaiya, but I hope so."

Looking her straight in the eyes, I wait for her to say something. To tell me what the hell happened.

"I tried to help. I spoke to Sam and begged him to let her go. When she was out from the tranquilizer, he wanted to have some fun, but I hit him in the back with a chair. I got this for my trouble and she still got hurt." She gingerly touches her black eye.

Nodding, I look back down at Hadley. She seems paler and again fear courses through my veins. Before I can ask the question, we come to a dead stop. Looking up through the windshield, I realize we are back at our clubhouse. Pope opens the back doors and I scoot forward to get out. Straightening myself, I walk toward the door.

Storm comes running out into the parking lot and a wail is ripped from her as her legs give way and she collapses to the ground. I can imagine what she's seeing.

Her dearest friend is cradled to my chest, covered in nothing but my cut and a pair of soiled jeans. She's pale as a sheet of paper and I'm saturated in blood. She must think her friend is dead and if I were in her position, I would think the exact same thing. Pope comes running past me and picks her up too.

Walking into the clubhouse, I realize that sometime during all the commotion, Pope put the club on lockdown. All the old ladies, kids, club whores, and club friends are inside. People stare at me but make way to let me through. Luna comes toward me and I can see that she's in professional mode. Never have I been so glad in my life to see her, knowing that with her training as a nurse she'll be able to assist Doc.

"Your blood or hers?" she questions.

"Hers. Seems to be a bullet wound in her left side. Just under her ribs. I didn't check to see if it is a through and through." I walk and talk at the same time with Luna following behind.

"Doc is in the conference room." Luna steers me by the shoulder in the direction she wants me.

"Pope texted that there were two women and a brother that needed tending. It's easier if they're all in the same room at the same time so that we can access them all together and see who needs the most help."

Kicking the door to the conference room open, I see that the meeting table has been moved against the far wall with all the chairs on top of it. Someone—I'm assuming one of the hang-arounds—has carried three cots from upstairs and put them alongside each other.

Doc looks up at me upon my noisy entry. "Middle bed, Wolf. I have a feeling she might need the most urgent care from the amount of blood on you."

Nodding at Doc, I lower her carefully to the bed. Her eyelids flutter but her eyes never open. Mad Dog comes in with Kaiya and lowers her to the cot on the right and stands to leave.

"Doll." He stares at her until she looks at him. "If you need anything, anything at all, you come find me. Everyone knows me. My name is Mad Dog and I'm going to take care of you until you ready to fly on your own, little bird. You got me?"

She nods and a smile tugs at the corner of his lips. He turns and walks out of the room. I turn my attention back to Doc and Hadley.

"Does anyone know what happened to her? If I

have a better idea of what happened, I will know the best course of treatment."

Doc looks at me as he asks the question but I don't have any of the answers he needs. For the first time in a long time, I feel utterly useless, so I just shake my head. "The only thing I saw was Viper kicking her in the head."

It's all I have to offer. The feel of a small hand on my shoulder has me looking up to find Kaiya standing beside me. It's remarkable that she's even able to stand, let alone try to comfort me. She has a question in her eyes, likely wanting to know whether she can trust Doc. I nod my head. She turns to Doc and starts talking.

"My brother did this. He brought her in yesterday knocked out cold and tied her to a chair. Left her in the dark alone for about two hours. He went back later and talked a lot of shit about you." She looks me in the eyes as she says this.

"Says if he knew you were so hung up on her, he would have taken her sooner. Then he ripped her clothes and smacked her around a bit before jacking off on her. They argued and he knocked her out with Midazolam." She stops for a moment, as though to gather her thoughts.

"He had me bring a mattress in and move her over. I asked him to let her go. He wanted to rape her while she was out, so I hit him in the back with a chair. I said he couldn't handle a fight with the Gypsy Bastards and he gave me this in reply." Again, she touches her shiner.

"He left us alone in the dark again and when he came back, Squid came down to fetch me. That's where you found me fifteen minutes later." She looks up at me with those emerald-green eyes and I nod.

"Thank you, Kaiya. You did all you could and could have been seriously hurt. But thank you for looking after her," I say softly.

Doc clears his throat to get our attention. While Kaiya was speaking, he was assessing Hadley to see what needed to be done.

"Okay, the bullet wound is a through and through, but it nicked something, so I am going to have to open her up to stop the bleeding. Wolf, I need you to go down to the clinic and get the portable x-ray and the portable sonar. I need that so that I can determine what, if anything is broken."

"I'll go to the clinic." A voice from behind me makes me jump and spin around. Behind me is Viking and he seems both heartbroken and pissed-off, gazing down at Hadley.

"Give me the codes and the keys and I'll have two prospects help me. Wolf will stay here and look after the girls and help where needed."

I nod at him in thanks and he turns to leave. Doc is hard at work and Kaiya takes a seat on the bed beside me. She looks up at me sadly with the greenest eyes I've ever seen.

"Thank you for helping me. I know that I'm not a Gypsy girl or any of your problem, but I do appreciate it."

"Kaiya," I sigh.

It feels like the weight of the world is on my shoulders and I'm unsure if I'll be able to hold it up much longer. "I don't have any idea what was going on in that fucking place, but I don't care if you are my worst enemy. If I see a woman being treated the way they were treating you, I will do something. Always. It's who I am and how I was raised. All of us are like that. We don't treat women the way you've been treated."

She looks at me thoughtfully and nods, returning her gaze to Hadley as Doc works. He and Luna are discussing everything that needs to be done and I'm confident in their skills. Luna walks over and lowers herself to her haunches.

"Hi, I'm Luna." She holds her hand out to Kaiya.

"Kaiya."

"Okay, Kaiya. We need to get you examined. I see you're only wearing one of the guy's shirts and we need to make sure you're okay," Luna tries to coax her.

"No need," Kaiya replies. Her whole demeanor has changed, and she sits still as a statue beside me. "Same shit, different day."

Looking at her, I cannot disguise my surprise or the rage that threatens to yet again overwhelm me. "Kaiya, you can't be serious. We walked in on you being held down and raped."

I'm shocked at her attitude. How can she be so calm about this?

"Wolf, I'm going to tell you something and I want you to listen to me carefully 'cuz I'm only going to say this once. Since the age of twelve, I have been living with that club. My parents died, and my brother was awarded sole custody. Since I was sixteen, I have been passed around the Mongrels MC. I have been fucked every which way from Sunday. I have been beaten, kicked, branded." At this, she stands and lifts the shirt she's wearing to show me a cattle brand with the letter M on her right butt cheek.

"And I have survived. I have been raped at least once a day for the last three years. I have never had consensual sex and I will never have children. They made sure of that. I'm a survivor and I will not have your goddamned pity. Do you hear me?"

She stands over me with her hands on her hips, scolding me like a three-year-old. I like the spunk she has and I appreciate her candor and the fact she's decided to trust me with this information. It breaks my heart that she has been through this, but there's nothing I can do to change her past.

"Yes, ma'am." I smirk at her.

We hear a roar from outside the room and something connecting with the wall next to the door. Then there's complete silence. Luna is crying, streams of tears running down her cheeks, but she averts her gaze and walks over to assist Doc.

"Also," Kaiya says softly as she takes a seat beside me, "if you can put in a good word for me with the guys, I would like to stay on. I cook and clean and obviously fuck. Also, I can tell you everything I know about the Mongrels."

She takes a deep breath. "They need to die."

Chapter Seventeen
Hadley

Jesus, every part of my body hurts. I thought when you die, the pain is supposed to end. Did I die? Am I still in that room? God, I hope not. Carefully, I force my eyes to open.

The room is filled with light. Turning my head to the right hurts like a bitch. My head feels like a fucking watermelon that weighs fifty pounds. I see a wood-paneled wall and a large table stacked with chairs. Gingerly, I turn my head in the other direction. Against the wall is a large couch with Wolf sleeping on it. In his lap lies a small woman with flame-red hair. Her eyes are open and she's watching me intently. The moment her green eyes connect with mine, she starts crying.

Haltingly, she leaves the couch and crawls over to the bed I'm lying on. She takes my hand in hers and presses it tightly to her forehead. She has a black eye that's starting to fade. Her body is wracked with sobs. She starts mumbling and I lean closer to hear.

"Thank you, thank you, and thank you. I was so scared. I'm so glad you woke up." She looks up through tears. "I'm so sorry. Words can never express the regret I have for not being able to help you."

"Where am I?"

"The Gypsy Bastards' clubhouse. You've been unconscious for six days. Doc said you would wake up when your body was ready, but we were so worried," she replies.

Tears still stream from her face. Watching her intently, I try to remember what happened. Realization dawns on me as I remember who she is. As the memories come flooding back, all I feel is anger. Anger at Viper for taking me, for hurting me, for making Kaiya part of what he was doing and for making her feel guilty over something she had no control over.

"You don't owe me an apology. I know you were just as much a victim as I was. Actually, I know you had it worse than I did."

Her shoulders fall as she relaxes. This was clearly a great weight for her to carry around. I squeeze her hand until she looks at me again.

"But I could use a favor?"

Hopefully, she will help me because I feel like I'm going to burst. She nods her head and I feel a slight smile tug at my mouth at her willingness.

"I need to pee. Can you help me to a bathroom?"

"I'll help you," a sleep-roughened voice answers.

Looking up, I find myself staring into Brandon's storm-gray eyes.

"You can't walk until Doc gets here to clear you and his text says he still has two clients left for the day, so it might be a while." He looks right at me as he explains all this to me and I am completely under his spell. I can't answer him, so I just nod.

"Okay, I'm going to pick you up, so tell me if anything hurts. I don't want to pull any of your stitches. Okay?"

Again, I nod, still at a loss for words. He leans down and picks me up gently. For such a big man, one would think he couldn't do anything gently, but he doesn't even jostle me. He takes me into the bathroom across the hall and sets me down on my feet. He looks me over and nods.

"I'll be right outside, so just holler when you're done. Don't try to walk. Please," he implores me with his eyes. "I don't want you hurting yourself."

"Okay."

He leaves the bathroom and closes the door. After doing my business, I flush the toilet and then just sit on the lid for a while. How did they find me? How did I get here? All this swirls in my mind when there's a knock on the door. He enters immediately after knocking, not giving me a chance to answer.

"What are you doing? Why didn't you call me? I thought something had happened."

I watch him run his hand through his hair as the panicked look on his face starts to fade. Tilting my head to the side, I study him for a moment. "I'm just thinking. Trying to get all the pieces together in my mind."

He strides up to me, picks me up again, and starts moving back to the room. He doesn't just hold me for the sake of carrying me, he holds me against his chest so I'm close to him. Like I'm somehow something precious to him.

He looks down at me and his eyes darken. I see him scan my face and then shake his head and continue to the room. As soon as he puts me down on the bed, hurricane Storm rips into the room.

"Oh my God, you're awake. Fucking finally!"

I laugh at her exaggerated gestures as she expresses herself.

"Don't laugh at me!" Her face falls and her demeanor changes. She starts crying. Never in the four years that I've known her have I seen my best friend cry.

"Storm. No, don't cry. God, please." I try to move toward her but a large hand holds me down. I glare up at Brandon, but he just shakes his head. Turning back to look at her, I find her sitting in the lap of the club president, Pope. Her head is buried in the crook of his neck as she continues to cry.

"Storm? Honey, talk to me. What's wrong?"

Storm sniffles into Pope's neck as he watches me

intently. Brandon makes me move forward and gets onto the bed behind me. He pulls me to his chest and I feel comfortable and immediately relax into him. Pope has his eyebrows raised into his hairline while looking over my shoulder. They must do that silent communication thing that men do because his face relaxes into a smile.

"Hi, Hadley, I'm Colin. But everyone just calls me Pope. I don't know if you remember me."

Of course, I remember him. That accent is enough to make any woman swoon.

I yelp as I get pinched on the butt. Storm stares at me while trying not to burst into a fit of giggles.

"Shit, did I say that out loud?" I can feel the heat from my full-face blush

Storm and Colin burst out laughing. I roll my eyes at both of them and even that fucking hurts.

"Urgh. At least you're not crying anymore," I tell Storm.

She instantly sobers. She leans forward and takes my hand while looking me in the eyes. "When Wolf got here with you—" She inhales deeply, like she's trying to gather her courage. "There was so much blood. You were so white and I, I thought you were dead. Doc wouldn't let me in to see you until they were done working on you. Only this stubborn ass and Kaiya were allowed in and it was driving me insane."

Tears run down her cheeks again. "I thought I was going to lose my best friend."

"Shit, Storm. I'm so sorry you had to go through that but I'm fine, girl. Viper is a fucking asshole and if I ever see him on the street, I'm going to run his ass down with Justice's truck."

Folding my arms over my chest, I huff. Silence envelopes the room and just as I'm about to ask what is going on, an older man walks in.

He's short and a little pudgy, balding on the top of his head, in the center of his snow-white hair. When he sees me, he smiles brightly. "Hadley, it is absolutely wonderful to see you awake." His smile falters and he glares behind me. "Wolf, get your damn ass out of her bed. Jesus Christ, man. She's fucking injured."

Wolf laughs behind me, but he slides out of the bed. The strange thing? I want to pull him back. The doc checks me over. Temperature, blood pressure, my stitches, and all the rest of me. I watch him as he makes notes on a clipboard.

"Any questions?" Doc looks at me with a grandfatherly smile on his face.

"Yeah. What was the damage?"

"Oh, well, I don't know if it's necessary to talk about all of that at this moment." He blushes and looks anywhere but at me.

"Well, Doc." I wait until his gaze returns to me. "I want to talk about it now. And I have a feeling everyone in the room already knows the answer to that except me."

I glare at him. He seems uncomfortable and starts to squirm.

"Hadley." A deep growl from behind me raises goosebumps all over my arms. "Leave the old man alone. He just doesn't want to discuss the intimate details in front of everyone. He doesn't know how much you want us to know."

Brandon frowns at me and I have this insane urge to take my finger and smooth out the frown lines between his eyes. Instead, I flip him the bird, earning another growl from him.

"Brandon." I sigh dramatically and hear a snicker from the other side of the room. I'm quite sure it was Pope, but I'll find out later. "If you found me after fucking Viper shot me"—I raise my eyebrows at him—"there isn't much *intimate* about me you don't know. Especially since you've seen me naked. I go shopping for underwear with Storm and Pope, as club president, probably knows more about me medically than I do 'cuz that's his job."

Looking to Pope, I wait for affirmation. He smiles and nods. Storm is trying not to laugh and Doc looks relieved. A growl sounds over my shoulder and I sigh.

"Don't you fucking growl at me. I have a right to know anything and everything that asshole did. If you don't want to be here, fucking leave." Twisting in the bed, I look up at him.

"You're not my brother or my husband or my damn father. You rescued me and for that, I will be forever grateful, but you can fuck off if you think that gives you some fucking claim over me."

He stares at me with his mouth gaping open. As I look around the room, my gaze falls on all their shocked faces. Truthfully, I am shocked myself. Usually, I let everyone walk over me and just accept the decisions made for me. Brandon is the only person who can rile me up to the point of becoming a raging bitch.

"Out." He growls yet again. Everyone, including myself, just stares at him.

"I said get the fuck out," he bellows so loudly I am sure he's heard in every room.

Everyone starts leaving and I simply glare at him. My eye catches Storm leaving and she shrugs.

"What the fuck is your problem?" I shout at him.

His nostrils flare. "You're my fucking problem. I'm trying to be nice here and give you some privacy and you just shit on it."

Shit, I didn't think of it that way. Now I feel like a

complete bitch. He runs his hands through his hair again. I'm coming to realize this is a frustrated gesture.

"I didn't fucking find you, I found what was left of you. I thought you were fucking dead." He sits down in the chair that Pope vacated and looks over at me.

"I was fucking terrified of moving you because I could hurt you worse. I covered you with my cut to keep the guys from looking at your tits. It was one of the top three worst goddamned moments of my fucking life." He inhales a deep breath. "So please, for me, no more talking about this shit when there are other guys around? It's too personal and it will drive me fucking insane if they think about you that way."

His elbows rest on his knees and he lowers his face into his hands. He looks so defeated. I'm trying to understand what's going on, but I feel like I'm missing a major piece of the puzzle. Slowly, I lower myself out of bed in front of him. I am on my knees when I touch his hand. His head jerks up and he focuses his steely gaze on me.

Chapter Eighteen
Wolf

Even bruised and full of stitches, this woman is fucking magnificent. She's a goddamned hard-ass, which is probably good. Everything could have been so much worse if she was a softer woman.

"What's going on?" She stares straight into my eyes. Piercing me and seeing down into my soul.

"Can this wait until you're better?" I implore her. I have never begged anyone for anything, ever. But at this moment, I am begging this wisp of a woman.

"No." Her gaze never strays from mine and I know she won't waver. She will not let this go.

"I can't handle the thought of anyone touching you or knowing anything too personal about you. Finding you like that nearly snapped my mind. Every time I think about it, it takes everything I have not to burn down the whole goddamned town looking for him. It's driving me up the fucking walls, *Blue*." I end my little speech on a sigh.

This woman, she's going to think I've lost my ever-loving mind.

She takes my face in both of her hands. Her palms are warm against my face and my skin tingles. "Okay."

"Okay?" I must look confused because she smiles. Even with all the bruising on her face, that smile lights her up. She's fucking spectacular.

"Yeah, just let me know when you figure it out. You're very domineering and apparently, I need to watch what I say and who I let close to me for a while. Your hero complex will fade, and then we can just go back to avoiding each other."

She takes her hands away from my face and moves to get back on the bed. How easily she dismisses me. My feelings—whatever they may be—are legitimate and I don't appreciate her dismissing them. Instantly, my blood heats and I'm pissed off.

"Will you tell me?" She asks this so softly that I almost miss it.

Her soft voice instantly cools my temper. She looks fucking terrified and so small sitting in the middle of the bed. Moving to sit behind her again, I gently pull her to me and with her back to my front, I tell her.

"He shot you on your lower left side. Luckily, he's a shitty shot. He missed everything vital. There was a lot of bleeding but Doc put a stop to that real quick."

Her hand goes to her left side. Instinctively, I cover her hand with mine. There's a moment of silence between us before she nods and I continue.

"Cracked a couple of ribs and Doc says you have a hairline fracture in your skull from where I saw him kick you. Doc says he can't do anything about either, but he did prescribe some kick-ass pain meds. And then basically lots of bruises and some scrapes. Two or three of the cuts needed stitches. You have three stitches above your left eyebrow. But in total, after Doc went in to stop the bleeding, forty-eight stitches altogether."

I wait quietly while she digests the information.

"Did he … um…"

Her voice fades away and I know what she's asking and shake my head. "No, babe. Kaiya says he was about to, but she knocked him on the back with a chair."

Her entire body relaxes. "That's good. At least there's that."

We sit in silence for a few moments. Just being there. I wonder what she's thinking about and feel glad that I could give her that tiny amount of good news.

"So you saw me naked, again?" she asks over her shoulder.

The question catches me off guard and I don't answer her. Looking up at her, I can see the smile she's trying to hide. Clearly, she's trying to alleviate the tension of this moment.

"Hello? Are you still there?"

"Yeah, I'm here. I didn't see you naked. You were still dressed. Your shirt was just torn to shit."

"Okay. So you saw my boobs. Can I ask another favor?"

"Sure, babe. What can I do for you?"

Watching the side of her face. I see her chewing her bottom lip as if she's still deciding if she really wants to do this. I wait patiently for her to tell me what to do. She moves forward on the bed and turns to me.

"I want to see. I just need you to help me get the shirt off." She sits there staring at me, probably waiting for me to deny her. God only knows I want to deny her. I don't want to fucking see her that way. But she has gone through something traumatic and needs to deal with it in her own way. Nodding, I get off the bed. I take her hand and lead her from the room to the bathroom she used earlier. There are no words between us. We both know what's going to happen.

We walk into the bathroom and I turn to lock the door. Stepping forward, I turn her to the mirror. I take the hem on my shirt that she's been sleeping in and find her eyes in the mirror.

"Are you sure, babe? This can wait a while."

With conviction in her eyes, she nods. "Yeah, I'm sure. I need to see what you all saw so that I can understand."

Unhurriedly, she lifts her arms above her head. Gathering the shirt, I lift it gently, giving her the opportunity to stop me at any time. Her eyes are closed and her breathing speeds up. Lifting the shirt over her head, I look at her in the mirror. Rage courses through my veins at what I see. This beautiful fucking creature is black and blue all over her body. I have seconds to school my face before she opens her eyes and I pray to God she didn't see my reaction. I know the look I wore was disgust. It wasn't disgust at the way she looked but at what had been done.

She studies herself and turns from side to side, touching places and bruises and then moving on. My hands rest lightly on her hips and I feel her silky skin beneath my roughened hands that mold perfectly to her. She turns around and presses her breasts to my chest. There's nothing sexual about it. She simply wants to see her back.

As I try to control my dick, I look over her shoulder and I'm amazed. Her back is one of the few parts of her I haven't seen before this moment. It's almost a full back piece. A full color phoenix rising from the ashes.

"Goddammit. Now I'm going to have to go see James again."

She's talking to herself and living in her own head at the moment. All I want to know is who the fuck James is.

"That's a trip to Louisiana. Going to have to work three months to save for a trip like that. Fucking expensive. If I could find that prick, I would beat the money out of him." She's mumbling to herself under her breath as she turns to face the mirror again.

"Damn fine piece of art ruined by an idiot." She frowns at the mirror and her image reflected there and bursts into tears. Turning her further into me, I hold her as she cries, damn near breaking my heart.

Chapter Nineteen
Hadley

For two solid weeks, I sleep and eat and heal. When I wake, either Brandon, Storm, or Kaiya is there. We talk and everyone avoids the topic of what happened. I'm never left on my own, I feel like I am being babysat, and each and every one of them grates on my nerves. When I ask when I can go home and back to work, no answers are forthcoming and that just serves to piss me off.

The upside to this is that I now know most of them really well. Sometimes other members will come in and just shoot the shit. I enjoy Sparrow and Luna but Gage hasn't been allowed to see me yet. We all decided to wait until all the bruising has faded from my face. He does call me every day to tell me all his news. Mad Dog is indeed mad but that's what I like about him most. Kaiya is beautiful, sad, a broken little bird—as Mad dog continually refers to her—but she's willing to fight for what she wants, and she wants a normal life.

Viking brings me books and chocolates and usually tells a joke or two before he leaves. We play twenty questions sometimes and I know he's only trying to get me out of my own head. Most of the questions get asked repeatedly, but I do appreciate the effort. I always feel like I assume I would after visiting with my dad or granddad after he leaves.

Brandon is altogether another story. He doesn't share overly personal information. I know what his favorite colors and food are, but I don't know if he has kids or a wife or even just a girlfriend. I look at the ink on his body and see a story. But I don't have all the information so it's an incomplete story. He's funny when he wants to be but most of the time he is focused and serious.

He likes to cook although I was forbidden to tell any of the guys. He has a house about fifteen minutes away and a custom paint shop that specializes mostly in motorcycles.

Every day, I speak to him and still feel like I don't know him. Every day, he leaves for two hours and when he comes back, there's an anger radiating from him. He doesn't tell me where he goes or why he's so pissed off. Club business is the only answer I get out of him.

I know the rules. *No* club business discussed with women and outsiders. *No* women in church. The list goes on and on.

Kaiya and I have bonded through our traumatic experience. We have talked through what happened to me from the moment I got to the house until the moment I woke up. She offers a lot of details nobody else is willing or able to offer and for that I am grateful. We always make sure the door is closed and to speak softly, both knowing that Brandon would lose it if he ever heard us. She has also told me about her history. We sat for hours, crying together and the only thought repeating in my mind is that it's unfair to know her story and she doesn't know mine.

Sitting with Kaiya outside at a picnic table, we watch as Sparrow plays with his little boy. The sun is setting over the horizon and it makes the moment they have together even more beautiful.

"I don't know if you realize this, Hadley, but the Gypsy Bastards are a completely different club from my brother and his idiot friends."

Kaiya doesn't turn to me as she speaks, but I know this is important to her. Guilt slams into me. If she knew my story, she would be aware that I know this just as well as she does.

"I know the difference, Kaiya."

Exhaling sharply, I ask the question before I can lose my nerve. "Do you know who the Iron Disciples are?"

Kaiya turns to me with a look of pure fear on her face.

Chuckling, I continue. "I grew up on their compound. My daddy was their vice president for many years and one day, he lost control of his bike on a run. He broke almost every bone in his body and died from internal injuries on the way to the hospital. I was ten years old. My mom, my brother, and I then became *property* of the club. Lucas was seven years older than me and although it would have broken my dad's heart, he was prospecting before the funeral."

Feeling the tears track down my cheek, I wipe them away with the back of my hand.

"My mom was made to cook and clean the clubhouse and offer her *services* as needed. Around the time I turned sixteen, the guys started noticing me. My brother was always there to keep them at bay and to get shit back under control. By then, he was a full member and could pull a little rank. But when their president, King, set his sights on me, there was no escape."

Breathing deeply to get my emotions under control and to keep the memories at bay, I stop talking. I want to tell Kaiya this, I want her to know that she can survive and that she can have a normal life again. She sits beside me, not moving, not speaking, and just giving me the time I need to finish my story.

"On my seventeenth birthday, King came into my room. It was dark out and there was a party going on somewhere in the clubhouse. He pushed me down into the bed using his massive size and covered my mouth with his hand. All the fighting in the world wasn't going to stop him, but that didn't stop me from trying. He had torn my pajamas from my body and just as he was undoing his belt, my brother came into the room. He grabbed King and ripped him away from me. They were fighting and shouting and my brother pulled a knife and stabbed King. The next moment, a gunshot went off and my brother was on the floor with a hole in his head."

Kaiya sobs beside me and her whole body is wracked with the emotions she must be feeling. I know without a doubt her story is similar to mine. Wrapping my arm around her, I pull her close. The sun has set completely and now we're just two women sitting in the dark, sharing secrets.

"Shh, don't cry, girl. My story isn't over yet. I don't know what happened after or how I managed to get away, but I know that I did. I lived on the street for about two of the longest weeks of my life before James found me. I was huddled up behind a trash dumpster, trying to find something to eat when the door across the alley opens and out comes this huge guy. I mean, he was bigger than Viking, with tattoos from his head to his toe. He gave me one look and turned to go back inside. Thinking he would leave me alone, I continued on my nightly routine. But James didn't leave me alone, he sent Devon to fetch me."

Laughing, I recall the memory... "She is tiny. Smaller than Luna, with this neon-pink hair and full sleeve tattoos and had a baby bump that made her look like she was going to topple forward at any moment. She walked right up to me and held out her hand. 'Come on,' she said to me, 'I have food inside and we will sort you out. We won't hurt you.' I remember thinking at that moment that she looked like some kind of rocker angel and gave her my hand. For four years, I lived with James and Devon. They finished putting me through school, their little girl Casey calls me her sister, and James taught me everything I know about how to defend myself, how to cook, how to work with finances, and even how to be a truly great tattoo artist. Those people saved my life and they didn't even know me. These people saved your life because the first thing they knew about you was the kindness of your heart."

Kaiya holds me close to her and mumbles, "Thank you for telling me all that."

Something out of the corner of my eye catches my attention and I see Brandon standing there. He looks furious and heartbroken at the same time. Knowing he was within hearing distance of our entire conversation and not knowing what he heard has fear coursing through my veins. Patting Kaiya on the leg, I get up and move over to where he's standing. He takes my hand and leads me into the club up to the bedroom I have been using and closes the door behind us. He doesn't say a word, simply lifts me off the ground and places me on the bed. He climbs in behind me and pulls my back to his front and holds me until we fall asleep.

****

When I wake, it's still dark out. Sitting upright in bed, I wait for my eyes to adjust to the dark. Brandon isn't in the room with me anymore. I don't know when he left but I do know that I don't want to be alone tonight. The memories are clawing at the surface of my mind and being alone will only make it worse. Anxiousness flows through me. Standing, I slowly make my way to the door, open it, and peer down the hall. Rock music can be heard from somewhere inside the clubhouse. Re-entering the room, I switch on the light and look around for some clothes as I'm yet again only dressed in one of his shirts. I find a pair of leggings and a clean shirt folded on the chair beside the bed.

Opting to keep on my current shirt and just add the leggings, I leave the room and make a slow trek down the hall. The closer to the end of the hallway, the louder the music. The music is not overly loud and it sweeps over my bruised and battered body to soothe my soul. Music has always had this effect on me. Looking around the large room the guys use as a get-together area for the club, my gaze drifts over the bar where three people are seated in a conversation, couches where two women are staring daggers at me, and empty pool tables. When I turn back around, at the foot of the stairs, Viking stands, staring at me with a look of horror on his face. I feel dirty and unwelcome and turn to make my way back to the room. Clearly, this wasn't one of my better ideas.

"Girl." The word comes from behind me and freezes me in my tracks. Frozen, I stand there, waiting for more to be said.

"Come here." His voice is raspy and I don't remember it having that quality the times we spoke before. He moves over to the bar and pulls out a chair for me and then one for himself.

"Viking." His name is the only thing I can get out of my mouth as I take my seat. He nods at me and taps the bar. A woman with bleached-blonde hair and overly large fake breasts sidles over to us. Her smile is huge as she leans forward, presenting her breasts to Viking and anger surges through me. What the fuck? Am I suddenly invisible? I might look like shit but I'm still sitting here right next to the man. Perhaps, overreacting a little.

"Get me a bottle of tequila and two glasses and then fuck off. I need to talk to my girl." He says all this while not taking his eyes off me. I stare back at him and offer a slight smile.

The woman huffs and marches off to do what she

was told.

"Don't worry about Tessa. She's one of the club girls. Just a little pissed at me, I suppose. Doesn't like not being the center of attention."

He talks as he pours us each a shot. I raise an eyebrow and he leans in closer. "You and I are friends, right?"

I nod as he hands me a shot. He clicks his glass against mine and we swallow down the shots. The tequila burns going down my throat. Slamming my glass down, I look at Viking.

"Okay." He looks me in the eye as he explains. "You and I are going to have a chat. I will answer your questions and you will answer mine, and neither of us will lie to each other. If a question is something we can't or don't want to answer, we can just tell the other person. Do you agree?"

Silence stretches between us as I consider what Viking could ask. Looking around, I see that most people are watching us but trying to hide the fact that we have their full attention. I nod, and conversation flows from both of us. There has always been a bond between me and Viking. It's not something weird or something sexual, it's just comfortable. We chat like we've known each other forever but all the questions are meaningless information.

"So." Viking eyes me closely. "You clearly have experience with bikes and club life. Want to tell me about it?"

His question catches me off guard. People usually find me hard to read, but Viking is able to see right through me. Taking a deep breath, I look straight into his eyes as I lay out my past. "My dad was the VP for the Iron Disciples. Spent a lot of time around the guys growing up."

Viking watches me closely before asking his next question. "What's your dad's name?"

Pain slams into me with the memory of my father. Lowering my gaze to the empty shot glass in my hand, I take a deep breath before looking back into his eyes. "Phillip Freeman."

"You're Juice's little girl? Damn." Viking pours us each another shot of tequila which we quickly slam down. "I saw you at the funeral, although you couldn't have been more than ten or eleven years old. How are your mother and bother doing?"

"No idea on my mom but my brother is dead."

Taking the bottle, I pour us each another shot. If this line of questioning is going to continue, I'm going to need some serious liquid courage.

"Shit." Viking scrubs a hand down his face. "This conversation is way too heavy. How about we play twenty questions again?"

The pity he feels for me is written clearly on his face and it pisses me off to an extent. But I'm happy for the change in subject. Slamming down the shot of tequila, I nod at him.

"You start."

"Favourite color?" he shoots right away. I roll my eyes at him. He always starts with the same question.

"Blue. Favorite food?" I return with a smile.

"Pasta. Especially Alfredo. Favorite drink?"

"Bourbon. Always."

The questions and answers continue way past twenty with shots of tequila flowing in between.

"We might need a breather from all this tequila, Viking. I can't drink the way you all do." Feeling myself listing to the side, I put my hand out to steady myself, only realizing too late that I've placed it on Viking's denim-clad thigh. Quickly removing my hand, I look away, so he won't be able to see the blush on my cheeks. My eye catches someone at the door and I do a double-take. Brandon stands there with murder in his eyes. About the exact moment I lay eyes on him, so does Viking.

Viking rises from his spot at the bar and holds out his hands in a placating manner. "Now, boy, you need to calm down and lose that look in your eyes. Nothing untoward is going on here. Just having some tequila."

Viking sways on his feet and if I'm not mistaken, he's just as drunk as I am. Before I can focus my gaze on Brandon again, he has Viking by the throat and has pushed him against the wall. He slams Viking's head against the wall before pulling back and slamming his fist straight into Viking's face. I hear the crack of his nose breaking as crimson blood spurts everywhere.

"Jesus," I shriek at Brandon.

Jumping up, I grab the arm that's holding Viking to the wall. All this bullshit has sobered me up considerably. "Wolf, what the fuck is wrong with you? Let him go!"

The grip he has on Viking is unbreakable and I watch in horror as he hits him again. Looking around, I see that no one else is going to intervene. Ducking underneath Wolf's arm, I place myself directly between Viking and the fist flying at him for a third time.

Time seems to slow as the fist comes flying at my face, but at the last instant, Brandon redirects and hits the wall beside me. He's panting and watching me through crazed eyes. His nostrils flare as he looks over my shoulder. He turns and stomps away up the flight of stairs. A door slams and can be heard all through the compound before the cursing starts, which is shortly followed by items being thrown around.

Turning, I look at Viking only to find him smiling

like a maniac. Blood runs down his face and discolors his teeth. Frowning, I turn away from him. This night has been too much for me and I'm going to bed. He takes hold of my arm until I turn to face him.

"Go see the boy. He needs to talk this out with you." He then proceeds to take a huge swig of tequila from the bottle and swaggers away like none of this shit ever happened.

Crazy old man.

Chapter Twenty
Wolf

I have lost my motherfucking mind. I just attacked one of the original founders of this club. I attacked him in front of most of the club, in the clubhouse. Because of what?

Because the fucking asshole has been grating on my nerves for the last two weeks. It's not enough that he already knew Hadley before I did, no. He had to know her better than I did. He knew her favorite chocolate and what kind of books she liked and what her favorite food was. The fucker kept rubbing it in my face. Always showing up to her room just as I was leaving.

He was doing it on fucking purpose and I knew it.

Picking up the desk chair, I sling it across the room I'm currently pacing. It hits the wall with an unsatisfying thud. Glaring at the offending piece of furniture at my feet, I wonder what it will take for it to break. Pacing the room from side to side, I feel like a caged animal.

The room is small and square with a single window. The walls are painted a generic beige color and a double bed stands in the middle, pushed against the wall with a bedside table on each side. One side has a lamp with a black shade and an ashtray beneath it. The bed has a blue bedspread covering it and against the wall beside the door is a chest of drawers. It's simple but it's all I need. I have a house but I use this room when I've had too much to drink or when the party starts to stretch for days. Currently, the only use for this room is Hadley. Everything around me smells like her and that only serves to amp me up further.

Amber hated the club. She never came out for a

party or a BBQ or any other club event, and I was willing to offer up anything for her, but I could never give up my club. Often, I've wondered if she had survived if I would have given up the club. The answer is always yes. I think if she survived, I would have given up anything for her and my little girl. Lost in my own mind and the anger swirling around me, I almost miss the soft knock.

Glaring at the door I roar, "Go the fuck away," and fume at the person on the other side.

"Wolf?" There's hesitation in Hadley's voice, and it shreds my insides.

After striding to the door, I fling it open. The momentum causes her to fall forward into me. The realization hits me that she was resting her forehead on the door. She places her palm on my chest to create some distance and I allow it.

Blue eyes stare up at me, filled with apprehension. "Can we talk?"

Turning away allows her space to enter the room. She looks around and sees the turned-over chair. Leaving it on the floor, she moves over to the bed and takes a seat in the middle. She crosses her legs and looks at me expectantly but says nothing.

"What did you want to talk about, Hadley?"

"I was hoping you would just talk to me. I mean, maybe you could explain what just happened downstairs." Again, she leaves me with that look that says she's waiting for me to say something.

"Well, I don't want to talk about it. You were there and you saw what the fuck happened so what more could there possibly be to say?"

Pacing the room again, I run my hand through my hair. I need her to leave. I need her out of my space before I do something irrational that I can't take back.

"Yeah." The sarcasm drips from her voice. "I was

there. You attacked Viking without provocation, broke his damn nose, and wouldn't fucking stop."

Her spine is ramrod straight as she glares at me. "What I want to know is why the fuck you would do that."

As we glare at each other, my hold on reality finally snaps. I lose my shit and she's the person I spew my venom at. "It really doesn't fucking matter, does it? I just need you to get the fuck out of my room, out of my goddamn head, and out of my fucking life."

Raging at her, I watch as her temper spikes. Being an asshole isn't something I do often. I should be ashamed of myself but I really can't find it in me to give a shit.

She unfolds her legs and smirks at me. This fuels the fire running through my veins. Leaning back on her elbows, she watches me patiently. "Want me out, huh? Well, I'll make you a deal. Tell me why you're being an asshole and I'll leave your room. Tell me the truth, hell, I'll be out of your life in the next five minutes."

Lying there on my bed, pushed up on her elbows and wearing only a pair of tights and one of my Gypsy Bastards shirts, she has never gotten to me more. Clearly, I'm fucked in the head. I scan her body from her painted toenails up her calves and over her thighs. The shirt is too big on her but I can see her figure and she's clearly not wearing a bra. Again. Her nipples harden under my gaze. I move my view over her exposed shoulder where the shirt has slipped off and then up the column of her neck. When I reach her face, I can see she's breathing harder and her lips are parted. She wets her lips with her tongue and I have to suppress a moan. This woman is like cocaine running through my system and my cock is so hard I could hammer nails with it.

"Well?" she keeps pushing. Her voice has taken

on a husky quality.

Watching her carefully, I decide that laying my cards on the table is the best option. At least then I'll be rid of her. I cannot handle the whiplash of emotions anymore. One minute I'm beating a brother to a pulp and the next I can think about nothing but fucking this woman into submission.

"You were touching him." It comes out on a growl.

I don't want her touching anyone and I don't want anyone touching her. Except for me.

"And?"

"I don't fucking like it."

Taking a step toward the bed, I stop myself before I move any closer. She watches me closely and licks her lips again. The room is badly lit and I have never been more grateful. Even through my jeans, she would be able to clearly see my erection if the lighting were only slightly better. She shakes her head and comes to sit upright.

Watching every move she makes, I realize how sensual she is. The way she moves is fluid and so goddamn sexy that I can't help but stare. She tilts her head to the side, studying me.

"So how do we fix this problem? You are a very important person to me and I don't want to lose you. I care for you deeply." Sighing, she continues, "But Viking is my friend and old enough to be my grandfather."

No reply is the best way to go. Grunting, I shove my hands into the pockets of my jeans. Too late, I realize she has tracked the movement and sees my erection clearly. A grin forms on her face and I know that I'm seriously fucked. She crawls on hands and knees over to the edge of the bed.

Looking up at me through her lashes, she breathes in deeply. "Do you want me to touch you?"

Chapter Twenty-One
Hadley

Watching his face close down on me is one of the most heart-breaking moments of my life. Realizing that I've pushed him too far nearly breaks me in half.

"Never mind." Moving from the bed, I straighten and walk toward the door. "You answered my question. I'll make sure to be gone by morning."

I know he heard me talking to Kaiya. I know he was pissed about what he heard. Seeing his erection push against his jeans, the only logical explanation I have is that after hearing everything, he doesn't want to deal with broken goods.

Before the handle can twist in my hand, he grabs my wrist, spins me, and slams me against the wall. My other wrist is captured and both are held above my head while he stares down at me intently. His breathing is harsh and my nipples are painfully hard as he pins me against the wall with his chest. I wish I didn't have this reaction to him, that I could be disgusted with him too, but it simply isn't the truth.

"Christ, woman." The quality of his voice is raw and honest. "What is your fucking problem?"

"I don't have a problem, *Wolf.*"

The amount of sarcasm is daunting now. I want him to do something. I've been on pins and needles around this man for two weeks. They won't let me leave the damn club. Wolf doesn't like it when there are too many people around me if he's not here, so I am isolated. They won't let me leave and go back to my own life, which in turn makes me beyond irritated.

I have no outlet for anything, and my vibrator is at home in a drawer, so I'm frustrated. All of this has apparently caused me to turn into a raging bitch. But I want him to show some balls and make a fucking move.

Day in and day out, I watch him watch me. Even when I was black and blue, his gaze never wavered. He never treated me differently. Now, when he has the chance, he won't do it because he heard my story. My past. No one wants damaged goods. Feeling tears pricking at my eye, I try to convince myself that it's the anger fueling those tears, not the heartbreak.

He slams my wrists against the wall to get my attention then proceeds to lift my hands higher. I'm now on my tiptoes and this causes me to arch my back, pushing my breasts harder into his chest. He's deadly serious.

"Don't fucking call me that!"

"It's your name, isn't it, *Wolf*?" I challenge him yet again.

I won't call him by his name. Brandon is someone I care for and might even love if I let myself. Wolf is an asshole and I need to remind myself of that at this moment.

"Brandon."

"Well, that's not what everyone else calls you, now is it?" I keep poking at him, hoping if I piss him off enough, he'll let me go, and I can get my shit and return to my regular life.

His eyes are dark, like storm clouds over the open ocean. He leans his head in and whispers in my ear. "But you're not everyone, are you?" He finishes the sentence with a nip to my earlobe.

A moan escapes me and my body goes lax in his hold. I don't understand what the hell is happening here. I'm so turned on I feel like I might spontaneously combust any moment. I thought he was disgusted after hearing about my past but that's not what's happening right now.

Only the hand holding my wrists and his chest pressed to mine keep me vertical. I want this man so bad. I have since the first time I laid eyes on him. My pussy is slick with need for him and I can feel my tights getting wet down my thighs. He releases one wrist to clamp it together with the other, using only one of his hands. His hand caresses down from my wrist, over my elbow to my shoulder. He doesn't stop or pause because he knows he doesn't need to. He skims it lightly over my right breast, barely grazing my nipple and then down my side and around the back to grab my ass. He lifts my leg and hooks it around his hips and grinds his hard-on against my pussy.

The moan that escapes me is wanton and I can't find the will to care because I don't.

"Do you really think I don't want you?" he asks, grinding his cock harder into my pussy. "Do you really think I'm just going to stand by and watch some other man touch you? Have what's mine?"

My eyes are closed and I hope to God that's a rhetorical question because I simply cannot answer him at this moment

"I'm giving you space." He pulls away from me and gently sets me back on the floor. My eyes open and I find his gaze intently on mine.

"I'm giving you time to heal. I can't be another person who hurts you. So I need you to be healthy and happy before I take you. Because when I take you, babe, I'm never letting you go. Understand?"

Watching him take a step back, I feel like I'm losing him. "Help me heal then."

His eyes find mine and they are filled with confusion. He doesn't understand what I want. I lift my shirt and reveal my body to him for the first time since the day I woke. I know there are still fading bruises and that the mark from the bullet wound will never completely fade. His gaze is like a caress on my body and he seems to be holding himself back. He's rigid from head to toe, but I see the desire on his face.

"Take it away, Brandon."

His eyes return to mine and I know that he sees the tears that are ready to spill yet again.

"The last hands I had on my body were his. The last memory I have with a man is with him. Help me change that."

I've barely finished speaking when he is on me. He cups my face in his hands and gazes at me before planting his lips on mine. This isn't a soft or romantic kiss. This is a claiming. He holds me to him and plunders my mouth. Fucking in and out of it with his tongue. Running my hands up his back, I push them through his hair, dragging him impossibly closer. He pulls back, breathing hard and staring straight in my eyes.

"If I knew that's what you needed, I would have done it the minute Doc cleared you." He grabs my ass and lifts me effortlessly into the air, and my legs automatically wrap around his waist.

Chapter Twenty-Two
Wolf

We take a seat on the edge of the bed and her pussy presses directly on my cock. I move my hands from her peach-shaped ass to run up her back. My hands tangle in her hair and pull her head back to expose her throat. Skimming my nose along the length of her neck, I take in the smell of her. She smells like me, like my shampoo and soap. I've been giving her my stuff for the last two weeks, clothes, shampoo, and soap. It was the only way to get close to her and although I felt like a creep, I don't regret one moment of it.

As I trail my lips along the path my nose just followed, the only thought running through my mind is that I'm going to take my time and savor her. This time, I want to make it all about her and her pleasure. Later, I'll take her hard and fast. Just as I've been dreaming of doing these past weeks.

Running the hand not holding her hair down her back to grip her ass again, I shift us, getting her underneath me. The need to be able to see her, her face, and her body consumes me to the point of madness. Slipping the hand encircling her throat down her chest to her breast, I feel the weight in my palm. She moans and goosebumps break out along her body when I graze my finger over her nipple. I do it again and again until her nipple peaks hard before I lower my mouth to capture it between my teeth. I bite down before laving at it with my tongue. The sound that escapes her makes pre-cum bead on my cock and slide down the shaft. The zipper presses harder into my cock and I fear I will come in my pants like a damn teenager.

After leaving her breast, I make my way further

down her body, pressing feather-light kisses to each fading bruise. Every touch of my lips causes her breath to catch further but when I kiss the mark where the stitches from the gunshot were just two days ago, a mewling sound slips from her mouth. When I look up at her, I see her watching me intently. I grab hold of the elastic band before slowly rolling the tights down. Observing her closely, I make sure she's with me every step of the way when she lifts her hips, giving me access to roll the tights down her legs. Her pussy is bare and I idly wonder who she went to the effort for. Before I can question her, the smell of her arousal reaches me, and I feel like an animal unleashed. Tossing the tights over my shoulder, I spread her thighs as wide as I can without hurting her to see her glistening cunt in the pale lamplight. It's just as I imagined that first night in my bed while I masturbated to thoughts of her.

"Fuck." I growl before clamping my lips to her pussy. Her pussy tastes like her. A unique taste that's instantly imprinted in my mind, and I can't even think about being gentle. Running my tongue from her slit to her clit, I eat her like she is my last meal, suckling her clit hard before letting go. Her moans fill the air around us and echo off the bare walls of the room, flowing over and through me. The need to pleasure this woman and make sure tonight is the pinnacle of her sexual experience is the only focus I have at the moment. I suck her clit deep into my mouth again before pushing a finger into her. The walls of her pussy pull me further into her and I add a second finger. Feeling her grow close, I nip at her clit with my teeth. She thrashes her head on the bed and lifts her back from the mattress. I slowly move up her body, nipping and kissing and licking until I reach her face. Intently, I watch her orgasm build and just as I see it becoming too much for her, I add a third finger.

I lean into her ear. "Come for me, babe."

Ecstasy shows in her face as the orgasm takes over and she reaches her peak. Continuing to thrust my fingers in and out of her, I prolong her orgasm for as long as I can. My forehead is resting on her chest as my fingers slowly leave her still contracting cunt. Her hands go to my hair and she gently strokes it. She entangles her fingers in my hair and uses it to lift my head away from her.

"Brandon." Her voice is hoarse, her eyes are heavy-lidded, and there's a beautiful flush across her chest. "Fuck me, please."

Her voice turns pleading, as do her eyes. Watching her closely, I see her eyes fill with tears and although nothing would give me greater pleasure than to stuff her to the brim with my rock-hard cock, I pull back.

Before I can open my mouth to speak, she turns away from me, covering her breasts. "Never mind."

The words come out so soft, I almost miss them. Grabbing her, I yet again have her hands captured above her head in one of mine. My temper snaps and I get right in her face. Again, I am back to this mood roller coaster. I simply needed a moment to make sure this is truly what she wants. I won't be able to let her go if I fuck her. If I mark her, she will be mine. But before I could get a word in edgewise, she freaked out about some perceived notion which she probably has all wrong. This woman might just be the fucking death of me.

"What the fuck is going on?" My mind is telling me to calm down, but my temper has taken the lead and I'll be damned if this woman is going to walk away from me.

"What the fuck just happened?"

She doesn't look at me but at my chest as she speaks. "I shouldn't have asked. I know you don't want me, you're just trying to help me. I know you heard me earlier with Kaiya and that you can't feel anything but disgust for me now."

She tries to pull her hands from my grasp and I finally lose my goddamn mind. With both her hands tightly clasped in mine, I move my other hand down to my jean-clad erection. I undo my belt, button, and zipper in record time, and before she can utter another word of this bullshit she's spewing, I thrust my cock in her to the hilt. She's tight and strangling me with the grip of her pussy.

"Does this feel like I don't fucking want you?" I snarl down at her, thrusting hard to get my fucking point across.

"Does this feel like I'm trying to make you feel better?"

Watching her eyes roll back into her head as I continue to thrust in and out, I can't help myself, I can't stop talking. "The only thing I think about from the moment I wake until the moment I close my eyes is you. What you're doing? If you're okay. I think of you and fucking you and holding you and just talking to you every moment of every fucking day. I dream about fucking you and keeping you and making you mine, and you don't think I want you?"

A tear spills down her cheek and I freeze. Jesus, I've hurt her. What kind of man am I? She pushes against the hold I have on her wrist and I let go immediately. I am shocked and disgusted by the animal I am because I'm clearly not a man. Going to move out of her, I feel her legs come around me and lock behind my thighs. Her hands go to my shirt and start lifting it over my shoulders.

"Don't stop, please," she pleads with me. "Fuck me. Make me yours." She pulls my face down to hers and runs her lips lightly over mine. Her tongue peeks out to coax my lips open and I'm lost to the moment. Kissing her is like being inside her body. It's something I never want to stop doing. As I plunge into her slowly, her moan spills from between our joined lips. The sound makes my balls draw up tight to my body and I know I won't be able to last. Rocking into her body, I feel her tighten around me, drawing me deeper and holding me tighter.

"Fuck, Hadley, I'm not going to last long." My thrusts become harder and faster as my orgasm creeps down my spine. "Tell me what you need. I need you there with me."

The smile on her face is the most beautiful yet wicked thing I have ever seen. "Make me yours."

Lifting her right leg over my shoulder, I thrust deep. My orgasm is barreling down on me, but I refuse to finish without her. Pulling back slightly, I look down at where we are joined. Pushing back in, I cause her back to arch off the bed. I lower my hand from her shoulder to her clit and start rubbing in small circles, using a featherlight touch. Her pussy clamps down on my cock so tightly that I don't even know if I'll be able to move. I thrust forward hard and she shatters around me.

Feeling her come around my cock is the thing that tips me over. I fuck into her like an animal. Four, five more pumps of my hips, and I explode inside her. Black dots dance in front of my eyes, and I swear I've never come so hard in my entire life.

I roll off her and pull her back to my front just as I did earlier tonight.

"You're mine now," I whisper into her ear. But she doesn't hear me because she's already out for the count.

Chapter Twenty-Three
Hadley

Waking up the next morning, I find myself alone in bed. The space where Brandon lay last night is already cooled. Standing from the bed, I make my way over to the shower to start my day. I stand under the spray and relive every moment of last night, every word he said and everything he made me feel. My body aches in the most delicious way possible. After not having sex for three years, I'm feeling it today.

Getting out of the shower, I give a shriek at seeing Brandon standing at the doorway.

"Looking good, Blue," The smirk on his face is unmistakable.

"You almost gave me a fucking heart attack." Clutching my towel to my chest, I inhale deeply. Brushing past him, I head toward the clothes I left on his bed before my shower. Brandon watches me get dressed with a hungry look on his face and desire in his eyes, but he makes no move toward me.

"Something on your mind?" Continuing to dress, I don't turn toward him.

"Just watching my woman." His posture is relaxed as he leans his shoulder against the door frame.

"So now I'm your woman?"

"You have been since you fell off the bar downstairs. We just had some details to iron out."

The look on his face can be described as nothing but pure confidence.

"Like?" Making myself comfortable on the bed, I wait anxiously to hear his answer. Things need to be sorted out on both sides and I want to know if he's able to see his own faults.

"Well, I need to chill the fuck out. I can't go around beating the shit out of my brothers all day long. I know you said you need your independence, and I couldn't grasp what you meant. But after hearing the story you told Kaiya, I have a better idea. I would never want you to feel like you don't have freedom just because we are together."

My eyes sting with the tears I'm trying to hold back but one escapes and tracks down my cheek. Brandon moves to his knees beside the bed, softly cupping my cheeks in his roughened hands.

"Don't cry, babe."

"It's a good cry." I shake my head from side to side. "You're doing good."

"Okay. You had me worried for a second." After taking a deep breath, he continues. "With all that said and done, you need to realize that I'm extremely jealous. I don't like you touching other men and I fucking hate them touching you. As long as we can both try our best to work on those things, everything else will fall into place."

Brandon looks nervous, waiting for my answer.

"I think I can live with that." The words have barely left my lips before Brandon crashes his mouth to mine. As I stand, he follows my lead before I turn him toward the bed. Pushing him down, I straddle him in only a t-shirt and a pair of lace panties. I press my core down on his semi-hard cock, and rolling my hips, I can feel him stiffen beneath me. Suddenly, I find myself on my back with Brandon staring down at me.

"Woman, you are playing with fire," he says with a growl, lips hovering above mine.

Rolling my hips again, I try to create some friction. Remembering last night in the shower, having his heated gaze on my while I got dressed, and then the emotional conversation, has me all worked up. "I'm your woman, right? Prove it."

He stares down at me with heat in his eyes and before I can utter another word, he flips me over on the bed. Teasingly, he runs his hands down my legs as he positions me on the bed. His calloused hands caress over the lacy underwear I'm wearing, over to push my shirt up my back and over my head. His hands caress my breasts and pull me back toward his chest as he plays with my nipples, tweaking and pulling, moans spilling from my lips. His phone rings and he stops momentarily to answer while still holding me to him.

"Tell me you have some news." He listens intently to the conversation on the other end of the line before replying.

"Great, give me twenty minutes and I'll meet you outside."

He doesn't wait for a reply, only tosses his cell phone onto the chest of drawers.

"Babe," he says, nibbling at my earlobe. "I don't have time to prove I'm your man the way I want to. But I'll be giving you a taste of what's to come." Pushing me forward, he smacks my ass. "Hope you aren't too fond of these," he says before a rip echoes through the room and my pussy is bared to him.

Like an unleashed animal, he ripped my panties before thrusting two fingers into me.

"Jesus." The word sounds torn from his throat. "How are you already so wet? Does your cunt long to be filled, babe?" The dirty words wash over me and although it has never been something I enjoyed in the past, it clearly is now.

"Fuck."

Pushing back onto his hand, I urge him to thrust deeper, more, anything.

Knotting my hair around his fist, he pulls my head back again to speak directly in my ear. "Your pussy actually got wetter. You like the dirty talk. Let me tell you something. Right now, it's going to be hard and fast and dirty. I'm going to fuck you until you scream my name and every man in this fucking club knows who this juicy little cunt belongs to." He adds a third finger and pumps into me hard, making me moan and writhe. "And then I'm going to leave you in my bed where you belong before sorting out some club shit. But when I get back, I'm going to take my time with you."

Releasing my hair, he pushes me forward again before another slap lands on my ass. His fingers pump in and out of me and I am so wet, the sounds are obscene. Just as my orgasm rips through me and crashes down, he removes his fingers and I hear his zipper. Before I can voice a complaint, he slides his cock into me in one smooth, forceful stroke, ripping a scream from my lungs.

He grabs my hips as he pounds into me from behind and all I can do is hold on to the duvet to keep me grounded as one orgasm flows into the next. Behind me, his thrusts become ragged and I know he's close. Pushing my ass out toward him, he seems to come unhinged and the pounding becomes more intense. An unexpected orgasm rips through me, causing me to scream again, and then he stills and pumps me full of his cum. Both of us are breathing raggedly as he slowly pulls out of me.

Falling to my side, I simply stare at him with what I can only assume is a lazy satisfied grin on my face as I watch him tuck his penis back into his jeans.

"Blue, I've got to go. I really wanted to show you my house today and maybe take you out for lunch but it will have to wait." Brandon levels me with a serious look before continuing.

"I'm going to tell you straight, because this isn't just club business but it involves you as well. I have a solid lead on Viper and I'm going to finish this today."

Shock courses through me but I try my damnedest to school my features. Nodding my head, I remain silent.

"Right now, we have to leave, but I'll be back soon and then I'm taking you to my house and keeping you there for the foreseeable future." Smiling at me, he helps me from the bed to my feet before kissing me again. His kiss is luxurious and full of promise. Twining my arms around his neck, I deepen the kiss for a moment before pulling away.

Brandon is not only doing this for his club but also to make sure I'm safe as well. Even though I fear for his safety—and I probably always will—I have no choice but to respect him for protecting what's his. Brandon moves toward the chest of drawers, strapping on his guns before throwing on his cut. Moving back to me, he kisses my forehead before walking out the door. He doesn't say goodbye and neither do I because he'll be back soon.

Chapter Twenty-Four
Wolf

Justice has insane computer skills for an eighteen-year-old. He mentioned something about being in trouble with the law because of it a while back but I didn't ask too many questions. That's decidedly a conversation for another day. Having Justice successfully do this favor for me will unquestionably get him off my shit list.

"Tracked his phone to the other side of town. He's holed up in the warehouse district."

Justice wastes little time telling me the information I need from him as we make our way out of the clubhouse.

"Great. You ready to ride? Everyone else is busy at the moment."

"Sure."

Striding over to our bikes, I cannot help but appreciate the fact that he doesn't ask any questions. He's simply ready to ride and that's a great quality to have in a member.

Heading to the other side of town, a feeling of foreboding hits me and I wonder if I should perhaps wait for a couple of the other guys. Anything could be waiting for us and usually, I'm more careful, but I just want to get this done. I want my woman safe and I want Viper gone. Permanently.

****

The outside of the warehouse looks decrepit. There isn't an unbroken window in sight, the side door has been ripped from its hinges, and most of the building has been tagged with spray paint. Making my way from my bike to the side door, I constantly scan my surroundings. The air is stale and cloying, there are no cars around, and an eerie silence wraps around us. I move through the door into the warehouse and look back toward Justice for confirmation.

"Just checked the tracking app on my phone and the signal is coming from the left-back corner of the building." His voice is pitched low, but in the empty building, it sounds louder.

The walls and the floor are bare concrete. There's a smell of piss permeating everything. In a corner is what I'm assuming to some homeless man's belongings to which he will probably return at sunset. This is the type of place you would expect to find junkies shooting up, but I'm lucky I don't see any.

Nodding, I move in the direction Justice specified. As we enter the back office, I instantly realize the mistakes we have made. We never knew the total number of members in the Mongrels MC and we assumed that we had taken out most of their members at the clubhouse the night we rescued Hadley. The second mistake we made was assuming they were working alone. They aren't.

In the center of the room, like a fucking king is Viper, his president—Mutt—beside him. He smiles at me with malice in his eyes.

"Welcome, Wolf."

Taking in the room around me, I try to formulate a plan. At least twelve men have their guns trained on us. There's no other door or even a window that we could use for an escape if the opportunity arose.

"Viper. Mutt." I nod at both of them in greeting, returning my gaze to them.

"Let's keep this simple. You have things that belong to me and I want then back."

Slowly, I take notice of him. He looks better than the last time I saw him. He's better dressed but the clothes are ill-fitting, like he's trying to be something he's not. Viper has also clearly been sampling his own product. His eyes are sunken, his skin has a greyish pallor to it, and his arms are covered in scabs.

"Nothing we have belongs to you."

Justice catches me off guard with his reply but the thing that scares the shit out of me is the gunshot that echoes through the small room we're standing in. Justice falls down beside me, clutching his thigh as blood seeps through his jeans.

"Wolf," Viper barks at me. He waits until my full attention is focused back on him.

"Call Pope and hand me your phone. It's time for us to negotiate a hostage exchange."

"No," Justice replies from beside me.

Watching Mutt, I see the nod he gives before another shot goes off in the small room. My ears ringing, I take a deep breath. Mildew, gunpowder, and blood blend and make my stomach roll. Looking down, I see Justice has been shot in the shoulder by a man I don't recognize.

"Make the call," Viper repeats from his spot.

Justice opens his mouth to say something, but I silence him with a shake of my head. He has balls—I'll give him that—but if he doesn't keep his fucking mouth shut, he won't live to walk out of here. Facing Viper, I pull my phone from my back pocket, select Pope's burner phone, and hold it out to Viper. There's nothing I want less in this world than to have Hadley anywhere near this tweaked-out motherfucker. But I don't have a choice. Viper and his men will simply kill us and go after the girls. There will be no one to warn them of what's coming because we all thought they were done. We weren't looking for an entire crew, we were only looking for one man. This is simply making the best of a bad situation. At least if I do die here, my brothers will know to look after her.

"Pope," Viper drawls into my phone. My sole focus is on him at this moment. How he breathes, moves, talks, even the slightest twitches of his eye.

"Well, I'm calling you because I have your boys." He responds to what I am assuming is a question on Pope's part. I wish I could hear their entire conversation but I'll have to make do with what I have.

"Well, I have your enforcer." He winks at me. "And a black boy bleeding out on the floor in front of me." Talking about Justice causes him to scrunch up his nose in disgust.

"What do I want? I want what your fucking boys took from me!" His voice has gone up in volume. His inner tweaker is front and center for all to see. Taking a deep breath, I can see him focus on whatever Pope has to say on the other side of the line.

"Great. Bring the girls to the farmhouse you took them from. Just you and one other man. No weapons."

He laughs at Pope's response. "Have some faith. See you in an hour."

My phone gets thrown to a man behind me before I hear it shattering.

"Great." Mutt claps his hands together. "Let's get the fuck out of here, get shit set up, and end this fucking nightmare. King wants that fucking girl before noon tomorrow."

King? What the fuck does he have to do with this? Before I'm able to vocalize anything, darkness envelopes me as someone hits me from behind.

Chapter Twenty-Five
Hadley

Sitting at the bar and having a drink with Kaiya, I watch as Pope enters, followed closely by Sparrow, Mad Dog, Beast, and Viking.

"Hadley."

His voice carries a tone of worry and regret. If it's a club-related problem, I can understand the worry, but the regret catches me off guard. But if it's strictly club business, he wouldn't be talking to me. We may be friendly with each other but I'm not an old lady or someone who gets to be privy to club business.

"Pope, can I do something for you?"

The slight amount of confidence I project is all a façade, but I need him to think, if only for this moment, that I'm capable of handling whatever he's about to tell me.

"I'm not going to bullshit you, either of you." His gaze lands on Kaiya before returning to me. "Viper and his cronies have taken Wolf and Justice hostage and want to trade you for them."

From the corner of my eye, I can see Kaiya has gone white as a sheet, but I don't give away any of my emotions. My mind runs in a million different directions, but I won't let them see that.

Pope continues to speak. "Wolf is going to have my ass for this, but I need to ask you what you want to do. He would never willingly allow me to risk either of you, but if it's your choice…" His voice trails off.

Turning toward Kaiya, I allow my full attention to settle on her. She breathes in deeply before nodding with a look of resignation on her face. From behind me, someone growls, but I choose to ignore this.

"Kaiya, you don't have to do this," Mad dog all but growls at her.

"But I will." Kaiya's reply is more confident than I was expecting. "The Gypsy Bastards have been nothing but good to me and if it hadn't been for Wolf walking into that farmhouse to rescue Hadley, I would still be bent over that fucking table."

"Give us five minutes and we can leave."

Not waiting for the men to respond, I take hold of Kaiya's hand and lead her toward Wolf's room. Turning my body slightly, I look directly at Viking.

"Can we have a moment with you before we head out?"

He nods and follows us up the stairs. He's the only person I can ask, the only person who will trust me to do this right. Getting to Brandon's room, I fling open all the drawers and hand a navy hoodie to Kaiya before taking a black one with the club logo on the back for myself. Brandon's hoodies are huge on both of us and hang mid-thigh.

Viking clears his throat while he stares at me. "Pretty girl, you know Wolf is going to shit himself about this, right?"

"Yeah, but he isn't here to stop me."

In the distance, I can hear the rumbling of motorcycles getting closer and assume that Pope has called for reinforcements.

"You're not going to stop me either. You're going to help me so we can all get home tonight."

Viking booms out a laugh. "And what do you need me to do?"

"I need a gun."

Facing him, I see the shock blanket his face before he can school his features. A laugh pours out of me. "You knew my dad. Do you honestly think I don't know how to handle a gun?"

Viking hands me the Beretta from his side holster. Checking the clip, I engage the safety and shove it into the back of my jeans. Turning around, I show my back to Viking. "Can you see it?"

"Not a thing, doll."

"Let's do this."

Grabbing Kaiya's hand again, we move out the door and downstairs. The guys have clearly already made their way outside and we move to follow. The moment we step over the threshold, I freeze. Before me stands Sway, the President of the Immortal Saints MC and behind him are at least fifty bikers, mounted to ride.

Sway stares at me before scooping me up into his arms. He holds me tightly to him before whispering into my ear. "Good God, girl, but you've grown. Haven't seen you since your father's funeral."

Putting me down, he holds me at arm's length while scanning me from top to bottom.

Wiping a tear from my eye, I smile at him. "You look exactly the same."

"I'll take that as a compliment." He winks in reply.

"Sway, Hadley. Didn't know you knew each other," Pope interrupts.

"Hadley is my goddaughter. Haven't seen her since her daddy's funeral. King and I had our falling out in those days and I haven't seen her since. But I sure am grateful for the opportunity to reconnect."

"Great stuff," Viking jumps in, "but can we please get this shit done and do happy reunions later?"

"Yes, yes, do we have a plan?"

Looking him straight in the eye, I lay out *my* plan before Pope can even begin to speak.

"Kaiya and I are going to be exchanged for Wolf

and Justice." Holding up my hand, I silence them before they can argue. "I have a plan and if we can all just work as one, we can all be back here later tonight enjoying a beer."

Gathering my resolve, I look around at all the shocked faces. Some of the men I know and some I don't, and few know me. Raising my voice, I run my gaze over the crowd of rough-and-tumble bikers gathered around us.

"My name is Hadley Freeman. My father was Phillip 'Juice' Freeman, VP to the Iron Disciples. Some of you knew him and those who didn't do know his reputation. I'm my father's daughter, and so help me God, I will do this with or without you."

Looking back at Pope, I see the surprise on his face, but he nods his accent with something akin to admiration before he heads to a black van and gets in the driver's side with Mad Dog beside him. Silently, Kaiya and I climb in the back before Sway closes the door with a wink and a look of pride in his eyes.

"Let's do this," Pope says as he starts up the van.

Chapter Twenty-Six
Wolf

My head hurts like a bitch, but at least I'm alive and awake. Beside me on the ground lies Justice, but he's barely awake and I know he's lost too much blood. Concern for his health courses through my veins. We're back at their dirty-ass clubhouse. Behind us stands a beat-up tan van with its lights on full blast, pointing in the direction we're facing. Our shadows are elongated on the ground before us. The crunch of tires on gravel is clear and coming closer toward us. If Pope is dumb enough to bring my woman to this meet, I'll kill him with my own bare hands.

The black van we often use for transport pulls to a stop about fifty feet from us. Pope exits from the driver's side with a nod in my direction. Mad Dog exits from the passenger side but doesn't look at me. That seals it for me, they brought the women. My heart pounds so hard in my chest that I'm sure Viper can hear it from his spot beside me.

The only light in the area is supplied by the two vans now pointed toward one another. My heart sinks and my stomach rolls as Hadley and Kaiya step from the van. They slowly make their way around the van toward Pope before Hadley lifts her eyes to mine.

There's a look of determination in her eyes that I wasn't expecting. There's no fear or hesitation, only determination. Wishing I knew what was going through her mind at this moment, I say a small prayer to a god I long since stopped believing in to keep her safe.

Pope made the mistake of showing up without any backup. He trusted that the Mongrels would actually honor the agreement, but I know they haven't. In between the trees surrounding us are at least twenty men armed to the teeth. Having no idea on how to alert Pope and Mad Dog to the situation, I remain silent, biding my time.

"Send those bitches over," Viper yells to Pope.

"Not a chance, you fucker. We do it at the same time." Pope stares down Viper and Mutt.

"Fine." Viper nudges at my shoulder, propelling me forward.

Helping Justice to his feet, I support his weight as we move down the gravel driveway. Hadley hugs Pope before moving toward me. There's no jealousy as I witness their hug because my ass is too confused by the look on the face of my president. Kaiya moves over to Mad Dog and he cups her face before kissing her. A moment later, they break apart and he leans his forehead to hers, talking to her in a hushed tone. Behind me, I hear Viper growl.

"Get your hands off my sister, you fucker!"

Mad Dog simply smirks at him as he smacks Kaiya on her ass and sends her on her way. Kaiya and Hadley link hands and make their way toward Justice and me. Hadley turns to Kaiya, hugging her before Kaiya moves past me toward Viper. Justice pushes my hand from his waist.

"Talk to her," he says before hobbling his way forward.

Before I can speak or react, Hadley throws her arms around my neck and kisses me. My hand circles her waist to hold her to me. She has a gun in the waistband of her jeans. Feasting on her, I remove it slowly so as not to alert Viper or his men.

Hadley smiles at me as she pulls away. "I love you and you can show me the house tomorrow." She pulls away and moves past me, twining her hand with

Kaiya's again as they continue to make their way toward Viper. As I watch them slowly walk away, something in the dark catches my eye. Just out of sight, beneath the dark cover of trees, Sparrow slits the throat of the man who was stationed there.

With eyes that I know are round with surprise, I look back toward Pope and he nods at me. He has a goofy grin spread on his face for a moment as tense as this. Taking the nod to mean that the men have all been taken care of, I flip the safety off the gun I took from Hadley and turn around. Pointing directly at Viper, I'm lucky enough to see the moment Sparrow creeps up and slits Mutt's throat before stepping back with a smile. Viper raises his hands in the air as he realizes he's alone. Hadley and Kaiya are about ten steps away from me and still holding hands. Slowly, I move toward them.

"Do something, Kaiya!" Viper tries to move toward her but likely thinks better when he sees Mad Dog move in beside her.

Kaiya shakes her head as she moves toward him. She has steel in her spine and we all watch her closely. Stopping in front of Viper, her brother, her only living relative, she squares her shoulders.

"No," she practically spits in his face before hitting him with a right hook any man would be proud of.

"This is for me. And every other woman you have ever abused. This is for Hadley and everything that you put her through. This is for letting your club beat me and rape me and take things from me that I will never get back."

Mad Dog wraps an arm around her shoulder as he leads her back toward us. Viper curses up a storm behind them but Kaiya is smiling even as tears track down her face. Reaching Hadley, they hug each other for a long moment before parting.

Kaiya tilts her head back to look me in the eye. "I don't give a fuck what you do with him, but I want this over."

Hadley smiles at me and nods. Kaiya waits for my response and I don't have words, so instead, I simply nod. Viper starts begging and trying to strike a bargain as soon as my long legs stride in his direction.

And there beneath the stars on a cloudless spring night, I use the gun my woman brought when she came to save my dumb ass to put a bullet between Viper's eyes. No one flinches. There are no regrets. There's just us.

Chapter Twenty-Seven
Hadley

Sitting on Brandon's lap in his ugly green chair in the clubhouse, I have rarely been this happy. Everyone is here and safe and although some of the Immortal Saints preferred to return home, Sway has opted to stay a while and reconnect with me. Everyone's in a good mood, enjoying a couple of drinks and just shooting the shit. Cherry has come out from Dusk and is dancing for the guys and even that isn't enough to ruin my good mood. The one thing no one can miss is the way Kaiya and Mad Dog keep glancing at each other. I hope it won't take too long for them to get their shit together.

Turning in Brandon's lap, I straddle him.

"So ... how does it feel to be saved by a girl?"

A swift slap lands on my ass before he answers me. "Very grateful, but if anything had gone wrong, I would have been pissed."

"Nothing could have gone wrong. I had the best guys in the world supporting me."

My plan worked perfectly. All the guys made their way by foot about a half-mile from the farm. We had Kaiya, after all, and she knew the property and all of her brother's dirty tricks. We sat in the van and waited patiently for ten minutes before we made our way up the gravel drive, giving the other guys the opportunity to get into place. We were never in any real danger and the plan worked perfectly. And finally, we are rid of those assholes.

"Did Pope tell you yet?" Brandon frowns as he asks the question.

With my index finger, I lightly rub at the frown line between his eyes. "Tell me what?"

"The cuts on the guys who were helping Viper belong to the Iron Disciples."

He watches me closely for a reaction. This cannot be good. Not for me or for the Gypsy Bastards.

"That means that shit is going to get bad around here eventually. So I want you to move in with me."

"So." The silence between us stretches before he looks at me. "Do you want me to live with you because you want me there or because you're trying to keep me safe?"

"Jesus, woman! Both reasons."

Clearly, I've exasperated him.

"I fucking love you and that means I want to keep you safe. So yeah, both reasons."

Spearing my hands into his hair, I crush my lips against his in a bruising kiss. After a catcall goes up behind us somewhere, I pull away. "Perfect answer."

"Thank God." Relief fills his features as he grips my ass and stands. Wrapping my legs around his waist, I wait for him to tell me where he's taking me. There must be a questioning look on my face because he leans in to whisper in my ear.

"I just told you I love you and you agreed to move in with me. I'm going to fuck you against every surface in my room."

Smiling, I think to myself, that's just fine by me.

Epilogue
Hadley

Three months later

Pulling my dad's car into the driveway, I look up at our home. Life is good. During the day, I run my tattoo parlor, which has been open for the last month. Business is booming and my appointments are filled up two weeks in advance. It helps that all the Gypsy Bastards have gotten something inked there recently. I even had to hire some help at the shop since it's started getting so busy.

For three months, I've been living with Brandon at his house. Knowing when I walk down the hall, or use the kitchen, or sit on the back porch that he bought this house for Amber and Rose. He finally told me about them. But I don't feel like second best. I feel like a queen.

Amber was his first love and will always be that. I don't want to take her place. Rose will always be his daughter and I would never try to replace her. But me? I'm different. I'm his first chance at happiness after losing his entire world and I feel honored. Wanting to make him happy, I try to do that through cherishing both of their memories. Standing out on the deck, having a cup of tea and watching the sunset, I feel lucky to have this opportunity. To start this life with him. Feeling his hands on my hips, I turn and smile at him. "Hey, babe. How was your day?"

"Great, actually. Finished the paint job on Mad Dog's bike. Just missed you."

The love shining from his eyes fills me with hope. Hope that we'll be able to have a long and happy life together. Hope that no matter what happens, we'll face it together.

"You?"

"Well, actually, you might want to sit down so we can talk."

Moving out of his grasp, I take a seat at the table we put on the deck just last week. My hands are knotted in my lap and sweatier than I ever remember them being. Brandon frowns at me but leans back against the railing.

"I think I'll stand. Don't know what this is about, but I have a feeling I might need to leave." His eyes have gone dark and that damn frown line is back between his eyes. With the sun setting behind him, he frowns down at me and that only makes me more nervous.

"I was hoping we could talk this through like adults. But you haven't even heard what I have to say and you're already on the defensive?" Instantly, my anger spikes.

Lowering my head, I feel tears well up in my eyes. I knew this was going to be hard, but I was really hoping for some sort of miracle.

"Well, I know how this conversation goes. It's not you, it's me … yada, yada, yada. But let me make one thing perfectly clear. If I don't make you as happy as you make me, that's fine. But if you think for one second that I'll let you move on with one of my brothers, think again. I'll kill him." His tone is deathly low.

My head snaps back as tears course down my cheeks. "What?"

It doesn't come out as a question but a squeak.

"Are you insane?" I ask.

He stares at me blankly. There's no movement, no reply.

"Maybe I should fucking move out!" My temper spikes instantly, again. Standing from the table, hands on my hips, fuming at him, I watch as confusion spreads over his face.

"You're an asshole, Wolf! I'm trying to do this the nice way because I'm afraid you're going to freak out and run and your first instinct is that I'm fucking around?"

"Wait…"

"Don't fucking *wait* me, you goddamned prick. I'm trying tell you that I'm fucking pregnant and you think I'm cheating?" My voice has gone high-pitched and my ears are ringing. A hiccup escapes through the tears and the screaming. Finally, enough is enough and the toll this day has taken on me becomes too much. My legs give out.

Before I land on the floor, he has me in his arms and is lifting me against his chest. Pushing against his chest, I try to get him to put me down.

"Jesus. Babe, I didn't know."

Regret is rife in his tone, but I am way too pissed to care about that at this moment. "Of course, you didn't know, you dickhead. You didn't let me tell you."

Brandon carries me through the house and up the stairs to lay me down on the bed in our room. The moment I roll over and try to get away, he turns me onto my back and pins my hands above my head. Usually, this move would inspire many things in me but at this moment, all I feel is rage. Trying to buck him off me, I yell. "Get the fuck off me. Now!"

"Not until you listen to me."

"Like you listened to me?"

Both of us stare at each other, breathing heavily. For a moment, neither of us speak, but the fight leaves me as fast as it started.

"Babe, I'm not going to run. Christ. This might be the best thing I've heard since the day you told me you love me." His right hand moves down my body to rest on my still-flat stomach. My insides flutter at the gesture.

"I don't think you're cheating. But it's my greatest fear. Knowing I'm not good enough for you, and that you could do better. I know I should probably let you go, but I'm a selfish bastard and I won't be doing that."

Looking him straight in the eyes, I wait. I want to make sure his full attention is on me. "I love you. You're the best man I know. You're the best man for me. You're the only man for me."

"I love you too, babe. I'm going to do my best to prove that to you every single day. I'm so sorry I fucked up your announcement, but I will love this baby with all my heart. I can't imagine my life without you."

"You won't ever have to."

The End

Gypsy Bastards MC—The Wolf Playlist

Three Days Grace - "I Hate Everything About You"

Pop Evil - "Monster You Made Me"

Seether - "Fuck me like you hate me"

Charlie Daniels Band - "The Devil Went Down to Georgia"

Evanessence - "Bring Me Back to Life"

Scorpions - "Rock You Like A Hurricane"

Shania Twain - "Black Eyes, Blue Tears"

Judas Priest - "Private Property"

Marilyn Manson - "Sweet Dreams"

7 Kings - "Born For This"

Bishop Briggs - "Dark Side"

Thutmase + Nombe - "Run Wild"

Pink - "Happy"

In Flames - "Not Alone"

Meatloaf - "Rock and Roll Dreams Come Through"

Bad Wolves - "Zombie"

3 Doors Down - "Duck and Run"

Death Cab For Cutie - "I Will Follow You Into the Dark"

Five Finger Death Punch - "I Refuse"

Red Jumpsuit Apparatus - "Your Guardian Angel"

ACKNOWLEDGEMENTS

I would like to thank the following:

First, My mother for instilling a love of reading from a young age. The same love that I am currently trying to instill in my daughter. Thank you for allowing me to read whatever I wanted no matter what. Thank you for giving me books and music instead of making me play outside. You are the best.

My husband, who often gets ignored when I am reading or writing and whom I drive insane with references he knows nothing about. Thank you for letting me do my own thing and never letting me quit. Love you tons. J4Z143TDDUP

My girls, my beta readers, of whom there aren't many as I didn't tell a lot of people I was doing this. Caroline Gerber, Christel Paxton, Jessica Kuhn, Marsha Botes, Celia Botes, and Surita van der Merwe. Thank you for having infinite patience with me, reading this book more times than is probably necessary, fixing my spelling, and generally just being there. Thank you for listening and allowing me to bounce ideas off you all. But mostly thank you for making me believe I could do this when I didn't and suffering through my special brand of insanity.

A special thank you to my daughter for making sure the dogs got fed and I remembered to feed her and her dad. Also for the copious amount of coffee and cold drink that she kept me supplied with. You are more awesome than I will ever be able to put into words. I love you to the end of time.

For all the strong men in my life. You have shown me what a hero should be based on. Just because you're a badass doesn't mean you have to be an asshole. Jacques Visagie, for always championing me and everyone else, always pushing me to dream and to never set my bar too low. You are missed always.

Thank you to everyone at Evernight Publishing for taking a chance on me. Thank you to Audrey for editing this book with me and showing me better ways to get my point across. A special thank you to Stacey for answering all my questions and putting my fears at ease.

To each and every person who has liked a Facebook or Instagram post, has listened to me rant, or just smiled at my crazy, thank you for the bottom of my heart. I haven't mentioned you all by name but each and every bit of support is felt and appreciated.

DEDICATION FOR *THE POPE*

To the boy who made my first kiss memorable
To the young man who made my first love something
that I will never regret
To the man who won my heart and completes me every
day
143TDDUP

GYPSY BASTARDS MC: VOLUME ONE

THE POPE

Gypsy Bastards MC, 2

Jade Marshall

Copyright © 2020

≺•••◆•••≻

Prologue
Storm

Growing up in foster care, I have very few memories I can look back at and remember fondly. Except for Colin and Faye. The one constant through my youth was them. Living in the house beside theirs, my older sister, Winter, and I would often end up at their house. Faye, Colin's mom, took us under her wing and treated us like the daughters she never had. Everything I know about being a woman, from boiling an egg to how babies are made, and even how my menstrual cycle works, I was taught by Faye.

Winter and Colin, being five years older than me, quickly fell into a fledgling relationship and were inseparable. I spent a lot of time playing the third wheel or reading. But things change as you grow and by my thirteenth birthday, I realized I was in love with Colin. The problem with being in love with your sister's boyfriend is the accompanying guilt. I started avoiding both of them, hiding in my room when it was possible and trying to make friends of my own. Being on my own for the first time was exhilarating, and I made many, many mistakes along the way. Let it be known far and wide that I can own up to my mistakes.

Mistake one: Falling for my sister's guy.

Mistake two: Making friends of my own.

Even at the tender age of thirteen, I got into more trouble than most people do in a lifetime. From things like petty theft and smoking weed to getting arrested for breaking and entering and getting blackout drunk. My youth was spent in a drug and alcohol-induced stupor, running from my own emotions. The consequences reverberate through me to this day.

At sixteen, I left the only home and family I'd ever known after finally declaring my love for Colin and being gently rejected. In the last ten years, I have not seen nor spoken to my sister. I spent months living on the street and struggling to survive, and even after all this time, I still love Colin.

The only difference is now we call him Pope.

Chapter One
Storm

"Who do you think of when you masturbate?"

I turn my head so quickly in my friend Hadley's direction I can feel my vertebrae crack. We are sitting outside the Gypsy Bastards clubhouse in the early-morning sunshine, at one of the picnic tables beneath an oak tree, enjoying the last remnants of summer. On my rare days off, I try to spend as much time with my best friend as possible, but at this moment, I seriously have to question my judgment.

She truly is a beautiful woman and has only become more so during the progression of her pregnancy. It's like her blonde hair shines and her blue eyes sparkle more the further she gets along. Although she looks super-cute in the baby-pink maternity dress she's wearing today, her stomach is huge. Across from me, she rests her left hand on her swollen stomach while the other holds a bar of chocolate.

"Jesus, Hadley. What kind of question is that?" I ask.

She furrows her brow at me before taking a bite of her chocolate. After swallowing, she sighs before returning her attention to me.

"When I was single, I used to think about me when I flicked the bean. What the hands touching me made me feel, or the mouth on my body would feel like for me. Me and a nameless, faceless person. But now that I have Wolf in my life, I think about him, words he would say, his voice in my ear, stuff like that. I was just wondering if it was the same for other women. I'm not friends with anyone besides you, Kaiya, and Luna, so I picked you to ask. So, who do you think about?"

My mouth hangs open at her explanation. Since Hadley and Wolf have fallen sickeningly in love and she became pregnant, every thought in her mind seems to pop out of her mouth.

But to be honest, the moment she asked the question, I knew the answer. Red hair, green eyes, and an Irish lilt run through my mind on a constant loop. Colin. Pope.

Fucking president to the Gypsy Bastards MC and the only man to ever hold my heart. He is also the only man to ever break my heart. Fucking Pope.

Looking back at Hadley, I find she's still waiting patiently for my answer.

"Okay. Because you're pregnant, I'm going to humor you, but don't make a habit of asking me sexual shit. I don't need to know the details of your sex life with Wolf." Waiting, I stare directly at her until she nods her head in acceptance.

"Mostly, hot famous guys. Maybe a musician or even just some hot guy I see when getting coffee or something. It differs from time to time, depending on my mood."

"So none of the guys around here?" She arches her eyebrow at me.

"What do you want from me, Hadley? You know the guys are all gorgeous, but there is nothing that could persuade me to get together with any of them."

The lie flows from my lips without much effort. What I feel for Pope is in the past and he already broke my heart once. I won't create an opportunity for it to happen again.

"Fine, I'll leave it alone. But let me tell you, anyone with eyes can see that the two of you want each other."

My forehead creases as I glare at her. Hadley lifts

her hands in a gesture of surrender before she bursts out laughing.

"Okay, let's talk about something else. Have you picked a name for the baby yet?"

"Well, since we found it it's a girl, it made it somewhat easier to decide on a name." She smiles as she rubs her hand over her swollen stomach.

"So? The suspense is killing me here."

"Ainsley. Our daughter's name will be Ainsley." Hadley's eyes sparkle with unshed tears which in turn causes me to tear up with her.

"It's beautiful, Hadley."

"Thanks." Abruptly, she rises from her spot before moving toward the clubhouse. After a few steps, she looks back over her shoulder. "Are you coming? I'm craving some pancakes."

Nodding, I rise and follow her inside.

Chapter Two
Pope

Having coffee at the kitchen table in the clubhouse, I watch as Storm and Hadley start whipping up a batch of pancakes. Delicious aromas waft around the kitchen and infuse the clubhouse with a feeling of home. It might not be that for many people, but to me, the Gypsy Bastard clubhouse is home. A long time ago, just after we bought the property and the building, I had a contractor come and renovate the upper floor, creating rooms and a communal bathroom for the guys. But I had the loft renovated into more of an apartment space for myself. The guys and club ass refer to it as the president's quarters and no one is allowed in my space, I don't even fuck women up there. I sank every cent I had into this place and I haven't regretted it one single day.

In front of me, I watch the women cook. The last space we renovated, and this was only last year, was the kitchen. All new cupboards, counters, and even new appliances and crockery. One of the guys who used to hang around the club was a carpenter, so we got everything at a steal.

Laughter tinkles from Storm and even though I try my hardest not to, my gaze travels to her. I wonder what Beast said to elicit that sound from her. Standing there, her black hair with purple streaks, her almond eyes sparkling with mirth, her hand lands on his chest as she continues to laugh at whatever he said. My gaze is glued to her hand as my jealousy spikes. Shaking my head, I look back toward the newspaper I was reading. Beast has no interest in Storm and even if he did, I couldn't do a thing about it.

I gave up my opportunity to do that years ago.

A stack of blueberry pancakes is placed in front of me. Looking up, I smile at Storm.

"Thanks, sweets."

She winks at me before she turns and walks away. My gaze is instantly locked on the curve of her ass and the way her hips sway as she walks back toward Hadley. My thoughts drift and I find myself fantasizing about grabbing her by the ass and lifting her into the air.

"Pope?"

Storm stares at me from the other side of the table.

"Shit, sorry. I have a lot on my mind. What were you saying?" I need to get my mind out of the gutter and focus on the conversations around me.

"I want to know if Hadley and I can borrow Justice for a while. We want to get the crib I bought and set it up at Wolf's house, but we need someone to carry it up the stairs. Probably won't be more than an hour."

I look toward Wolf, who nods his agreement. Even though he was overly jealous of the friendship between Hadley and Justice in the beginning, he soon figured out they are more like siblings and constantly give each other hell. It helps that Justice would probably die to protect the woman who belongs to my sergeant at arms.

"Yeah, that shouldn't be a problem. Wolf has to get down to the shop to see a new customer and Sparrow is on his way to Dusk. Everyone else is busy and I have a meeting, so use the prospect for whatever you need, but have him back by noon. He needs to clean out and stock the bar before the party tonight."

Dusk is the strip club where Storm works. The Gypsy Bastards also owns a percentage of it and Sparrow does the books. Wolf owns a legitimate business doing custom work on motorcycles, of which the club also owns a percentage and recently, the club helped Hadley start her tattoo parlor, which means we get a cut from that as well.

Storm nods at me and then rises to rinse her plate and load the dishwasher before walking out of the room to presumably talk to Justice about their plans. Everyone around me continues to talk and finish their meal before heading out.

****

My meeting with McLaughlin goes well. They are completely satisfied with the last shipment of AR15s they received. Throughout the years, we have built up quite the name for ourselves. Although we try as a club to keep most of our businesses legitimate—the strip club, custom bike shop, and tattoo shop—we weren't making enough money. An opportunity presented itself to us and we jumped at the chance. We now run guns across the border for the Mexican cartel and have quite the network of people—not always good people—who are very happy to buy their hardware from us. From the Italian mafia to the Irish mob, we sell indiscriminately as long as the cash is right, and McLaughlin and the Irish mob have the right money.

Riding down the freeway from my meeting, I head toward Wolf and Hadley's place, hoping to spend some time around Storm. Although I pushed her away years ago out of a sense of loyalty to her sister Winter, it has become one of the greatest regrets of my life. I constantly keep her at arm's length because I don't want to hurt her again. The last time almost killed her and if I let her in, this time might kill me.

Storm ran away from home, ran away from me, and from the little she has told me about that time, I know it wasn't good. She lived on the street for a while and even though I don't know all the details, I do know something bad happened. Something bad enough that she has taken self-defense classes for years to ensure she's never in that position again.

And then there are the drugs. When she first came back into my life, it was with less of a strut and more of a stumble. She was hooked on heroin and in a bad place when I saw her at Dusk. Luckily, with some help from Doc, she went through rehab and detox and has been clean for about four years. Thinking back on those dark days breaks my heart, knowing what she went through. Fearing she may relapse and end up killing herself this time keeps me from baring my feelings to her.

That doesn't stop me from wanting her, though, and the longer she's around, the more my feelings for her grow. I thought about going up to Kilkenny in Ireland to visit my mom for a while and get my head back on straight, but with everything going on, there isn't a chance for me to get away. Instead, I sulk around and keep a watch on her, trying to remain sane. There's no way to explain the pain in my chest when other men look at her or she gives one of my brothers attention. The hardest part is going to Dusk and watching her dance. Don't get me wrong, she is a goddamned goddess on stage, but every time, I just want to jump up on stage and carry her away from all the other gazes locked on her body.

Deep in thought, I almost miss my turn and have to correct quickly. The car behind me honks loudly but I don't have an opportunity to change course before I feel the car clip my rear wheel. An image of Storm smiling flashes in my mind as my Harley swerves but at the last second, I regain control and keep her upright. My adrenaline spikes and I thank all that is holy that I didn't wreck. For the rest of the drive, my attention is focused on getting there safely.

A near-death experience is exactly what I needed to get my ass in gear. No more running. No more pushing her away. It's time to claim the woman I have always wanted but have been too afraid to go after.

Parking my Harley beside the curb, I wave back at a blond-haired kid down the street. The suburbs make me itch and feel out of my depth, and I very rarely come here, but this where Storm is and I need to see her right now. Reaffirm that I'm still alive and start the long road to fixing everything I've fucked up between us. Striding with purpose, I push open the front door without knocking and move through the house, entering the kitchen just in time to watch Storm crumble to the floor.

Chapter Three
Storm

You always think there will be time. Time to apologize, to make things right, or to say sorry. But that isn't always the truth. Sometimes, your time runs out before you are ready. And you lose the chance to fix things.

My phone clatters to the floor as Hadley screams, but she sounds so far away. Like my head is underwater and I can't hear properly. Hands cup my face and tilt it up to look into bright-green eyes. The concern is etched on Pope's face.

How did I end up on the floor? Where is my phone? And then it hits me like a ton of bricks. My sister is dead.

My sister died.

My sister, who I haven't spoken to in ten years, the only family I had, has left me alone in this world.

My body is no longer under my control as a gut-wrenching, soul-shattering scream is torn free from my lungs and tears stream down my face. My body is wracked with tremors as I sob uncontrollably. Panic consumes me and although I can hear Pope speaking to me, there is no way to hear him above the shattering of my own heart or the unstoppable sobbing. My chest feels like an anvil is pressing down on it and I can't seem to catch my breath. As the world goes dark around me, I see the panic clearly in Pope's eyes and it breaks my heart just a little bit more.

****

I wake up with a start and bolt upright. Looking around, I'm unable to recognize the room or bed I am in. The walls are painted a dove gray and the bedding is the same color. Color accents in differing shades of red are scattered around the room. Rising from the bed, I look around. In the corner is a burgundy reading chair and a bookshelf most people would be jealous of, stacked with all the greatest horror and thriller writers. Black curtains hide a window from view but as I draw them back, I can see the parking lot for the Gypsy Bastard compound.

In the back of my mind, a thought niggles, something important, something I need to remember. Yet, every time I try to grab on to the thought, my mind pushes it away, trying to protect me from something I instinctively know will be painful. Instead of trying harder to remember, I leave the room. As I walk into the lounge area, I know exactly where I am. The presidential quarters, where no woman or man, besides Pope, is ever allowed. Turning in a circle, I take in my surrounding with a new perspective.

As I turn again, a blown-up photo catches my eye. In the middle of the living room wall, where any other man would usually have a big-ass flat-screen TV, Pope has a blown-up canvas of a photo I took on a run. All the guys are together, some of the wives and girlfriends as well, having a beer. Tears prick my eyes as I stare at it, remembering what a great day that was.

He has large chocolate-brown couches set about the room with an open plan to it. The kitchen is off to my left with beautiful black granite counters. The thought strikes me that his place is a lot cleaner and tidier than I would have expected for a guy living alone.

"You're awake."

Spinning around with my hand clutched to my chest, I stare at Pope.

"Jesus, make a fucking noise or something. You nearly scared me to death." The accusation flies from my lips.

Pope looks pained. "You did scare me to death." He holds my gaze, and the torment in his eyes helps the memory my mind was fleeing from to come back instantly.

My sister is dead. Tears start streaming down my cheeks again as I stumble backward. Pope rushes toward me, wrapping me in his embrace. I bury my face against his chest and sob.

"She died and I never got the chance to make things right between us."

Pope soothingly runs his hand up and down my back, trying to comfort me. He leads us toward the couch in his living room before taking a seat and pulling me into his lap. He doesn't ask questions, simply holds me and lets me cry.

Sometime later after the tears have subsided and I have calmed down, I take a deep breath. Knowing me well enough, Pope reads this as his opening to ask me questions.

"Love, who died? What's going on? You are freaking me the fuck out. I have no idea how to fix any of this and seeing you this way is driving me insane."

Scanning his face, I see the worry and frustration. He has never been the type of person to just let something go. When Pope cares for you, he cares for life.

"Winter."

The word leaves me on a whisper. My voice won't cooperate, no matter how much I want it to.

"Winter died. Her lawyer called me to assist in the final arrangements. I don't know anything other than she died."

"Oh, love." The emotion in his voice fills me with an ache for more than we can ever be. "I'm sorry that you're going through this. You know that we are all here for you, me and the guys, and if you need anything, you only have to shout."

"I need my phone. I need to call him back and find out what's going on. There's so much to do and I have to get started."

Pope reaches into the inner pocket of his cut and hands me my phone. "Let me get you something to eat while you call him. Give you some privacy."

His voice is pleading, as if me eating is something really important to him. Even though I'm not hungry in the slightest, I nod and move off his lap. I pull up the last number in my call log and dial.

"Murphy," a gruff voice answers.

"Hi, this is Storm Lin. We spoke earlier in regards to my sister, Winter."

"Yes, Miss Lin. Again, I am sorry to be the bearer of bad news. But we need to discuss the arrangements."

"Okay. But I have some questions before we move on."

"Shoot. I will answer anything I have the information for." His reply puts me at ease, but I only have one question.

"What happened?" The words sound weird but it's hard talking while you are trying to keep a fresh batch of tears at bay.

"Yes, you are unaware of everything. Let me start by saying that I had known Winter for the last eight years, and I was well aware of the fact that the two of you were not on speaking terms. That said, she did put you in charge of her last arrangements. There is a will that will be read after the service as there are two other parties included." Mr. Murphy takes a deep breath before continuing. "Winter got sick two years ago. Breast cancer. She started to make all the arrangements but didn't want to contact and bother you. Although she went through all the therapy and had the heart to fight a war, she didn't win the battle."

Tears stream down my face and a hiccup escapes me.

"Let me get your email address, and I will email you all the information. If you could get down here by tomorrow or the day after, I will be able to assist you with all the arrangements."

A moment of silence passes between us while I regain my composure.

"Where is here, Mr. Murphy?"

"Louisiana."

From: amurphy@murphyattorneys.com
To: storm.lin@yahoo.com
Re: The last letter of instruction
To whom it may concern

I, Winter Lin, being of sound mind leave the following directives in the case of my death. Please contact my sister, Storm Lin, in the case of my demise. I request that she is the person to handle all my affairs. Including my funeral, estate, and any other matters that may arise.

If she is unable or unwilling to accept the responsibility please contact Irene Willis. She is a dear friend and will be willing to perform the task if necessary.

This is not my last will and testament, which will be read after my funeral.

I would like to be buried in Baton Rouge, Louisiana, where I have been living for the past eight years.

Thank you,
Winter Lin

Chapter Four
Pope

This is fucking horrible. I spent about six years in my youth in a relationship with Winter. And I know I should feel something akin to loss at this moment, but all I feel is the worry. Worry about Storm. She won't eat anything and she wants to leave tonight. The drive to Baton Rouge is over five hundred miles and I won't let her go alone, but I can't go with her and I don't have anyone I can spare. We have the gun run for McLaughlin tomorrow morning, and it's something we can't miss.

Following behind her as she heads downstairs, I try to reason with her.

"Please, let me do the run tomorrow and then we can leave tomorrow night. You can't drive all the way alone. Not with the way you're looking right now."

She turns on her heel so fast I almost run into her. Hands on her hips and fire in her eyes, it's the first sign of my Storm I've seen since she got the news.

"And what exactly do I look like, Colin?"

All the eyes in the clubhouse turn to us. No one calls me by my given name except my mother and although I love the way it sounds coming from her lips, now isn't the time for her to be sassing me.

"Relax, love. I didn't mean anything by it. Just that you are emotional and haven't eaten anything yet. You driving all that way by yourself is dangerous."

She huffs at me and walks away again, making me follow her like a lost puppy. Abruptly, she stops and turns toward me.

"She was my sister and I will honor her last wishes. I will be heading to Baton Rouge as soon as I get a fucking car and there is not a damn thing you can do to stop me, so stop trying. All you're doing is pissing me off."

When she turns away from me again, I grab her arm and pull her back. She glares down at my hand, steps into my personal space, and stares up into my eyes.

"You are not my boyfriend, father, or even family. You aren't my president, you aren't even my boss. I left her. I didn't fix it between us. This is my last chance to make amends. I left you both ten years ago and don't for a second think because we are friends again that I need you. I will leave you behind me so fast you'll wonder if I was ever here."

Her voice is loud enough to carry clear across the clubhouse and I release her as if touching her burns my skin. Every word she said hit me like an arrow, none of them missing their mark on my heart. Behind me, I hear a woman gasp but don't turn to see who it is. My temper spikes and the urge to hurt her with my words starts to overwhelm me. Before I can spew one word of poison in her direction, a small hand lands on my shoulder. Turning, I see Kaiya beside me.

"Mad Dog took me for my license last week. I'll go with her. I can drive."

Her gaze darts to Storm, who nods.

"You have five minutes to pack and then we'll leave. Give me your car keys and I'll wait outside."

Storm takes the keys from Kaiya and heads outside without saying another word as Kaiya heads to her room to gather her shit, Mad Dog following behind her. I'm bristling and boiling with the need to inflict damage. My ego is bruised and my heart is torn to shreds. Turning, I head to the bar counter, deciding to drink instead of doing or saying something I might regret later.

"Whiskey. Just give me the bottle," I order

Justice.

He doesn't argue or ask me any questions. He simply reaches beneath the bar and hands me a bottle.

****

When I wake, I find myself on Wolf's couch with a hangover from hell. I'm lying on a tan suede sectional with a large flat-screen mounted to the wall. The only light in the room comes from a floor-standing lamp at my feet. My shoes and socks have been removed and a comforter was thrown over me. Sitting up, I cup my face in my hands when I hear clothing rustle. Looking up, I spot Hadley curled up on a comfy-looking chair reading a book.

"You didn't have to watch me."

"Really?" She arches a brow at me. "Someone had to do it. Besides, last night, you declared me the only decent female on the planet beside your mother. You said that all women are succubi that want to rip men's hearts from their chests and wither their souls. You're quite poetic when you're drunk out of your gourd."

She tries to hide her smile as she says all of this.

"Damn, how much did I drink?" My skull throbs.

"About two bottles of whiskey and a ton of tequila shots. There are water and aspirin beside you for the hangover."

"Dear Lord. Thank you for being an understanding woman." My eyes are cast toward the ceiling as I mutter the words, "What happened last night?"

"Well, except for the drinking?" A laugh tinkles from her. "Not much. You played pool, arm-wrestled Viking because he said you had scrawny arms, and made me stop at the twenty-four-hour diner for greasy cheeseburgers on the way home. Which we both enjoyed immensely. Apparently, your drunk cravings and my pregnancy cravings are the same."

Shaking my head, I laugh before gripping both sides of my throbbing skull.

"What time is it?"

"Just after four. This young lady is trying to kick her way out of me so I decided to read a book instead of keeping Wolf awake. But—" She hesitates while looking at me.

"Speak your mind, Hadley. You're going to do it either way."

"You know she didn't mean it. The moment those words came out of her mouth. You know her better than I do and even I know she regrets it. It's the grief. She had to inflict pain to try to lessen hers."

Her face is stoic, giving away no emotion. This woman has adapted so well to us, knowing if she shows me any pity, I will shut down and the conversation will be over.

"You're right, and I know you're right. But that doesn't take the sting away or soothe my bruised ego. Maybe when she gets back, I'll be over it. I sure hope so." Looking away, I grab the aspirin and water and swallow them down.

"So, we had an amazing conversation last night."

Looking at her again, I can see her trying to hide a smirk. Dear Lord, what did I say?

With the biggest smile I've ever seen on her face, she drops a bomb on me.

"Are you still going to tell her that you've been in love with her since you were a kid?"

Chapter Five
Storm

Driving with Kaiya is an interesting experience. She doesn't talk or ask questions or pry at all. She does, however, sing along to every country song that plays. I never would have figured her to be a lover of country music, but she knows all the songs by heart.

About two hours into our eight-hour drive, she pulls up to a gas station. Kaiya gets out of the car, fills up the gas tank, and proceeds into the store. We haven't spoken one word.

When she gets back in the car, she puts two full bags in my lap before driving away.

"And this?"

"Can't have a road trip without munchies." She smiles at me quickly then turns her attention back to the road. "I know this is not a road trip and it's a sad time for you, but it's my first time out of the state. I've never driven further than from the grocery store close to the clubhouse and I always have Mad Dog in the car with me watching everything I do."

"Oh, Kaiya, I keep forgetting that you are experiencing a bunch of firsts with us. I never even thought about it that way."

She waves her hand in the air in a dismissive gesture. "Don't even worry about it. But I do have an idea?"

"Okay." I don't know whether I have to be wary of what she is about to say or not.

"You're sad and that makes sense from what little I heard back at the club. Sorry. But we could take your mind off of it. I mean, let's pretend, just for a little while before we reach Baton Rouge and everything gets dark and sad again, that we are just two girlfriends driving across state lines for a road trip?"

"You know what, Kaiya, I think that's an amazing idea!"

For the first time since I got the news, I feel something other than utter despair.

"What kind of snacks did you get?" I ask while rummaging through the bags.

****

The rest of our drive is spent talking about nonsense. What kind of snacks are our favorites, what kind of music we like and hate and even movies and TV series we like. Kaiya and I have a lot more in common than I initially thought we would. After jumping on my phone and ignoring my messages, I search for a breakfast place in Baton Rouge. We watch the sunrise over the Red River while sitting on the hood of her car, eating a greasy breakfast burger we picked up along the way.

Looking out over the water, I steel myself for what is to come today. After finishing our breakfast, we book into a motel and grab a quick shower before heading out to see Mr. Murphy.

My first impression of him is mixed. He's an older gentleman who has a look that might have had the ladies falling over him in his youth. Dark hair and bright-blue eyes, a chiseled jaw, and a good physique for someone I'm assuming is in his late forties or early fifties. Although he looks attractive enough, he has a way about him that gives him an unapproachable air.

"Miss Lin. Sorry to meet under these circumstances." He shakes my hand firmly. "Let us get down to it."

He isn't one for idle chitchat and works through everything quite quickly. We meet the funeral director, pick out a coffin, and even get all the arrangements set for the wake. The funeral will take place the day after tomorrow and her testament will be read later that evening.

****

The funeral is a beautiful gathering. A lot of people are there to pay their last respects and most of them are friendly and supportive. One woman, though, is distant and standoffish. With her son at her side, they are stoic throughout the proceedings, although I do see the boy wipe away a single errant tear.

After the funeral, everyone gathers per Winter's request at a local pub to enjoy a drink and toast to her memory instead of only being able to mourn her loss. People are constantly giving their condolences and it is a whirlwind of activity. I watch most of the people approach the young woman and her son to pay their condolences as well, and I assume they were close to my sister.

By the end of the entire affair, I am bone-weary and want nothing more than to head home. The last couple of days have given me a lot of time to think things through. I have started to type messages to Pope at least ten times a day to apologize for my horrendous behavior the night we left, but I think that maybe I should apologize in person. And I will be apologizing. Life is too short to live it angry or with regrets, so when we get home, I am going to beg for forgiveness and then I am going to tell him how I feel. Put my heart on the line again and hope for the best.

When we walk into Mr. Murphy's office for the will reading, the young woman and her son are already seated.

"Have you all been introduced yet?" Mr. Murphy asks.

"Not formally," the woman replies.

"Okay. Storm, this is Irene and Brogan. Irene, Brogan, this is Winter's sister Storm and her friend Kaiya." He nods his head before pulling out a thick folder.

"Storm, this letter is for you, which you must read, and then I can continue with the proceedings." He hands me a sealed envelope.

My heartbeats escalate as I consider what could be inside. The weight of it should feel like nothing but instead, it feels like a ton. As I look at the people around me, I find all their gazes glued to me. Slowly, I slip my nail into the lip and open the envelope, retrieving the letter.

Upon seeing Winter's handwriting, the tears already start to flow down my cheeks.

My dearest Storm,

Today I got the news that I have breast cancer and it is one of the top three aggressive types. Although we haven't spoken in many years, you are the only person that I want to talk to. I know that we have had our differences but you will always be my little sister. The love I have for you will never change no matter the miles or the years. About six months ago, I had a private investigator seek you out. He found you and wanted to initiate contact, but I asked him to wait. Upon seeing the photos of you, I knew I was right. I am glad that you and Colin have found each other all these years later. I never told you, but even as children, I always knew you were meant to be together. Perhaps if I had said something all those years ago there would have never been a rift between us.

You truly look happy in the photographs and I wish nothing but the best for you both. If you are reading this, you have agreed to be the person who handles my final affairs and I'm grateful for that. In this room with you are two of the most important people in my life. My dear friend Irene who has been part of my life since just after you left. She is the closest thing I have to family beside you and has been with me through thick and thin these last years.

With her is a young boy named Brogan, he is seven years old and is my son. He is also Colin's son. I know that this might be uncomfortable for you, but I want you to raise him, introduce him to his father. If that isn't something you want to do, please just tell Mr. Murphy you can't accept the gift and he will leave with Irene.

I love you more than words can say. Please don't feel any pressure to honor my last request of you. I only want you to be happy.

All the love in my heart,
Winter

Chapter Six
Pope

Three weeks. She has been gone for three goddamned weeks sorting out her sister shit. I'm going out of my ever-loving mind with worry. Our last conversation was more of a screaming match and so much unnecessary shit was said. She won't answer when I fucking call. I need to hear her voice, just to be sure she is okay.

The only news I have heard about her is second-hand from Hadley. Thank God she has taken pity on me or I wouldn't have a fucking clue what was going on. But something is wrong, I can feel it in my bones. The fact that Hadley is a terrible liar doesn't help. She's hiding something from me and even Wolf can't seem to pry it from her.

My guys are wary of me and keep their distance. I'm like a bear with a hurt paw and anyone who gets too close is liable to get their head bitten off. The worst of all is Mad Dog. I constantly catch him watching me. There is pity in his gaze, and I know Kaiya has told him what is going on, but when I ask him, all he does is shake his head and walk away. This has caused us to almost come to blows many times over the last couple of weeks.

I need Storm to get back to town so we can smooth things over. The need to fix things has become a nagging in my mind, like an itch I just can't scratch.

But all that will be resolved today. Storm and Kaiya are on their way back. This isn't something I was told, but something I overheard Hadley and Luna talking about. And even though it's driving me up the fucking wall to wait, I am going to. Well, I'm going to at least wait until the sun starts to set before making my way to her apartment.

Enjoying the peace and quiet for a minute, I drink a cup of coffee and try to get my thoughts in order for tonight's conversation. Kaiya walks in and takes a seat beside me.

"Pope."

"Kaiya."

I turn toward her, looking at her closely. She is a beautiful woman, especially now that she has been away from her brother and his fucked-up club for the past couple of months. Beautiful green eyes and porcelain skin. She changed her hair while they've been away, cut it shorter and dyed it a red that's close to that of a stop sign. Those people put her through the wringer. Raping and beating her for the better part of four years. But she has been with the Gypsy Bastards for a while now and looking a lot better. It helps that she is finally in an environment where she doesn't constantly fear for her safety.

Arching an eyebrow, I ask, "What does Mad Dog think of your hair?"

Raising her hand, she touches it quickly, and pulls her hand away. A serious look falls over her face as she answers me.

"Bohdi is not my brother, father, or husband. I am a free woman and entitled to make my own decisions. That said, I don't really give a flying fuck what he thinks."

I consider her for a moment, nodding my agreement. Her words aren't those of the woman I have come to know these past months, but at least she doesn't look afraid of her own shadow anymore.

"But that is beside the point." She stops to take a deep breath and if I didn't know better, I would think she was gathering the courage to give me the worst news of my life.

"Storm is still in Baton Rouge. She still hasn't been able to finalize everything but should be back at the end of the week. She asked me to tell you that she's fine and she will talk to you as soon as she gets back. She sees all the calls and messages."

The words fall from her lips like a waterfall and she doesn't look at me when she speaks. She's hiding something and it's driving me insane.

"Fine."

I stand from my spot, leaving my coffee on the bar, and head up to my apartment. This shit is starting to grate on my nerves and I am done. We will all be having a club meeting as soon as Storm gets her ass back to Gypsy Falls. Women, children, club ass, hang-arounds, men, everyone. No more fucking secrets in my goddamned club.

Chapter Seven
Storm

Arriving at my apartment with a kid in tow is a brand-new, really nerve-racking, experience. Although I know that Hadley and Luna have been to my place and fixed up my spare bedroom for Brogan, it's still scary. We have gotten to know each other these past weeks but always had Irene as a buffer. He's a nine-year-old boy who acts more like a thirty-year-old. He is way older than his years and I think it has a lot to do with Winter's disease. It made him grow up a lot faster than he ever should have.

At least I don't have to worry about Pope for the time being. I know full and well what I'm doing is wrong. He should have been my first call when I found out about Brogan, but I didn't call. I needed time to work through everything that happened in such a short period. And then, when I finally had my head wrapped around everything, I just couldn't do it. I had a conversation with Brogan about what he wanted and the fear on his face tore my heart to shreds. But he does want to meet Pope, he wants to know his dad. He just isn't ready yet. So we will wait.

As I walk into his room for the first time, tears fill my eyes. I have the best friends anyone could ask for. The room has gray walls with some framed pictures that Hadley called for. All of them are of Brogan and Winter and some even include a few of Irene. They have a television mounted on the wall with a game station beneath it. A desk for him to study at and a single bed with a nightstand beside it. His bedding is black with lime-green accents as well as gray curtains in front of his windows.

Clearly, a lot of thought and attention has gone into this room and again I am more thankful than I can express at the moment.

"Storm, is this my room?" Brogan asks softly from behind me.

"Yes, buddy. I know it's not much and if you want to change anything, we can."

"I really like the green. It's cool the way it is." He walks past me and takes a seat on the bed.

"Do you want something to eat?"

"Yeah, I'm a little hungry."

"Okay, but this is something we haven't discussed yet. I have no idea what you like to eat." I give him a sheepish grin and a smile spreads across his face.

"I love pasta."

Relief fills me at his answer. Pasta is one of my favorite dishes to cook and to eat so we should be just fine. Cooking isn't really a strong point for me, only cooking the basics because I have to eat to live. But if he had asked me for a triple layer chocolate cake with salted caramel ganache, I would have been more than happy to jump into the kitchen for him. I love baking, creating beautiful desserts. It is my secret passion and few people are aware that I spend hours watching cooking shows, teaching myself every trick and technique there is. But I can't raise Brogan on only desserts, so I will be adding some new recipes to my arsenal. A boy cannot live off pasta alone.

"Great, get settled and we can eat in a little while. If you want to clean up after the long drive, there is a bathroom across from your room that you are welcome to use."

Brogan nods but gives no other form of reply. I close the door behind me, offering him some privacy as I go to the kitchen to make us something to eat.

****

After dinner, Brogan helps me clean the mess I call a kitchen and then heads to bed. I will have to invest in somewhere bigger for us to stay in the long-term. My apartment is way too small and I hate my kitchen. Heading to bed, I think through all of the stuff I need to get done tomorrow, and I need to do it without being spotted by Pope or one of the guys. Luna is picking us up early so Gage and Brogan can try to get to know each other. There's an age gap but maybe they will bond just by simply being boys.

Lying in bed, I worry. What if I have made the wrong decision by taking him away from everyone and everything that he has ever known? But Irene assured that it would be fine. After all, kids are resilient. I hope to God that she's right and that I'm not just another person who is about to fuck up this poor kid's life.

I'm mostly worried about Pope. He likes kids just fine as long as he can give them back. What I fear most is that he will simply reject Brogan and walk away. And although that boy is a lot stronger than he should be, I doubt he'd be able to handle that.

****

Brogan is enrolled in school and got the laptop he wanted. A welcome present from Luna and Gage. Brogan and Gage seem to have struck up quite the friendship. Gage tells him about everything. From the guys in the club to the best place for ice cream in town and everything in between. Hadley joins us for a while and we have lunch at a local restaurant with a play area, although it goes against every instinct I have.

After finishing our meal, the boys head outside to play while we drink coffee and Hadley has hot chocolate. My mind whirls with everything that still needs to be done. And I don't notice him until it's too late. Pope strides right up to the table, pulls out a chair, and stares at me.

"Well, look at that. Back from Baton Rouge so soon?"

Luna and Hadley have the same panicked look on their faces but neither stand to leave. I look behind me, checking for Brogan before I say anything.

"It's fine. I'll catch you outside."

Hadley nods but Luna watches me closely. "Are you sure you're okay?"

Pope snorts and we all look at him.

"You're treating me like the fucking enemy. I'd love to know when that happened. All of you have been alone with me and nothing has ever happened to you. Besides, I'm not the one lying, am I?

Luna hangs her head in shame before standing and leaving with Hadley in tow. I haven't stopped staring at Pope since he sat down. I couldn't see it before, but the similarities between Brogan and Pope are so clear. The shape of their noses, the tilt of the chin, and those unmistakable eyes. Brogan is definitely his kid if I ever had a doubt.

"Explain."

Pope has his arms crossed over his chest and the look on his face is about as serious as I have ever seen it.

"Nothing to explain, Pope. You have your life, and I have mine. I knew the minute I got back to town you were going to corner me and I needed, no I need, time. I just buried my sister and I'm grieving. I'm processing everything." I'm not lying, I'm just omitting some details. Everything I just told him is the truth.

"Great. Why didn't you just fucking say that? Why all the lies and secrecy?"

"Have you ever considered that I just don't want to explain myself to you? This conversation is going to end the same way the previous one did, and I don't feel like doing that again."

Pushing my chair back, I walk away from him as tears threaten to spill down my cheeks. I almost make it to one of the side doors before Pope grabs me by the wrist and pulls me into the restroom. Pushing me in ahead of him, he locks the door behind us. I know there's no getting away from this. I'm either going to have to rip his heart out to get him to leave me alone—and I don't want to hurt us both like that—or I am going to have to tell him the truth. Hanging my head low, I hold on to the basin as I try to decide.

Hands envelop my hips from behind. turning me around. My gaze remains downcast, and in a move so gentle I didn't know he was capable of it, Pope grasps my chin and tilts my face up. He stares into my tear-filled eyes for a moment before crushing his lips to mine. His kiss is possessive as his lips and tongue plunder mine. For a moment, I forget where we are, everything going on outside, and all my problems, and just throw myself into kissing the man I have loved for more than half my life. After a few moments, Pope pulls away and looks down at me.

"I want to be able to argue about stuff with you. I want a right to have an opinion about your life. Don't you get it, Storm? Why there isn't a woman in my life, not even just one I fuck? I love you. I have been in love with you for a very fucking long time."

He stares straight at me as he waits for an answer. But all I can do is let the tears roll down my cheeks. My heart feels like it might burst. This is what I have wanted from him since I can remember, but I don't know if he will ever forgive me for keeping this secret from him.

"We need to talk."

Chapter Eight
Pope

We leave the restaurant and head outside after Storm composes herself. I head to my bike and watch as she goes toward Luna and Hadley. Gage is positioned on a swing and another boy is pushing him. Their laughter rings out across the little playground. I feel twitchy and hyped up. I know Storm feels something for me. But her reaction to me declaring my love for her isn't what I expected. She wants to talk? Doesn't she know there are no more frightening words in the English language? All that means is that she is going to tell me something I don't want to hear.

What if there is someone else? What if she doesn't feel the same about me? What if I have read the situation entirely wrong?

Watching me, Hadley heads to her car and drives off. Luna, Storm, and both kids pile into Luna's car and start driving. I assume the boy is one of Gage's friends, although he is a couple of years older. I follow behind and soon realize we are on our way toward Storm's apartment. As we stop, I shut down my bike and make my way over to Luna's car and open the door for Storm.

"I will see you in a little bit. Enjoy your time with Gage. This shouldn't take too long." Storm is speaking to the older boy in the car. My mind races as to why she would be reassuring this boy. His gaze drifts to me and for a moment, he stares before looking back at Storm.

"Okay. I will see you soon, Storm," he replies.

Storm gives him a small smile and nods. She gets out of the car and heads toward her apartment.

"Don't be too hard on her, Pope. I know you're pissed at all of us, but she's doing her best in a shitty situation." Luna looks at me with pleading eyes.

I nod as I close the car door and watch her drive away. Climbing the stairs, I formulate everything in my mind. Clearly, Storm is in trouble but that doesn't matter because I love her and will be with her every step of the way, no matter what.

Walking into the apartment, I see her sitting, legs outstretched on the floor with her back against the couch. A bottle of tequila is already open and standing between her legs. She looks beaten down and tired, but the thing that nearly breaks me is the fear in her eyes. She's terrified of whatever she has to tell me. Or is she terrified of me and my reaction?

"I need you to sit with me, no questions. I need to have a couple more big sips of this tequila to gather my courage, and then I will tell you everything. And then you can decide if you still want to be with me. If not, no hard feelings. I'll understand. But first, I need to drink." She nods her head as if agreeing with herself.

After closing the apartment door, I head toward her coffee table. I remove my gun and place it on the table. Next, I remove my shoes and take a seat beside her on the carpet.

"I know you said no questions, but are you going to share the tequila? By the look on your face, I might need some too."

A sad smile plays on her lips as she hands over the bottle. We spend at least ten minutes on the floor sharing the tequila before she rises and she holds out her hand to me. I rise from the floor and place my hand in hers. She leads me down the hallway to a room and opens the door. After walking inside, she takes a seat on the bed and watches me.

I stand just inside the doorway and take in the gray room with green accents, TV, and game station.

Nothing outwardly remarkable, but then I spot the photos against the wall. Walking closer, I see Winter. She's older, but it's her, and she has the boy from Luna's car with her. My heart starts to race as I carefully look at the photo and things start to fall into place. The kid in the car is Winter's and he's now living with Storm. This is what she's worried about, but I don't care. I don't care that she's suddenly a mother figure. It doesn't make me love her any less.

Turning toward her, I'm about to tell her all this when I see her shoulders shake as she cries. I join her on the bed, pull her into my side, and hold her for a moment. This whole scene is confusing the shit out of me.

"Storm?"

"His name is Brogan." Her voice is so soft I almost miss it.

But the name and the fact that he is Winter's child clicks everything into place. I send up a silent prayer to all that is holy that her next words won't be what I think they will be.

"He's your son," she whispers as another sob wracks her.

Of course he is, he has my granddad's name.

Chapter Nine
Storm

Watching Pope leave Brogan's room without saying a word splits my heart wide open and the tears flow faster. I don't know how I will tell that little boy his father has no intention of getting to know him. With my head in my hands, I sit on Brogan's bed as I try to figure out what I will do.

"It's okay. We'll figure this out."

My head snaps up at the sound of Pope's voice. In his hand is the half bottle of tequila we left in the lounge.

"Thank God." Even to my ears, my voice sounds hoarse. It doesn't sound like my voice at all.

Pope watches me closely as he drinks from the bottle. The silence is loud in its emptiness. I have no idea what he's thinking or what he expects me to say. His face is impassive.

Slowly, he lowers his gaze to me, but he still doesn't speak.

"We need to talk, Storm. Before Brogan gets home." His voice is even, like he might be discussing the weather.

"Okay. Let's head back to the lounge."

Following behind Pope, my nerves get the better of me. What if he wants to take Brogan away? I know I've only had him in my life for a short time, but I love that boy. Is he mad I kept this from him?

My palms are sweaty and my hands start to shake. I don't know how this conversation is going to go.

"Storm." Pope says my name like he might have already said it. I'm so in my mind that I didn't hear him. Looking up, I find him seated on my couch. He pats the space beside him, motioning for me to join him.

Instead, I take a deep breath and steel myself for what is to come.

"How pissed are you?"

"Oh, I'm plenty pissed," he replies, and I feel like crying. "But I'm not pissed at you."

His answer has my gaze colliding with his. I don't have a clue who he could be mad at besides me. He rises from the couch and starts pacing.

"I'm pissed at Winter for keeping this from me. How many years have I missed? Does my son think I didn't want him? What the fuck?" He roars the last part.

His gaze darts back to me, but I'm frozen to the spot. He shakes his head as he continues. "I'm pissed at myself for taking so long to tell you how I felt. If I had the balls and manned up earlier, you wouldn't have felt the need to hide this from me. You and I would have known where we stand with each other. But no, we have to deal with this first. And yeah, I am pissed at my club and all the fucking females for not telling me what was going on. So yes, yes, I am pissed, but not at you."

Relief courses through my veins, but at the same time, I have a pang of overwhelming guilt.

"Pope." I move toward him slowly, like he's some kind of rabid animal and I have to be careful. "A lot is going on at the moment, but I need you to listen to me."

He stares at me, waiting for me to talk.

"The top priority is Brogan. There can be no you and me if it's going to affect him in the long run."

"No."

"Pope." I soften my voice and try to make him see reason.

"No, Storm. I will not push you to the back burner again. You and I are going to sort this out here and now before we both go and fetch Brogan. Together."

I'm stunned. Never has Pope spoken to me this way. There has never been an *us* and I gave up on there ever being one years ago. But he seems determined.

"I love you." He doesn't give me a chance to speak. "I have always loved you and the biggest mistake I ever made was letting you walk away all those years ago, letting you think I didn't. So no, I will not accept us not being together."

He stares at me intently as he waits for me to reply, but I don't have one. So many things have been thrust upon me in the last weeks that I simply don't know how to answer him. I do know I love him, but it seems like we keep trying to do this at the wrong time. Maybe it just isn't meant to be.

Chapter Ten
Pope

My heart is bared, my soul laid out before her, and she remains silent? I feel like I am losing her without ever having had her. I can't let that happen, I can't let her be in my life without being mine. I never should have let her leave in the first fucking place. Closing the gap between us, I cup her face in my hands, and without giving her a chance to pull away, I kiss her. At first, the kiss is tentative, her full, soft lips pressed against mine. Her posture is rigid and I know she's thinking too hard. I need to get her out of her head. For the first time in my life, I might actually have to work for something I want.

Slowly, I part my lips and use my tongue to trace the seam of her lips. I gently ease my hand into her hair at the nape of her neck and tug. When she still doesn't respond the way I want her to, I fist her hair harder and tug again. She gasps and I take the opening I need, pushing my tongue into her mouth. She tastes like coffee and tequila and I know I will forever be addicted to the taste. Plundering her mouth, I move my hand from her face, down to her hip, and pull her body into mine.

Tentatively, she strokes her tongue across mine and I can't help the growl that escapes me. Her body goes pliant against mine and inside, I can help but celebrate. But before I take it too far, I pull away from her lips and rest my forehead to hers. Both of us are panting loudly in her quiet apartment.

"Storm." My voice is hoarse from the emotions I'm feeling, as well as the intense arousal.

"Don't let us both continue to live being unhappy. I know you want me, I know you feel something. Let's do this. Me and you and Brogan. We can all be happy."

She takes a deep breath and nods. She steps away from me but takes my hand as she leads me to her bedroom. Stopping at the foot of her bed, she turns to face me again. Slowly, like she isn't sure of what she's doing, she raises her hands to my shoulders and starts to work my cut off. When she gets it past my arms, she folds it with care and places it on the stool in front of her vanity. Returning to me, she lifts the hem of my t-shirt to remove it. I don't speak, don't tell her to take off her clothes the way I want to. She needs to be in control at this moment and this is me giving that to her.

She doesn't show the same care for my clothes as she did my cut, instead, tossing my shirt to the floor. As she stares at me, her breathing accelerates and she touches my bare skin. Her nails run over my tattoos and then my abs before she moves around me. She touches the tattoo on my back and plants a kiss between my shoulder blades. I always knew Storm loved the club, but her reverence to my cut and the tattoo of our patch on my back almost unmans me. It's enough to nearly bring me to my knees.

She turns me around so I'm yet again facing her. Pushing, she walks me back toward the bed where I wait on the edge. She has a plan and I'm smart enough to know not to interfere. Taking three steps back, she smiles at me, but it's not the smile I'm used to. Instead of the self-assured Storm I have always known, the woman in front of me is almost shy.

"Tell me what you want."

The words leave her on a breath, no louder than a whisper. She's dressed in jean shorts and a black halter neck top. She isn't wearing the shoes from earlier, having kicked them off somewhere along the way.

"Let me see you. Show me what is mine from today on out."

Chapter Eleven
Storm

Letting go is easier than I thought it would be. Even with our history and all the drama we have been through, when his lips touch mine, my walls crumble and I succumb to him. Not that I was really putting up a fight. And even knowing all the challenges we are going to face, I'm doing the selfish thing and taking what I have always wanted.

With Pope staring at me with hunger in his eyes, I lift the hem of my shirt over my head and toss it to the floor. Slowly, I undo the button on my shorts and slide down the zipper, allowing it to fall to the floor. I stand in front of the only man I have ever wanted, ever loved, in nothing but a set of neon-pink lace underwear.

I don't know why I feel self-conscious. I take my clothes off for a living, after all. Pope has seen me naked before. But this different. This is more personal than stripping, just me and him in my room. All the doubts I have ever had about myself and my body suddenly flood to the forefront.

"You are fucking exquisite."

The words rumbling forth from Pope have me forgetting everything. With newfound confidence, I stand in front of him. His hands find my hips and guide me between his legs.

He runs his lips along the lace cupping the underside of my breasts, causing a full-body shiver to work its way through me. Straddling his lap, I feel his hands go to my ass. His erection is pressed up against my center. I can't resist the urge to grind down on him, and he thrusts up toward me. I reach for the clasp in the front of my bra and undo it, allowing my breasts to fall free.

"Jesus, Mary, and Joseph." For a moment, he doesn't look at me, just stares at the ceiling.

When his gaze does return to mine, I can see the heat there. Before I can comprehend what he's doing, I'm thrown on my back with him standing between my legs. His hands skim from my hips to my breast, where he tweaks both nipples, my back to arching off the bed. His lips follow the same path his hands just took before sucking a nipple into his mouth. He growls against my breast, biting hard.

"I wanted to take it slow, I swear to God I did. I wanted to do right by you, but my control is slipping and all I can think of is fucking you so hard your headboard leaves a mark on the wall."

Goosebumps break out over my entire body at his confession. Cupping his face in my hands again, I look straight into his eyes.

"Who wants soft and gentle when they can have real passion?"

He pulls in a sharp breath then kisses me again. The passion and need he can put into one kiss steals my breath. His hands are everywhere as he grinds his erection into my center. He doesn't ask permission anymore and gone are the slow, soft kisses and touches. I permitted him to lose control and he has. This is a claiming.

He grips my underwear on either side of my hips, pulls, and the sound of ripping can be heard as the torn piece of material is discarded over his shoulder.

There's no preamble as he pushes two fingers deep into my heat. He works them in and out of me in quick succession and even though I would have sworn it wasn't possible, I only get wetter for him. The sound of him working his belt loose has me squirming on the bed. Every sound is amplified in our passion, the sound of his zipper sliding down, his belt buckle as it hits the floor, the crinkle of a condom wrapper.

He moves his fingers to make space for his erection. The thick head of his cock is poised at my entrance, but he doesn't move.

Taking a deep breath, he stares at me. "I need to be sure you want this. Because we can stop. It will probably fucking kill me, but we can. But if we do this, that's it, you're mine."

I don't answer because I don't have to. I have always been his. In a move he probably wasn't expecting, I twist my body, roll us over, and straddle him, impaling myself on his thick shaft.

"Fuck!" His curse is a shout as he throws his head back. I don't ever want to stop now that we've started and I intend to prove that to him. Slowly, I roll my hips, getting accustomed to his size. His hands grab my hips and hold me still for a moment before he pumps into me.

"Oh, God." I mewl, throwing my head back.

I can't remember a time I ever felt so full or felt someone so deep in me. His hands on my hips guide me back and forth, setting a pace that's bound to drive us both insane. Placing my hands on his chest, I ride him for all that I'm worth and soon feel my orgasm barreling down on me. He moves one of his hands from my hip to my clit and starts rubbing in small, fast circles with just the right amount of pressure applied.

"Come for me, love. Show me."

His words send me over the edge, and I'm screaming his name as I come harder than I have ever come in my entire life. He pumps into me twice more and roars his release.

Chapter Twelve
Pope

Storm lies on my chest with my dick still buried deep inside of her. Our breathing has evened out and at this moment, I know what it is to feel peace. She smiles against my chest before pushing up. Grinning, she gets off the bed and enters the en-suite bathroom.

"Where are you going, woman? I'm not nearly done with you."

"Well, you don't really have a choice. Your son is waiting for me to come and pick him up," she shouts from the bathroom. The sound of the shower starting has me moving toward the bathroom to join her.

"I have a son." The smile on my face couldn't be any bigger as I face her. "I have a son and I have my woman. I didn't think this was in store for me today."

Storm turns to face me as I get into the shower with her. She smiles softly as she places a kiss on my chest.

"I'm glad you're happy, Colin. I was really worried. And Brogan is terrified you wouldn't want him." Her eyes go sad at the thought.

"Don't you worry about that. I want him. I want to get to know him and I damn sure want to make up for the lost time. You'll see, everything will work out just fine. I promise."

Leaning down, I take her lips in another kiss. Slowly exploring her mouth with my tongue while running my hands all over her body. My cock is already hard again, but I need to prioritize. Pulling away, I stare into her eyes.

"I would love nothing more than to fuck you against the shower wall but we need to get going. So let's finish our shower and go fetch our boy. And I promise to make you scream later."

Smiling, she grabs the soap and we both get started on finishing our shower. We have somewhere we need to be.

****

Brogan waits quietly in the backseat of the car and eyes me wearily. Not one of us speaks and the silence is uncomfortable. I watch him carefully in the rearview mirror as he sits straight and stares ahead. Dark hair like Winter, which is a little longer than most boys his age wear it, and green eyes that look exactly like mine. His skin is tan, which I know he didn't get from my pasty ass but from his mom's side, and he's tall for his age. Like almost five feet tall, but I don't know if that's normal or not.

From the corner of my eye, I can see Storm wringing her hands. I reach out and grab one before giving it a light squeeze. She smiles at me but it doesn't reach her eyes. Her nerves are shot and the fact that we aren't talking doesn't help.

Getting to the apartment complex, I park her car in its designated spot and get out. I open the door for Brogan to get out, then move to Storm's side of the car. After closing the door behind her, I take a deep breath and turn toward Brogan. We need to get upstairs and start a conversation. There are tons I need to say to him and things that he probably needs to say to me. But he isn't there anymore. He was standing right beside the car and now he isn't.

Panic envelopes me and for a moment, I feel like I might not be able to breathe. Where is he? Where did he go? I turn to Storm to ask her, but she's smiling at me. What the fuck is she smiling about?

"Funny, isn't it? How someone so small can have

such a huge impact on you so quickly. You didn't even know he existed a couple of hours ago and now he's the center of your entire universe. Luna says it's normal to feel panic, in the beginning, every time you can't see them. Welcome to parenthood, Colin."

Taking my hand, she leads me around her car. Just beyond the car is my parked Harley, with Brogan standing beside it. He has his hands in his pockets as he stares at the bike. Storm releases my hand and walks away. "Go talk to your son. You don't need me for this. I'll start on dinner."

It sure as shit feels like I need her for this. What if we have nothing in common? What if he doesn't like me? What if Winter lied about me knowing about him? What if... Dear Lord, I have never been this terrified in my entire life and I have been shot at, threatened with knives, and almost blown up once. I do business with some of the scariest, most ruthless men on the planet, and the thing that terrifies me most is my nine-year-old son.

Every step I take toward him feels like I might be walking to my doom. I don't know a fucking thing about kids. What the fuck was Storm thinking leaving me alone with him? Standing beside him, I don't speak a word, I don't even look at him. I need to control the air flowing into my lungs, suddenly feeling like I might pass out from lack of air.

"Mom told me you liked motorcycles. Said since you were just a little older than me that you were always riding around on one trying to give Grandma Faye a heart attack."

Brogan's voice is soft and he sounds unsure of what he wants to say.

"Your mum told you about me?"

Brogan looks up at me, his green eyes identical to mine. "Yeah. She told me about you and showed me photos of when you were younger. She also told me about Aunt Storm. Said that no one knew about me but that one day she would tell you all and we could all be family again. But then she got sick."

He sounds so sad when he talks about her. I don't question the move as I lean in and hug him. He doesn't push me away, but he doesn't hug me back either.

"I'm sorry about your mum, bud. But I am glad you're here. We can get to know each other and make up for the lost time. There are a lot of things that I don't know about you and you don't know about me. And there are so many people here who are going to be part of your life now."

He nods, slowly moving away from my embrace. "I like your bike. Will you take me with you sometime? Mom said she never liked it, that you always went too fast and she was afraid of falling. But I think maybe she was just chicken."

Laughter bubbles forth from me.

"Well, that is true. Your mum was a chicken, especially when it came to speed. Let's get you a helmet this week and we can go for a ride one day after school. How does that sound?"

Brogan is doing all the work, all the talking, and making this easier for me than I would have expected. I'm grateful to Winter that she didn't say stuff like I didn't want him, which would have been something we might never get past. But knowing that she told him about us and then kept him away from us still pisses me off. There's nothing I can do about that now though. The past is in the past and we will all just have to learn to live with it.

Chapter Thirteen
Storm

Colin spends as much time as he can with Brogan and they quickly become best friends. During the day, Brogan goes to school, and at night, we act like a happy family. I suppose it's not acting when we all are happy. Colin stays over every night and sleeps in my bed. We lose ourselves in each other every chance we get. The sex is better than I ever could have imagined and we have very few challenges in our relationship. It helps that we have known each other for most of our lives and know what tends to set each other off. There is one thing that has been a bone of contention between us.

Colin doesn't want me to return to work. He hates the thought of other men watching me and says that it has always bothered him but that he didn't have a right to say anything. I told him that I wouldn't be some woman he had to look after and would continue doing my job. I don't want to be a stripper for the rest of my life, but the money is good. As soon as I have enough saved up, I will get a shop and start up my bakery, but until then, this will have to do.

I have started looking for another job because I don't want any of this blowing back on Brogan. Kids hear the wildest things from grownups and tend to be cruel with their words, and that's the last thing I want for Brogan.

But for tonight, I will be going to work.

Colin sits on our bed in just a pair of blue jeans and watches me finish getting dressed. He doesn't say a word, but I can see the emotions flashing through his eyes. He's pissed, but he knows if he pushes me on this it will just drive me to be more of a hardass. When everything is done perfectly the way I like it, I rise from my position in front of my vanity and go to him. He pulls me between his legs. Pressing his face into my stomach, he breathes me in while holding me tightly.

"I don't like this, but I know I can't stop you. I love you. You have to know that, but I made sure the guys know they can't go to Dusk on nights that you're working."

"Colin, you can't keep the guys away." I pull back from him so I can look in his eyes.

"The fuck I can't. If I could stop you, I would. If the club wouldn't kill me for loss in revenue, I would have shut Dusk down before I let you back on that stage, but I can't so this is the next best thing. No member of my club will see you naked again. It's bad enough that they already have, but you weren't mine then."

The tone in his voice is final and although I want to argue, although everything he has just said has me bristling, I turn to walk away. Just as I reach the door, he cages me in, pushing my front up against the door, stopping me from leaving the room.

"Feeling pissed off, love?" he asks right beside my ear.

"Whatever, you do you and I'll do me. I'm not going to fight you on this again."

Before I have the chance to move, his hand cups my breast.

"How about I do you and then you go to work? We can both just try to be a little less pissed at each other?" He grinds his erection into me from behind and I can't stop from moaning even if I wanted to.

Colin has tried this before, fucking me into submission, but it doesn't work. I push back against him, trying to turn around, but he doesn't allow it.

"You can't fuck me into submission, Pope. I have

a mind of my own and won't simply fall in line because you want me to. I'm not some piece of club ass you can command to do whatever you want."

The air in the room shifts, becoming thicker. Pope shoves me against the door again.

"You keep telling me you aren't club ass." His voice has an edge to it and suddenly, I don't feel so confident anymore. "But I have never treated you like club ass. In the years you have been back with me, part of the Gypsy Bastard family, I haven't even touched the club ass. But you always want to assume. Maybe I should show you how I treated the club ass before you came back into my life."

There's a threat behind his words, but I don't have time to figure it out, no time to apologize for being a bitch or to stop him. His left-hand leaves the door then tangles in my hair, pulling hard. He tugs my head all the way back, suddenly biting down hard on the pulse point in my neck. I try to slip out of his grasp, but there is no escape as he holds me as he wants me, keeping me trapped against the door with his big body.

"Colin?" The word leaves my lips in a whisper, so soft I wonder if he heard me.

"No, love. You called me Pope. That is clearly what you wanted and that is what you're going to get."

Before I can comprehend his next move, he has me turned against the chest of drawers, sweeping everything off the top in one harsh move. Glass shatters on the floor and I'm thankful Brogan is visiting at Gage's house until later. Colin, or should I say, Pope, pushes me down over the piece of furniture while still gripping my hair. My eyes tear up due to the sting and although I know I should be afraid, I have never been more excited.

He flips my skirt up, revealing my naked ass to his gaze, bared to him by the fact that I am only wearing a tiny red thong. I don't have a chance to speak as his hand lands on my left cheek. God damn, does that hurt! I try to pull away but he simply uses the leverage on my hair to push me down again.

"You asshole," I hiss at him. He only chuckles behind me, rubbing his hand lovingly over the spot he just smacked.

"You have no idea the kind of asshole I can be, but before you leave here to go and do the job we both know you no longer want, you will know."

He punctuated the end of his sentence with another smack to my ass before soothing over it. A moan slips past my lips and I know he wasn't expecting it because his whole body tenses. I don't want to react this way to him, to what he's doing to my body, but I can't stop myself. No man has ever touched me this way or treated me this way, and I am so turned on I can't help it. I didn't know this side of Colin existed. I didn't know I would like it, but it is driving me nuts.

He pauses for a moment, then continues to rub my ass. I can't turn my head to see him, but by the tone of his voice, I know he's smirking at me. "I love the way my handprint blooms on your ass. Showing my ownership. So pretty and pink. When you take your clothes off tonight, every asshole there will know that you belong to someone, that they can look but they will never have you."

While he talks, he uses his feet to push my legs further apart. I'm probably in the most obscene position of my life. Bent over a chest of drawers, my skirt flipped up to put my ass on display, his red handprint on my ass, and my hair in a tangled mess between his strong fingers. And even though I know I should be pissed, I should feel shame or that what he's doing is something I don't want, but I just can't find it in me. When his palm connects with my buttocks again, I can't help the gasp that leaves my lips, and when he caresses the spot, a moan tumbles forth again.

"You're enjoying this, aren't you?"

I don't answer, but he doesn't need an answer as he runs his hand between my legs to feel my soaked underwear. The moment his fingers connect with my wetness, he hisses.

"Fuck, Storm."

All coherent thought flees from my mind as another set of my underwear is snapped and two calloused fingers are shoved into me. An inhuman sound escapes me as I push back against his hand. He pumps into my pussy, using first two then three fingers, provoking my knees to feel like they might buckle beneath my weight. I can feel my orgasm approaching faster than I thought was possible. But Colin removes his fingers from me with such speed I'm left feeling dizzy and deprived.

Pulling back on my hair again, twisting my head to the side, he stares into my eyes. "I'm going to let go of your hair, but hear me, if you move a fucking inch, I will stop. Understood?"

I don't speak because I can't. I only nod in agreement. The Irish lilt he usually speaks with has become more pronounced. The color of his eyes has changed. Where they are usually bright green, they have gone so dark they are closer to forest green. His pupils have expanded to the point where they almost cover any color left.

His hand leaves my hair and I don't move. I'm terrified of him stopping at this moment. I need to know what will happen next. He runs his hands over my ass, cupping the mounds then moving on. His hands skim down my inner thighs only an inch from my pussy and I have to force myself not to move to get them where I want them. He runs his hands down my leg to my calves and I realize he's crouched behind me.

"You look like a fucking goddess. Legs spread wearing these fucking blue heels. My mark on your ass and your puffy, wet pussy on display for me. You have no idea what you fucking do to me." His voice is hoarse and even if I wanted to say something, I couldn't because he takes my clit into his mouth and sucks, leading me to shriek and my back to bow.

The smack to my other cheek is unexpected and I moan again.

"Stop moving," he says with a growl before biting my inner thigh hard enough I know there will be a mark.

Throughout my life, I have never thought anything could be as hard as standing still is at this moment. But as soon as I stop moving, Colin returns his mouth to my core and starts to eat me out like it's his damn job. I resist the urge to grind down on his face but the struggle is real. His tongue runs from my clit all the way back to my now sopping wet entrance, then going back to my clit. He sets a punishing tempo that drives me wild and pulls sounds from me that are foreign to my ears.

Again, he thrust two fingers into me. I go onto my toes as another smack lands on my ass. It's a warning not to move and he knows he doesn't have to say it, so he just continues to torture me with his mouth. My orgasm builds in my toes and moves through my body, and just when it starts to crash over me and I experience the best orgasm of my life, he removes his fingers from me. He doesn't stop the suction he's currently applying to my clit, only sucks harder. Just when I think I can't handle any more, he slips one of the fingers covered in my juices into my ass. I scream. My body trembles and a second more powerful orgasm overtakes me as my knees actually give out.

But I don't hit the floor. No, Colin has a hand around my waist, holding me up, pushing me into the fucking drawers again. His finger leaves my ass and I hear his belt and jeans hit the floor. With no preamble, he shoves all eight inches of his hard cock into me. I feel like I am losing my fucking mind and no longer care what he says as my body bows beneath his.

"If you stop, I will fucking kill you," I say with a growl once I've regained my breath.

"If I stop, I will fucking die," he answers.

His hands on my hips guide me as he takes two steps back. "Hold on to the edge, love. Hold on tight."

The moment my fingers curve around the edge of the piece of wood, Colin starts moving. His thrusts are punishing, moving my entire body with every shove. His hands leave my hips, traveling upward to the collar of the shirt I'm wearing. He grips it tightly, and rips it down the middle. I want to be upset that he has ruined two items of clothing in the last ten minutes, but can't find it in me as he unclasps my bra, freeing my breast. Not for one moment does he stop thrusting into me and I know every time I move, with every step I take, every shift of my hips when I dance later tonight, I will feel him.

"Fuck," he growls in my ear as another, unexpected orgasm sweeps through me. My pussy clamps down on him and he grunts in my ear. His hand travels from the breast he's fondling, over my stomach, and down to my overly sensitive clit, where he starts rubbing circles again.

"You are going to come for me again."

I shake my head because it's too much, but he just continues.

"You will come for me again." He punctuates the demand by pinching my clit and setting off another orgasm I didn't know I was possible of.

"Fuck yes." He stills behind me and I feel the moment his cum shoots out of him and into me. Feel it coating me and marking me his even more than I was a half-hour ago.

"Fuck, woman." His breathing is heavy as he rests his forehead on my back. "You're going to be the death of me."

A laugh bubbles from my chest and soon he joins in, holding me to his chest as we both laugh. Turning me to face him, he kisses me softly, almost reverently. "I have never done that to or with any other woman. I just want you to know that. But I do look forward to doing it again."

Me too.

Chapter Fourteen
Pope

After fixing her hair and getting dressed in a different outfit, Storm leaves to go to work. I don't let her shower before she leaves. I like the fact that she smells like me and hope that it will keep other men away from her. I'm not nearly as pissed as I was about her going to work, but that might have to do with the huge hickey on her neck she can't hide. Or maybe it's the smile on her face that she can't disguise that proclaims her to be a woman who is well fucked by the man she loves.

After getting my jeans and shirt back on, I grab my cut and both Brogan's and my helmets and head out the door. I'm going to pick up the little dude with the Harley, drive around for a little while, and then we can stop somewhere for burgers and ice cream. Brogan loves being on the bike with me and can't wait to be old enough to have his own.

Driving to Sparrow's house, I can't help but replay everything that happened between me and Storm earlier. She may think that I try to fuck her into submission, and sometimes I might even try, but she isn't the one submitting, I am.

I didn't want her to go to work, but I let her, knowing that if I pushed, it would only cause a fight. I know she's looking for other work even though she didn't tell me herself. She doesn't like to be told what to do and the harder I push this, the harder she will push back. I need to calm down and just let it be. She will be out of there sooner rather than later.

One thing that does help is the fact that Kaiya is now also working at Dusk. She took Hadley's place as a waitress, giving her some money of her own and the freedom to do what she wants. I know Mad Dog wasn't impressed but he couldn't do anything about it either. I mean, he doesn't have a claim on her as his woman, so he's totally fucked. But with Kaiya there, she has promised to keep an eye on Storm and let me know if there are any problems. Kaiya has taken to Storm and tends to treat her like an older sister. But because of everything Kaiya has been through in her life, she is also completely overprotective of the people she has in her life. That serves to give me a little peace of mind.

****

As I pull up outside of Sparrow's house, the boys both come running out to greet me. They are laughing and falling all over themselves and each other to get to me. Seeing Brogan just be a kid and enjoying himself brings joy to my heart. When he first came to us, he was such a serious child, always trying to be perfect and apologizing for everything. But now, after getting to know us better and spending time with hurricane Gage, he seems to have relaxed and is enjoying his life more.

"Hey, Dad." He waves at me as Gage crawls up my body in an attempt to hug me. Hearing him call me that always makes my heart skip a beat. He has never called me anything else. He says it's because I was never a stranger to him and it breaks my heart that I sometimes feel like he's still a stranger to me.

"Hey, bud." I smile over at him, hug Gage, and set him down. "Where is Sparrow?"

"On the porch drinking a beer," Gage answers while he pulls his face in distaste.

Laughing, I move past them into the house. Luna is standing with her cell phone pushed against her ear but smiles and waves when she sees me. Moving past her, I head toward their back yard where Sparrow is chilling on a blue garden chair. Crossing the deck, I grab a beer out of the cooler and take the seat beside him. For a moment, we both just watch the boys, who are now in the back yard running around playing. It's a companionable silence that wraps around us and we are both just happy to be there.

The door to the kitchen opens and Luna walks over to us.

"I have to go into the hospital. Someone just quit mid-shift and now they are short-handed in the ER. I should be home by nine at the latest because then the next shift will be in."

Sparrow's shoulders tense but he doesn't argue. He hates Luna working in the ER because it can be dangerous at times, but just like with Storm, the more he pushes Luna, the more she will push back.

"All right, *mi amor*. But if you're not going to be here and Storm is working as well, I think us guys should have a boys' night."

Luna laughs as the boys pick up on the conversation and come running toward us. "I think that is a great idea. Just the four of you doing all kinds of manly things."

The boys smile at each other and fist-bump as they excitedly start chatting with each other.

"Just going to get changed and I will come and say bye before I leave." Luna ruffles Gage's hair as she returns to the house.

"So, what would you guys like to do?" I look right at Brogan when I ask the question.

"Are we taking the bike?"

"Yes. I brought your helmet and there are jeans and a jacket in my saddlebag."

"Can we go to the lake?" He watches me closely to see my reaction, as though he's still afraid he will ask the wrong thing.

"Sure. Don't see why not. Maybe get a burger and eat out there for dinner?" My gaze drifts to Sparrow to ensure he agrees with my plan, but he simply smiles and nods.

"Yes!" both boys crow in unison, running off into the house to presumably get changed.

Before either Sparrow or I can speak, my phone rings and I fish it out of my pocket. Storm's face flashes on the screen and I have a mini panic attack as I put the phone to my ear.

"What's wrong?" The moment the question is out of my mouth, both Sparrow and I are up out of the chairs and moving through the house.

"Nothing." The pout in her voice is clear.

Giving Sparrow our signal to show that everything is fine has him stopping in the kitchen and grabbing us each another beer.

"Then why are you sulking?" As I'm speaking on the phone, I see Luna head down the hall from their bedroom toward Sparrow.

"You have to come and get me. I drove with Kaiya and she needs her car to get home later." She doesn't say anything more but I know her well enough to know there is a story. I head outside toward my bike as I wait for her to continue. Sparrow and Luna are short on my heels.

"I can't dance, okay? I feel dirty with all of these guys watching knowing what we did no less than two hours ago. Are you happy now?"

"Ecstatic. Just hold on a second." I press the cell phone to my chest and wait for Sparrow to finish kissing Luna. Luna walks over and gets in the car, rolling her window down.

"Brother," I call out to Sparrow. He turns toward

me.

"I'm just gonna get Storm from work and then I will be back for boys' night. You okay to watch the kids?"

I hear Luna's car turn over but it doesn't start. The second time she tries, there is an unmistakable click that has me and Sparrow running toward her as her car explodes into a ball of flames.

Chapter Fifteen
Storm

Walking into Dusk after the most explosive sex of my life is different. The regulars greet me, but where I always saw friendly smiles, I now only see lecherous looks. The air inside seems stale and for the first time, I realize there isn't really a way to make a strip club look classy or to keep the stench of desperation from clinging to everything.

Walking into the back area where all the girls get ready before going on stage, I simply look at them. I don't get along with most of them and even those I do get along with occasionally look different to me now. Most have plastic breast implants and all of us—including me—wear too much makeup. We are all trying too hard. And for the first time since I started two years ago, I feel uneasy.

Colin has fucked with my head. I love my job and am damn fucking good at it. With that thought in mind, I take a seat at my station and start to prepare myself.

About five minutes later, my headspace feels better. I rise from my seat and head to the back of the stage to wait for my song to start. Tonight, I'm wearing my schoolgirl ensemble. Black high heels with thigh-high white stockings, my white set of garters, white lace boy shorts, and my favorite white pushup bra. The skirt I chose is a blue plaid number that's as short as I could alter it while still wearing a skirt, with a white button-down blouse that is sheer enough to see through. My hair is pulled up into two ponytails and I know what I look like. I look like a tease. I am a tease! I look amazing but I don't feel amazing.

But I will not back down, as the bass of my

favorite song starts to pulse through the speakers. As I strut out on stage, the level of unease just climbs. I try my best to ignore it and continue. I grab the pole and do a rotation. I have always loved dancing, it lets me feel free. When I'm on stage with the bass assaulting me, the lights shining down on me, I'm the master of my universe. I don't need anything or anyone and I tend to shut the world out. But tonight, the harder I try, the less that feeling is enveloping me. The first thirty seconds of the song haven't even passed, and I have already decided to quit once my set is done. I simply can't do it anymore.

As I shake my lace-covered ass for the world to see, I slowly start unbuttoning my shirt. But a shout from the left has me freezing.

"Just take it off already, will you?" The voice is slurred and the person it belongs to is clearly drunk, but that's my final moment. I snap out of my daze and walk off stage mid-song.

I hear the crowd boo and the song change as another girl runs past me with a frown to take her place on stage.

Maurice is standing at my work station, waiting for me. He smiles sadly as he takes my hands that I didn't realize to this moment were shaking.

"It's okay, *cher*. I knew when you walked in here with that massive hickey on your neck that it would be your last night. A woman like you doesn't fall in love only to return to a place like this." He kisses my cheek, winks at me, and walks away.

I slump down into the chair and take a deep breath before calling Colin. Even over the phone, I can hear the smugness in his voice. When he asks me to hold on for a moment, I start pulling a pair of jeans up my legs while holding my phone between my ear and my shoulder, listening to him talk to Sparrow about the kids.

I'm waiting for him to tell me he's on his way as I knew he would be the moment I called him before I hear an explosion in the background and the line goes dead.

"Colin?"

There's only silence on the other end of the line. I know something is massively wrong. I pull on a black t-shirt and grab my sandals, handbag, and phone, dashing out into the front of the club. My gaze scans for Kaiya because I need to borrow her car but instead, I find Mad Dog. As I near him, I realize he has Kaiya caged in against the wall, using his arms.

"No, Kaiya, you don't seem to understand. This shit isn't going to work. You belong to me," Mad Dog all but growls at her.

Fire flashes in her eyes and for a split second, I reconsidered interrupting but simply do it.

"I promise you can chew him out about being a dumbass later, Kaiya," I interject into their conversation. Both of them train their gazes on me. "But at the moment, I need him to take me to Pope."

The last part comes out on a sob and both have their attention focused on me.

Mad dog takes my hand to get my attention. "Doll, what's wrong? Tell me and I can help you." Worry envelopes his face.

"Nothing is wrong with me. I was on the phone with Pope when there was an explosion and the line went dead. He's at Sparrow's with Luna and the boys. Please, I can feel it in my bones. something is very, very wrong." The tears roll down my face as I plead with him to take me there.

"Truck's outside. Let's go." Mad Dog looks toward Kaiya but doesn't get a chance to say anything.

"I'm coming with you." She hands her apron to

the bartender and we all leave.

****

The drive to Sparrow's house is pure hell. I keep staring at my phone, waiting for Colin to send me a message. I have sent tons but he isn't replying.

17:51 Storm: **Colin call me!**

17:54 Storm: **Are you okay?**

17:58 Storm: **WTF! CALL ME!!!**

I only lift my eyes from the screen when I feel the truck accelerate beneath me. Looking into the distance, I see the black smoke rising from the area that Sparrow and Luna live in. And then I hear the sirens.

The last half-mile feels like it takes hours. But as we pull up, I feel relief and at the same moment, my world falls apart. On the front lawn, Pope is working his best to pull Sparrow away from the wreck that used to be Luna's car. And in the doorway to Sparrow's home, a home that will never be the same after this tragedy, is Brogan sitting on the top step, cradling Gage to his larger body, tears streaming down both of their faces.

Chapter Sixteen
Pope

The spires of the local church loom above me and although I am far from a religious man, I always find it beautiful. The silence surrounds me and brings me the first semblance of peace I have felt in this entire bitch of a week.

After the explosion, everything fell to complete and utter chaos. Sparrow had to be sedated by Doc. When the shock wore off, he was hell-bent on burning Gypsy Falls to the ground, trying to find the person responsible for Luna's death. We've had to keep a close eye on him as his need for vengeance is currently overshadowing his grief. Gage is lost in his father's need to avenge Luna and is currently staying with us.

Every time I see Gage and Brogan together, the sadness claws at my heart, threatening to consume me. No child should lose their mother at such a young age, especially not to such unnecessary violence. Add into the mix my own son, who is still grieving for the loss of his mother, and the situation is unbearable. Having two boys living with us in Storm's apartment should be loud and boisterous and full of shenanigans, but instead, it is filled with sadness, heartache, and silence.

Brogan has taken Gage as his surrogate little brother and is constantly within the younger boy's reach. The first night Gage was with us, he had a nightmare. Poor kid woke up screaming with tears pouring down his face. Storm and I had been prepared for this to happen but didn't expect to find Brogan cradling the younger boy to his chest. When Storm tried to intervene, to offer comfort, Brogan only shook his head.

"I know what he's going through. I've got this."

At that moment, time stood still, and I realized again how much my young son had been through before I even met him for the first time.

I have no answers. I don't know who planted the bomb that ended Luna's life while she was still in her prime. I don't know how to help my brother process his grief or how to help him get his vengeance. And I sure a shit have no clue what to say to Gage when he asks where his dad is. What I do know is that after today, I will need to find answers, and Luna will be avenged. No one hurts someone I love and walks away from it.

Taking a deep drag from my first cigarette in three years only serves to piss me off further. But today isn't about revenge or anger. Today is about bidding farewell to a woman we all loved.

As the rumble of motorcycles nears the church, I grind the last of my cigarette into the ground with the toe of my boot. Proceeding to the front of the church, I watch the procession make their way closer.

More than fifty motorcycles lead the procession, driving two abreast. Behind them is the hearse carrying the coffin that contains the little of Luna's remains that could be found after the fire was put out. Vehicles follow behind, no less than fifteen, and I'm glad that so many showed up to pay their last respects to one of the best women I have ever known.

Slowly, everyone enters the church. The casket is carried in by Sparrow, myself, Wolf, Beast, Viking, and Mad Dog and placed in front of the podium where the preacher will give his farewell. For a moment, silence reigns as we all rest our hands on the gleaming wood before making our way to the pews. We all fill into in the front row as we wait for the sermon to start.

****

The preacher has given a beautiful sermon and

brought tears to many eyes. He spoke of the goodness that was Luna, how she always put others above herself, and never showed any person in need away. He spoke of the love she shared with all those she came upon and that loving each other would be the way to keep her memory alive.

Everyone exits the church and Luna's casket is lifted back into the hearse to be taken half a mile to the cemetery where she will be laid to rest for the last time. Watching everyone speak in hushed tones, I wait. Storm and Hadley are across the street with Brogan and Gage, trying to keep them away from the people who want to discuss what happened to Luna. I have no idea what I'm waiting for, but there's a feeling, call it a sixth sense, that tells me something more is coming.

My phone rings in my pocket. I remove it, stare at the blocked number for a minute then answer it, and hold it to my ear. I don't speak, I wait.

"Pope?"

The voice on the other side of the line isn't one I have heard before today. It is pitched low and the speaker seems to be out of breath.

"Yes?" Wariness is evident in my tone.

"You need to get everyone out of there. Riot has convinced King that the Iron Disciples need to exact revenge for what you did and take the property that previously belonged to the Mongrols as their own."

"Who is this?" I demand.

"My name is Calum Quince. But people call me Bishop," he replies sharply. "But that doesn't matter now. What matters is getting your people away."

He ends the call promptly. I turn and scan the throng of people in front of me, looking for Wolf. Even if I don't know or trust this man, I can't take the chance that he may be speaking the truth. I need to get to my guys and have them clear everyone out of here as fast as possible.

Keeping an eye on my surroundings, fearing that the Iron Disciples could strike at any moment, I slowly wander through the people gathered when three things happen almost simultaneously.

First, an ear-splitting scream is heard from across the street.

Second, Brogan is running in my direction, calling out to me.

Third, a hail of bullets sprays from a passing black SUV.

Chapter Seventeen
Storm

The funeral was beautiful. Luna was remembered as she'd lived. With love.

Standing across the street from the church, I watch Brogan sit beside Gage on a set of swings. Hadley stands beside me, dressed in black and holding her stomach. She keeps moving her hands, and she looks uncomfortable.

"Are you okay?"

"I'm fine." But she has tears in her eyes.

"Hadley, if something is wrong with you or the baby, you need to tell me." I hold her shoulders and look straight into her eyes as I say this. I know my best friend and she wouldn't want to draw any attention to herself, especially not today.

She nods at me as the first tear slips free. "I'm in labor. I have been since I showered this morning when my water broke." She sobs.

"Oh, my God, Hadley." Turning my gaze to the boys, I feel her body shake as she rests her forehead on my shoulder.

"Brogan, I need you to run across the street as fast as you can and find your dad. Tell him it's an emergency."

Brogan doesn't speak, he simply takes off running across the grass toward the church as a shriek tears from Hadley. Everything seems to be happening in slow motion as her knees give out and I am barely able to catch her before she hits the ground. Gage is beside me in a second with a panicked look on his little face.

"Don't worry, buddy," I reassure him as I lower Hadley and myself to the grass. "Hadley is going to be fine, but the baby is coming."

My explanation seems to soothe some of the worry from his face. He knows about the baby and has been really excited about it since he found out.

"Can I help?" his little voice asks.

It seems like Hadley is through the worst of the contraction as she smiles at him. "Yes, Gage. I need you to hold my hand until Wolf gets here. I need you to help me be less scared."

Gage smiles at Hadley for the first time in days as he plops down beside her, taking her hand in his and pulling it tightly against his chest. It's a gesture we all know well because Sparrow would hold Luna's hand the same way. Emotion crawls its way up my throat and makes it hard to speak.

I look up and see Brogan running across the street. There isn't time to scream and warn him as a black SUV hits him, sending his little body flying through the air. My world stops at that moment and everything falls away as I watch him hit the ground. I didn't recognize it earlier, but as my mind clears, I hear the gunshots being fired.

"Hadley, keep Gage with you. I will find Wolf and send him here."

"No, Storm, you can't go over there!" She grabs my leg of my pants and tries to stop me from walking away.

"I have to go." I shake my leg, dislodging her hand and running toward the anarchy that has broken out in front of the church. I don't run toward the men, I run toward Brogan. I near him as he lies motionless on the pavement, but he doesn't move. I kneel beside him and feel for a pulse exactly the way Luna taught me. His pulse is there and I don't see much blood except for on his forehead. But his arm is bent at such an odd angle that I know with complete certainty it is broken.

Pulling my cell from my pocket, I dial 911 and look around me. The SUV is no longer in sight, people are on the ground, screams are coming from somewhere near the church, and from the corner of my eye, I watch Wolf run toward Hadley.

"911, what is your emergency?"

"My name is Storm Lin and there has been a shooting at St. Angelicas on Broad Street. You need to send ambulances."

I try my best to speak clearly and slowly because I don't want to have to repeat myself.

"Okay, ma'am. Please remain on the line units have been dispatched to that area." The operator has a clear voice as she speaks calmly to me. "Have you been hurt?"

"No. But my nephew…" A sob chokes of the rest of the words.

"I need you to remain calm. What happened to your nephew?"

"He was hit by a car. The people who shot at the church hit him with their SUV." Taking a deep breath, I do my best to compose myself.

"Is he breathing?" she asks.

"Yes, he is breathing. He has a pulse too. But there is blood on his forehead and I am sure his arm is broken."

"Okay. I need you to not move him. Is he conscious?"

"No."

"All right. When he does regain consciousness, if the paramedics aren't there yet, you need to keep him calm. We need him to not move. We don't know the extent of his injuries, and him moving might cause more damage."

In the distance, I can hear the sirens approaching, and I feel a small amount of peace at knowing help will be here soon. I stay on the line with the woman until one of the ambulances stop beside me.

"Thank you for your help."

"It has been my pleasure," she replies as she hangs up.

The paramedics assess Brogan before placing him on a backboard and then in the ambulance. I see that Hadley is getting loaded into a separate ambulance with Wolf accompanying her. I haven't seen Pope through all of the chaos and pray that he is fine as I get into the ambulance and we race off to the hospital.

Chapter Eighteen
Pope

In a moment, the entire world around me exploded. The last thing I saw was Brogan's body flying through the air as the bullets started flying.

I wake up in a hospital, tubes and cables connected to me. Panic seizes me. Where are Brogan and Storm? Has anyone else been hurt? How long have I been here?

Pushing myself upright, I look around the room. In the corner, Beast is slumped uncomfortably, sleeping in a chair that is way too small to hold a body his size. I try to clear my throat, since it's dry and scratchy, but it doesn't help. Turning, I try to reach the glass beside the bed. The noise must have woken Beast as he appears beside me.

"Sit back, Prez. Just take it easy." He hands me the glass, holding the straw to my lips.

"Well." I try to clear my throat again. "Tell me what happened. How long have I been here?"

Beast takes the seat beside my bed and shakes his head. "You need to stay still and heal." He sighs. "But if I don't tell you, you're just gonna get out of that bed, aren't you?"

He watches me closely. I nod.

"After the shooting, everything was chaos. Storm got a call into 911 so it was fast."

"Brogan?" My voice is raspy and it hurts to talk

"He's fine. Broke his arm and had a concussion with a couple of cracked ribs, but he is doing great. Got released yesterday."

"How long have I been here?"

"A week. The bullet that hit you nicked your left

lung. We almost lost you." He breathes in deeply. "We did lose Ruger and two civilians didn't make it. Hadley went into labor and gave birth to their daughter in the ambulance on the way to the hospital. Some people are banged up and bruised, but for the most part, everyone is still alive."

"Get me a doctor. I want to be discharged."

Beast stares at me for a moment but knows better than to argue the point.

****

Beast drives me straight to Storm's place. Even though I'm in an immense amount of pain, I need to see her and Brogan. My stomach is in knots as I move to the door. Before I can knock, the door swings open and Storm is right in front of me.

"Just get inside, you idiot." She yanks on my arm, pulling me into the apartment. "People are trying to kill you, you almost died in the hospital, and you think it's a good idea to just sign yourself out and drive around with no backup?"

She pushes gently on my chest, forcing me to take a seat on the couch. Just seeing her has my heartbeat calming. Taking her hand in my own, I pull her down on the couch beside me.

"I'm fine. I needed to see you with my own eyes and make sure that you are too. Where is Brogan?"

"He wanted to stay at Wolf's for the afternoon. I think being there and helping them out with the baby makes him feel useful."

"Good. I'm so happy that you are all safe."

She stares at me but doesn't say anything more. I want to take her in my arms and hold her. I want to kiss her so badly, but what I need to do is going to be hard enough. I don't want to hurt her, but there's no other choice.

"I had to come to see you first. I woke up in that hospital and knew that we had to talk."

She looks at me expectantly, waiting for me to get what I have to say of my chest. But even without a word, I can see that she's wary.

"I can't do this. I thought I could, but now I see that it is impossible."

"What are you talking about?" She faces me head-on like she knows what's about to come and is going to take the punch straight to the jaw.

"I can't be with you. I can't be a father to Brogan. I can't be responsible for either of you." My heart feels like it is being torn from my chest. The words coming from my mouth taste foul on my tongue. This is the last thing I want to do.

"Okay." Storm rises from her spot and heads to the door. She opens it and looks at me expectantly. "You can leave now."

"Storm."

"No, Pope. This is the choice you made. You decided to push me away and Brogan too. I hope this doesn't do irreparable damage to your relationship with your son. But for me? I am done. The fact that you think this is okay just shows how little you know. I loved you. I loved the Gypsy Bastards, and I was willing to stand by your side, through the good and the bad shit, but that wasn't enough for you. So, yes, I accept your bullshit excuse, but I am done with you. I'm done being hurt by you. Let me know if and when you want to see your son and we can come to an arrangement, otherwise, get the fuck out of my apartment, and just stay the fuck away from me."

The moment I am outside, she closes the door and engages the lock. I thought this would be for the best, that I was protecting the people I loved. But right now, I know I have made a huge mistake.

Chapter Nineteen
Storm

Instead of staying home and wallowing in self-pity about the choice that Pope made on our behalf, I decided to get out of town. I pack a bag for myself and Brogan and head off to pick him up. I don't leave a message with anyone or explain where I am going, for how long or anything else. I pick up Brogan and say a hasty greeting to my friends before getting us both on the road.

At first, Brogan is silent and just watches me. But about fifteen minutes into the drive, he clears his throat and starts to speak.

"So, I know I'm a kid and all that, but you are upset and I know my dad did something stupid." He looks so serious as he says this that I can't help but burst out laughing.

"Yeah, Brogan, you are a kid but you are a very smart kid. You must have gotten it from your mom."

"Yeah, Mom always said men were stupid. They didn't know how to handle their emotions and because of that, they ended up making dumb choices. Is that what Dad did?"

"Buddy." I sigh. "Problems between me and your dad are just that. Our problems. You don't have to worry about anything. I love you and so does your dad. He's just being pig-headed. We'll go to the beach for the week. A friend of mine has a house there, and when your dad is thinking clearly, we can go home and sort this mess out. We all just need to take a step back for a moment."

"Okay, but if you are mad at him, so am I." Brogan tilts his chin out stubbornly and at that moment, he looks more like his father than I think he wants to.

"I can accept that. Before this is over, I might need you in my corner."

Brogan nods and gets comfortable in his seat.

****

A few hours later, just as the sun starts to set, we pull up outside a beautiful little wooden cottage, painted white with a deep-blue roof and shutters. From where we are parked, I can hear the waves lapping at the shore before we even step outside. Opening the doors, we both step out of the car. As I take a deep breath, I feel the tension that has plagued me the whole drive just start to slip away. The clean, salty air does wonders for my spirits and I feel a grin form across my face. Turning toward Brogan, I find him grinning back at me.

"We have to wait for my friend to bring us the keys and then it's just me and you for an entire week." I can't stop smiling. The fact that his smile gets bigger only reaffirms my decision to bring us out here. The last couple of months have been hell on us and we need a break.

****

For days, we do whatever we want. We go swimming in the ocean, not too deep because of Brogan's cast, pick up seashells, watch movies late into the night, and eat at local restaurants. We enjoy each other's company and get to know each other better away from everyone else. But it is time to return to our regular lives. Gage has been out of school for long enough and I need to find a new job. I don't think that I'll be able to return to stripping even if Pope and I are split up. I'm a mother figure and a role model now, and I need to remember that.

Resting on the back porch with an ocean view, I listen as the waves crash against the beach while drinking a beer. There are so many things that my mind keeps trying to figure out, problems it keeps trying to solve, but I shut those thoughts down immediately. This is my last night here, in this beautiful and tranquil place before heading back to the madness that is my life, and I will do my best to try to enjoy the last couple of hours.

Suddenly, a man jumps over the railing, and without giving me a second to react, he has me out of my chair and pressed to the white wooden walls of the cottage. One hand is closed over my mouth and the other is holding my hands above my head. I can't remember ever seeing anyone move that fast.

For a moment, he just stares into my eyes, watching me closely. He doesn't say a word and the longer he remains quiet, the faster my heart beats. The adrenaline is kicking in and I want to fight, but I can't. Brogan is in the house, asleep, and if this man were to know that, he might hurt him and I would never be able to live with myself if that happened.

"I'm not here to hurt you. I know Brogan is asleep in the house and I don't want to hurt him either. But we need to talk." The man doesn't lower his voice or whisper, he simply states it.

I now know that he has been watching us and that this isn't just a home invasion. The need to fight thrums through my veins and I have to work to tamp it down. Slowly, I nod my head. The man releases my mouth and my hands and steps away.

"Storm, I need you to listen to me. You may not know me, but I'm here to help. Will you at least just hear me out?" He has his hands lifted up, palms turned outward. But he's right, I don't know him and I sure as shit shouldn't trust him. As I look at him in the glow of the single outdoor light, I have a gut feeling about him. I need to listen to him.

"Who are you and what do you want?" I'm trying to put on a brave face, but I haven't been this scared since I was eighteen years old and living on the street.

"My name is Calum Quince, but most just call me Bishop. And I'm here to help you and the Gypsy Bastards before this gets any worse." He stares at me with pleading eyes.

"Okay, Calum, why would you want to help us?"

"I want to tell you everything, but you need to let me finish my story, then you can make your judgments." He no longer has his gaze trained on me but instead on the shoreline in the distance.

"You have ten minutes to convince me that you aren't some kind of psycho, and if I'm not convinced, I will shoot you."

A low chuckle escapes from him as he faces me.

"Why do you think I waited until it was dark out? Until you were relaxing with a beer? I know what you are capable of and I don't want to get my nuts shot off." He smirks and for the first time, I realize how attractive he is.

Now that I have decided he isn't an immediate threat—mostly—I can look at him more closely. He is of average height but there is nothing average about his build. Strong, muscular arms encased in a fitted red t-shirt. Muscular thighs that are hugged by the denim of his dark-wash jeans. He has a chiseled jaw and high cheekbones with just a little bit of scruff covering it. He seems to be in his twenties but looks like he might be carrying the weight of the world at this moment.

"So tell me." Stepping away from the wall, I take a seat on the opposite side of the table.

"You, Pope, Brogan, and the Gypsy Bastards are in danger."

I snort but before I can speak, he lifts his hand to

silence me.

"Let me finish, please. I know as an outlaw club the Gypsy Bastards always has some or other form of trouble, but this is different. King wants Wolf's head on a platter and he wants Hadley back. And that's just to start with. Riot is losing his mind because Sparrow killed Mutt, the president of the Mongrols, and also his brother. I have seen first-hand what happens to clubs and their families when those two go on a rampage, and it isn't going to end well."

"Well, thank you for the warning, but Brogan and I are fine—"

"But you aren't," he cuts me off. "In the four days you have been here, frolicking in the ocean without a care, one of Riot's men almost killed you. And if it weren't for me, you would both be dead."

He states this calmly, like reading a grocery list out loud. And although I want to argue, the look in his eyes tells me every word he is saying is the truth.

"Thank you for that. But I don't understand why you would help me or the club."

"Because it's the right thing to do. Because you don't run around killing women and children when you are trying to get to a man. Because I am tired of this bullshit."

Calum is clearly upset. I'm missing something important and I can't seem to put my finger to it.

"What bullshit, Calum?"

"Watching King and Riot do whatever they want." He runs his hand over his shortly cropped dark hair. "Since I can remember, this has been their M.O. Someone crosses them, sometimes without even knowing it, and then they start. First, they target family members, friends, loved ones. Then they go after the entire club and tear it down piece by piece. They will give the offending party the chance to hand themselves over soon in the game, but it's not what they actually want and very rarely happens. Usually, they wipe out everyone and everything before ending it all."

Dread fills me. They are doing the exact same thing to Sparrow.

"How do you know all of this?" I whisper, afraid of his answer.

He stares at me for a moment, clearly considering whether to tell me the truth or not.

"Riot is my Father."

Chapter Twenty
Pope

The last five days have got me going insane. I shouldn't have pushed Storm away. I knew it the moment I walked out of her apartment. But I'm stubborn and I have my pride. I didn't know how else to protect her or Brogan and it seemed like the only answer. I thought I would be able to control the ballgame, have her watched from afar to ensure that they are safe. But life doesn't work according to plan and Storm left town, taking Brogan with her.

I have no idea where she is or if she is safe. And I have no way of finding out because she isn't taking my calls, again. Every time I call and she doesn't answer, I leave a voicemail. They range from telling her I love her and I am sorry that I fucked up, to angry and threatening. I don't know if she even listens to them, but I hope she doesn't. I said things that I hope she never hears and the things I want her to hear should rather be said in person.

At midnight, I find myself standing at the foot of the stairs in the clubhouse, looking at everyone gathered. My club is in full lockdown mode. Again. Members, family, and friends are all staying at the compound until we can figure out this mess with Riot.

My eye catches movement at the side door and I turn to see who it could be. My breath catches in my lungs as Storm walks into the clubhouse. Relief washes over me for a moment before I see a man enter directly behind her, carrying my sleeping son. I feel my face heat as my temper spikes, and I cross the room toward them. Five days. Five days is all she needed to replace me.

I love her with everything I have and she can just replace me?

Striding across the clubhouse, I can feel everyone watching me, judging me, pitying me. I don't need their pity and no one here has the right to judge me.

"What are you doing here?" I growl at her.

Instead of shrinking away from me, like most other people would, she lifts her chin. There is a fire in her eyes and I ready myself for the fight I know is coming.

"Judging by the number of voicemails and the fact that you kept on calling for the last five days, I assumed you wanted to see me. But I can just as easily leave if that would suit you better?" Her left brow is arched in question.

"Just leave, Storm. Just get out and take your boy toy with you. You aren't welcome here anymore."

I hear a sharp intake of breath behind me but I don't take my eyes from Storm.

"First, he is not my boy toy. He is the man"—she emphasizes the word *man*—"who kept me and your son alive for the last five days. So you might want to show him some fucking gratitude. Second, I don't give a shit what you say. I will always be welcome here. Just because you don't want me in your life anymore doesn't mean I'm not family. And third, if you ever come at me with your goddamned attitude again when you have none, and I repeat none of the facts, I will use the gun you bought me to shoot you in the foot."

She stares at me, waiting for me to say something. I feel like a chastised child.

On one hand, I want to roar and rage at her. Who is this man she suddenly trusts with her life and my son's? On the other hand, I am simply relieved to see her and Brogan, alive and well. I have a million questions flying around in my mind. Where has she been? But I can't ask her anything, as she turns away from me.

"Justice, can we put Brogan in your room? He is exhausted and I don't know how clean any of the other rooms will be."

Justice nods his head, leading the man, the stranger, into the bowels of our clubhouse. Around me, people pretend to do things but I know everyone is watching us.

"What are you doing here, Storm?" I ask again.

"Where is Sparrow?" she counters.

I look around, trying to find him in the sea of faces, but don't see him. I turn back to Storm to tell her that he might be in his room but find her talking to the stranger.

"I think I should head out, let you settle things here, but I will see you in the morning," he says to her.

Storm nods, reaching out to hug him around the neck. I have no idea what possesses me, but I yank her back and place her behind me. Grabbing the stranger by his throat, I walk him back against the wall and bring my fist down into his face. Everything happens so quickly, and before I know it, Beast pulls me off the man. Wolf is in my face, trying to talk to me, but I can't hear him over the sound of my blood rushing through my ears,

Looking over Wolf's shoulder, I see Storm staring daggers at me while the man leans against the wall, touching his bleeding lip.

"Typical," Storm says while moving closer. "You don't talk to me, just jump to your own conclusions about everything. Perhaps if you had asked who my new friend was instead of assuming the worst about me, thank you for that by the way, we could have avoided this whole mess."

She waits, staring into my eyes, for me to calm down.

"Who is your new friend?" I ask through

clenched teeth while Beast still holds me back.

"His name is Calum Quince, and he is the answer to all your problems."

****

As the sun rises over Gypsy Falls, we gather in church. For the first time since my father started this club in 1986, we have not only a non-member but a member of a rival club joining us. Every fiber in my being is screaming at me that this is wrong, that I need to get him out of here, but I can't do that. Twice now this man has saved the lives of someone I love. Twice now he has been there when I wasn't. He called me ahead of the church shooting and although there were still deaths, the number was significantly lower than it could have been had we not been warned. And then he kept Storm and Brogan alive for the five days they were out of town.

I pushed her away, basically sent her out of town to protect her, not knowing that I was putting her in more danger. If I had known, if I had even the slightest inkling that they would be in more danger because they were away from me, I never would have said those things, I never would have pushed her away.

Calling the meeting to order, I stand and look over my club members. Old members and new stare at me with questions in their gaze.

"Let's get this started. There is a lot to be done and we will need to be fast about it. This is Calum and he has some intel for us, so let's listen to what he has to say."

I nod toward Calum, giving him the chance to speak. I look at his split lip again, and although I should feel bad, I don't.

"Riot and King are coming for you. For all of you. Loved ones, family, members. They are coming to wipe you from the face of the earth and they have done this before so they know what they are doing."

"We know they're coming, boy," Viking speaks up from his spot. "They have been coming since Hadley became one of us. What changed?"

"Sparrow changed everything." Calum takes a breath. "When he killed Mutt, he escalated everything."

"I don't see what Mutt and the Mongrols have to do with any of this," Sparrow says. "We put an end to their shitty club. And they deserved it."

"Yes, Sparrow, they did deserve it. Storm filled me in, gave me the whole picture on both Hadley and Kaiya, and I agree with you, but Mutt was also Riot's little brother. And in his mind, blood will have blood. He will exact revenge for the death of his brother unless we stop him."

"Shit," Wolf mutters and shakes his head.

"Fine, I get the need for revenge," Sparrow replies. "But to wipe out families and clubs just to get that done is ridiculous."

"It may be, but that is the way he does things. You are not the first to be targeted by him and if we don't end this, you sure as shit won't be the last."

Sparrow rises from his seat and stares at Calum.

"Explain to me, boy. Who the fuck are you to walk into our lives, our club, and tell us how to take care of our business?"

Tension is thick in the air as everyone waits for Calum to answer. I already know the answer, but I watch him closely. He is completely relaxed in his seat as he answers Sparrow.

"First, I am not your boy. I may be younger than you and respect you for the patch and rank you wear, but do not think I am below you. I know how Riot's mind works because I have seen it first-hand when he killed my mother and her entire family for something she didn't even do. I am Calum Quince and I used to be a prospect for the Iron Disciples. They all know me as Bishop, but the one thing I am best known for is being a son to a sociopath. I am Riot's son and I watched him kill my mother in cold blood when I was thirteen. So yes, I am uniquely qualified to give insight into how to take him out."

Silence reigns in the room as everyone takes into account what Calum has just told us. I knew the basics of who he was but not everything. And although there may be a chance that he is here to lead us into a trap, I have a gut feeling that isn't the case.

"So tell us, Bishop, how do we take care of your father?" I ask, staring straight at him.

****

Four hours later, we all walk out of church with a plan. It is risky and the Iron Disciples have a hell of a lot more members than we do, but we have to take the shot. The club will remain on lockdown, protecting family and friends, and I even called in a few favors for an extra couple of hands. McLaughlin was willing to lend me a couple of guys to watch the compound while we take care of business. It will cost me a pretty penny when his next gun shipment comes in, but if this all works out, it will be worth it.

Moving through the lower part of the clubhouse, I search the bar area, looking for Storm. If anything goes wrong today, I need to have cleared the air between us. I find her on a couch between Hadley and Kaiya, holding Ainsley.

I watch from my spot, half-shrouded in shadows as she talks to the other woman and the tiny baby she is holding. She is a true beauty and seeing her this way, unguarded, has my protective instincts rearing up. I want to fix what I broke and put my family back together.

Some day in the future, I hope to be able to see her holding our baby with a smile.

Hadley is the first woman after Luna to have a baby with one of our members and I had forgotten how soft some of the guys could get around babies. And although none of them would admit it, Ainsley definitely has most of the guys wrapped around her little finger.

I approach Storm slowly, making sure that she sees me. She hands Ainsley back to Hadley after kissing her on her forehead. She turns an expectant gaze toward me.

"Can I have a moment with you?"

She doesn't say a word. She simply nods and starts to move toward the stairs. I follow behind her, but as we reach the top, I take her hand and lead her toward my private quarters. Closing the door behind us, I wait for her to turn around but she doesn't stop until she is in my bedroom. I walk in to find her rummaging through my closet. Neither of us speaks as she starts to place items on my bed.

Bulletproof vest, 9mm Beretta, knife. She places them all on my bed before removing a black shirt from my closet and handing it to me. She starts talking before I have the chance to apologize.

"I know you love me, and I know that you pushed me and Brogan away because you thought you were protecting us. Bet you're kicking your ass about that at the moment." She smirks while saying this last part.

Grabbing the hem of my shirt, she starts to lift and I help her by lifting my arms. I'm knocked on my ass by her words. I was fully prepared to apologize for my shitty behavior and thinking that I always know what is best for those around me, but she beat me to the punch.

"What we are going to do is this." She stares into my eyes, making sure that my focus is fully on her at the moment. Like it could be anywhere else. "You are going out with the guys to take care of business. You are going to take care of yourself and come back home. When all of this shit is said and done, you and I will sort us out. Until then, no talking about our relationship or what is going on with us at the moment. I will be here when you get back."

After getting my shirt on, she moves behind me and drapes my bulletproof vest over my shoulders and secures the straps. She pats me on the butt before making her way toward the door.

"I love you. And it will all work out. Finish getting dressed and go kick some ass. I'll see you later."

With that said, she leaves me alone with my thoughts. Fuck, I'm a lucky bastard.

Chapter Twenty-One
Pope

We have a plan that should work if everything goes according to plan, but first, I need to make a call. Raising my cell phone to my ear, I wait for the person on the other side to answer.

"Who the fuck is this?"

I remain silent for a moment, enjoying the upper hand before I answer.

"Pope."

"Fucking hell. Where did you get this number?" Riot growls back at me.

"From your son."

Silence reigns between us. Neither of us daring to be the first one to speak, both fearing the loss of the higher ground in this battle between us.

"So, let me get this straight. First, your Vice President kills my brother and now you think that it is a good idea to kidnap my only child, to do what? Do you want to make peace? Or are you simply trying to prove a point?" His tone is deathly calm.

"Neither. What I want to do is talk."

"So talk. You have two minutes or I will get my guys together and burn your entire world to ashes."

"I need this ended. Tonight. I will return your son to you unharmed, and Sparrow will give himself over to you on the condition that you will leave the rest of the Gypsy Bastards, their families, and friends alone. The debt will be paid."

For a moment, we move back to the silence.

"Why should I trust you?"

"Because I have honor. Your son is alive and well, right beside me. You are on speakerphone, so you can talk to him." I remove the phone from my ear and set it to speakerphone.

"Bishop?"

"Riot." Bishop doesn't say much. His face is stoic, giving away no emotion.

"Where are you? I'll be there in five minutes."

"Don't be stupid. Walking in here will get me killed and at least one or two of the guys that come here with you, too. Just take the deal and let's move on from this shit show."

"I need to discuss it with King first. I will call you back."

He ends the call abruptly, no niceties between father and son. Bishop stares straight ahead. He has nothing to say because we can all see it. He doesn't care for the man who is his father and has no regrets helping us.

We wait in silence for what seems like forever but is actually closer to ten minutes before my cell phone rings. Slowly, I lift it from the table and answer.

"Drive south out of town until you reach the old factory side. Bishop will know where to go from there. You have two hours. If I do not have my son and Sparrow at that time, I will be coming for you and yours first."

He doesn't wait for me to agree, he simply ends the call. Turning toward Bishop, I wait for him to talk.

"I need a pen and paper. I know the old abandoned warehouse and surrounding buildings well, and I have the perfect plan."

****

Bishop had split us into three groups before we made the initial call to Riot. He knows his father the best and assured us that the trade would take place at one of two places. We sent one group to the farm, one group to their warehouse location that Riot just chose as our meeting spot, and the third group is currently in the clubhouse around our table. Our group consists of myself, Sparrow, Wolf, Viking, and Bishop.

We will head to the warehouse with the van including myself, Sparrow and Bishop tied up in the back, with Wolf and Viking accompanying us on their bikes. The plan is very simple but it is better to keep it that way instead of trying to overcomplicate things.

Our team has already surrounded the warehouse and is hiding in wait. Mad Dog has gone ahead and scouted out the area for the best positions to set up as a sniper.

Everyone is strapped and everything is in place as we all head out to our bikes. On the way through the clubhouse, Wolf and Viking stop to say goodbye to Hadley, with Viking sneaking in a chance to cuddle little Ainsley, and Sparrow speaks to Gage. Storm is nowhere to be seen, but Brogan is waiting for me by the door.

"You are my father, and I'm grateful that I got to meet you. But Storm is all I have left of my mom and I don't want to see her hurt. If you hurt her again, I will act my age and throw a tantrum so big that we will move back to Baton Rouge. You won't see either of us again." He says this without looking away from me.

At that moment, I have so much pride that I feel like I could burst. The fact that he loves her enough to stand up to me, even though I know it must be scary, fills me with more pride than I thought possible.

But I also realize that my son is a lot more mature than anyone gives him credit for and that he is smarter than people would think for his age. Knowing that he would most definitely be able to guilt Storm into moving back to Baton Rouge scares the shit out of me. I stare at him for a moment without saying a word before nodding.

He nods in return and hugs me around my waist quickly, then walks away.

"Some kid you got there." Bishop watches Brogan as he walks deeper into the clubhouse. "And you are a good father. My dad would have knocked my ass out for saying something like that to him."

"I know that some would think he was being a disrespectful little shit, but knowing he loves her enough to come at me head-on fills me with pride. Besides, if he is like this at this age, I can't wait to see what he's like when he's all grown up."

Bishop chuckles as he moves past me toward the van. I retrieve some zip ties from the back and loosely tie his hands in front of him. He needs to be able to get loose and get to his gun if shit breaks out. I help him get into the back as Wolf, Viking, and Sparrow come outside to join us.

"I have a bad feeling about this, brother," Wolf says to me. "No offense, Bishop, but I don't know you for shit. Who says you aren't leading us into a trap?"

"Believe what you will, but I know the truth," Bishop replies. "Riot likes to believe he is smarter than everyone else, and that no one would ever go against him. The fact that I am the one person he believes will never do that is going to be his downfall."

Viking nods his agreement. "I have seen it a million times. The people closest to you, the ones you least expect, are the people that often cause your downfall."

There's something in his voice, something that niggles at me, and I know there's a story. And even though I want to ask him what's going on, now isn't the time nor the place for that.

"I don't care if it's a trap or not." Sparrow scowls at all of us. "Let's get this shit show on the road so that I can face the man who murdered my wife."

No one says anything against him. He has lost so much and deserves the chance to get some peace. The only problem is that I don't know if this is going to make it better or worse. We all think we want revenge and some even make it their life's mission to get it, but what then? What is left after you end the person who caused you more pain than any other person in your entire life? My greatest fear is that we will lose Sparrow after all of this is over.

Without another word spoken, we all pile into the truck and head out.

Chapter Twenty-Two
Storm

I told Pope the truth when I was standing in his room. I do love him and I know that he loves me. There's no question about those two things in my mind. They are facts and can be taken as holy writ. But I do have my doubts about how far love can sustain us, as people. Because the truth is, you can love someone with your whole heart, with every fiber of your being, and sometimes it still doesn't last. Sometimes, sadly, love just isn't enough.

I watch them from the window in Pope's apartment as they load up and head out. I know what is happening. Bishop told me exactly what he was planning to do, and although it scares the shit out of me, I know it has to be done. From what Bishop has divulged to me about his father, Riot is a complete psycho who will not rest until he has what he feels is his revenge.

My stress levels are through the roof and from previous experience, I know that I won't be able to relax before all of the guys are back and I can see them with my own eyes. Previously, I would have to pretend to have the same level of care and worry for Pope as I do for the rest of the guys, but with our relationship out in the open, I can show my true worry. It's not that I care less for the other guys, it is just a different type of caring.

A soft knock on the door draws my attention. I know who it is, and although I don't feel like talking to anyone, I open the door for Hadley and Kaiya to enter. I know they want to talk about what's going on but I don't have it in me. I don't want to talk about something that is out of my control, something I can't do anything about, and simply drive my stress up further.

"I don't want to talk about it. They have a plan, they went out, they will be back." I level both of them with a hard glare.

"Okay." Hadley doesn't look happy about it, but she doesn't press the issue.

I hold out my arms and she hands a sleeping Ainsley over tome. I cuddle her to my chest and breathe her in, calming my frazzled nerves a little bit. She smells of soap, sunshine, and love. Just like all babies should

"I don't care. Mad Dog told me to chill out, that they could handle themselves and that me stressing about it wasn't going to help anything." Kaiya rolls her eyes as she plops down on the couch. "Like him telling me not to think about something is just automatically going to stop me from doing it. Like my mind just jumps at his damn commands."

Even though I know she is being serious, I can't stop myself from laughing. Kaiya has grown so much in the last year and I find it entertaining that she finally found her voice. It drives Mad Dog nuts that she's learning to stand on her own and do things for herself. In the beginning, she was content to lean on him and have him there for support, but more recently, she has started wanting to do things for herself. She started talking to Irene, my sister's best friend who also happened to be a grief counselor, and since then has become more and more like a normal twenty-something.

She is constantly changing the color of her hair, trying to find her way in the world, including getting a job and covering her scars with tattoos. She is blooming into a beautiful, willful woman and I am so proud to be here for her during this transition.

"I mean, can you just sit here and not worry?" She stares at me with worry lining her face.

Shaking my head, I answer her. "No. I wish I

could just turn it off, but it doesn't work that way. Still doesn't mean I want to talk about it."

"I get that," Hadley says softly as she takes a seat on the couch.

Taking a seat beside her, I take her hand in mine while cradling Ainsley in the other and, in silence, waiting for the guys to return.

****

Pope

Pulling to a stop, I stare at the warehouse.

"Deja-fucking-vu, brother. This looks identical to the place they trapped me and Justice previously." Wolf speaks through the open driver's side window from his perch on his bike.

The place seems to be falling apart except for the fact that all the doors have recently been replaced. If you hadn't been looking for somewhere someone would be hiding illicit activities, you would miss this place for sure.

None of us says a word. The air is thick with the emotion and the adrenaline pumping through all of us. Anticipation thrums through my veins as I see Riot standing beside a pickup truck. Five bikes are parked beside him, riders straddling them.

"Let's get this show on the road," Bishop says. "No time like the present."

Sparrow and I get out the front and move around the van to open the back door and help Bishop out while Wolf and Viking shut down their rides. Bishop turns to Sparrow and stares at him.

"Remember the plan. Don't let my dad goad you into going off track. If you want to lose your cool, push me down or something, but don't deviate from the plan. We need him to fall for our charade."

Sparrow watches Bishop closely for a moment before nodding his head and escorting him around the truck. Viking and Wolf have already dismounted and are waiting for us to reach the front. Across from us, I can see Riot's jaw tense at the sight of his son with his hands tied.

"Send my son over," he hollers at us.

Sparrow lifts a booted foot, which he then plants behind Bishop's knees, forcing him forward and into a kneeling pose. Just as fast, he whips a pistol from underneath his cut and points it directly at Bishop's temple.

"How about I shoot your *puta* son right in front of you and you can know what it felt like to watch my wife blow up and burn?" Sparrow questions with an eerie calm.

"Don't you dare touch my son." For the first time since this mess started, I can hear the panic in Riot's voice. It seems that the psycho may actually have a weakness.

Placing my hand on Sparrow's shoulder, I stop him from speaking. The muscles in his arm ripple with the force he is using to try to contain himself.

"Perhaps we can do this more agreeably. The deal is we give your son back, and you and Sparrow will sort your shit out man-on-man and everyone else will be left out of this?"

"Correct," Riot answers. "You have my word."

Nodding, I signal for Viking to untie Bishop and help him to his feet. Sparrow watches everything closely and the vein in his forehead is visible to anyone with eyes.

"Relax, brother," Wolf whispers to him. "We won't let him get away."

Sparrow doesn't answer but watches Bishop and

Riot like a hawk, while Wolf scans the area around us. Taking a deep breath, I can smell the rain on the horizon. The clouds have been gathering since early this afternoon, promising rain.

We don't have a moment's notice as Sparrow draws his weapon and fires at Bishop.

"Motherfucker!" Riot roars from across the lot as he returns fire.

Everything turns to chaos in the blink of an eye. People are firing left and right as we all scramble to take cover. Wolf is beside me in a moment and already I can see the red seeping through his green shirt from the wound in his shoulder. Bikes start up and the rumble fades away as Riot's men hightail it into the distance. We have them outnumbered as our guys come from all sides, and they know it, choosing to beat a hasty retreat rather than die here.

Moving from my spot behind the van, I see the destruction in front of me. On the ground lies Bishop, Sparrow, and two of Riot's men. Mad Dog is crouched beside Sparrow, feeling for a pulse. His gaze collides with mine and sadness shows in his gaze as she shakes his head. Sparrow is dead, as is Bishop.

Slowly, we load Sparrow and Bishop into the back of the van and head back to the clubhouse.

****

As we drive up to the compound, our plan comes to fruition. I was starting to think this whole charade was a waste of time when suddenly the van is hit from the side, sending it skidding across the wet road. Everyone is disorientated for a moment before starting to right themselves. The back door of the van is wrenched open and Riot stands there in the downpour. His white shirt is stained with blood, though I'm not sure whose, and his gaze is wild as it tracks between the men in the van.

"I am taking my son. But be sure to say all your goodbyes, because I will come for each and every one of you. Nothing will stop me." Riot screams at us as thunder drones in the distance.

He grips Bishop beneath his arms and starts to drag him from the van. When he gets to the edge, he turns to lift Bishop out. Three men stand behind him, semi-automatic rifles pointed at us, keeping us in place. Before Bishop is completely out of the van, Sparrow rises from his spot and holds his blade to Riot's neck. The men facing us have no idea what to do so they wait for further instruction. Bishop starts to move and in his shock, Riot lets him go.

Bishop faces the men with the guns trained on us.

"Leave now and you may survive this. Get your men, go, and don't come back. Tell King the Gypsy Bastards are ready."

They stare at him for a moment, then hightail it out of sight. Clearly, they weren't expecting the turn of events. Bishop turns to his father.

"You did this to yourself." Riot spits in Bishop's face.

"No matter. Today the almighty Riot comes to an end. Do you have anything you want to say before Sparrow ends your miserable existence?"

"I regret nothing."

Sparrow slides the blade across Riot's throat, pulling him into the van at the same time. He doesn't release him, just sits there with his head resting on his lap as he bleeds out. Watching him, seeing the life leave him.

"Neither do I." Lightning flashes across the sky, showing Sparrow's vacant expression.

Chapter Twenty-Three
Storm

It has been two weeks since I last spoke to Pope. He stops at the apartment to pick up Brogan but doesn't talk to me. Perhaps I was wrong and the love I thought we shared was simply one-sided. But perhaps I was right and love really isn't enough to overcome all obstacles. I live in a perpetual loop of hopelessness, wishing he would show up and we could sort this out, but I'm too proud to go to him and fix it myself.

Today is the hardest day of all. I would love for nothing more than to spend my birthday at the clubhouse as I have done these past few years, but it just isn't reasonable. All the guys have been around to see me, telling me he loves me, they love me, telling me to come home. But I can't and I won't, not until he asks me himself. Although I am still pissed at him for pushing me away, and I know this isn't the feminist thing to say, I would run to him if he only asked.

A knock on the apartment door draws my attention. Hadley and Wolf have already been by today, bringing little Ainsley by to cheer me up, and Brogan and Pope left about an hour ago. Tonight is the first night that Brogan will not be coming home after visiting with his father. And although we are no longer together, I want them to have a good relationship. Brogan deserves to have a relationship with Pope even if I don't.

As I open the door, a smile forms on my lips. Bishop.

"Hey there, beautiful. What are you up to?" He leans against the railing.

"Not much."

"Well, do you want to help me out with a

problem I'm having? I'll feed you in return." His smile is infectious and I can't help but smile back.

"No problem, as long as it's sushi."

He pulls a face but doesn't protest. Moving into the lounge, I find my flats and slip them on, lock up, and follow him to his truck.

"Where are you taking me? And what is this mysterious problem?"

"Well, since the police found Riot's body, his paperwork has been moving along and I finally got the all-clear on my mom's farmhouse." He opens the passenger side door for me then moves around the truck and gets in. He starts it up and gets it underway. "It was her favorite place in the whole world and I have been doing some upkeep on it these last few years, so it's in pretty good shape."

"Okay, so what help do you need from me? Hadley is much better at decorating than I am."

"No, no nothing like that. I want to sell the farm, house and all. All my best childhood memories are there with my mom but she isn't there. My memories of her will always be with me, I don't need the house. Besides, it's way too big for me. I need an apartment like yours."

"A bachelor pad?" I laugh.

"Yup. But I need someone to tell me if it looks okay. I just want your opinion on if you think it is ready to go to market or if I should do some more work."

"Well, I'm not a pro on this or anything, but I can give you my opinion. You may want to get a second opinion though."

Bishop laughs as he turns down a gravel road leading to a double-story farmhouse surrounded by lush green trees. The garden is well kept and I can see a family living here. Kids and dogs running around the yard. For a moment, I can imagine it being me, Pope, and

Brogan living here. The thought fills me with longing and I'm instantly sad. Bishop must feel the change in me as he shuts off the truck and turns to me.

"Everything will work out fine." He kisses my cheek and jumps out of the truck, coming around to open my door.

To say that I am beyond shocked is an understatement, but I don't mention it, I only follow Bishop. The house has a beautiful wraparound porch with a porch swing. It is all painted white except for the shutters that are painted a bright, brilliant green. Bishop wastes no time leading me through the house.

All the bathrooms have been modernized and the hardwood flooring has been redone. As he leads me into the kitchen, I almost start crying. It's my dream kitchen. Beautiful dark countertops, cherry wood cupboards, and stainless-steel finishings and appliances. Before I can tell him what a beautiful house this is, how lucky someone would be to buy it, his phone rings. He pulls it from his pocket and checks the screen.

"I have to take this, but head out into the backyard. I know you're just going to love it." Turning away from me, I hear him speak as he heads back into the house.

Making my way to the sliding door, I stare outside and my breath catches in my throat. Standing in the fading sunlight are Pope and Brogan, each holding a bouquet of daisies. The first tear falls down my cheek as Brogan runs toward me and moves the door open. He takes my hand in his and leads me toward Pope.

"I love you both," Brogan says giving us each a hug, handing me the bouquet he was holding, and running back into the house.

Staring at Pope, I have no words. Thoughts tumble through my mind but I'm terrified to say anything at this moment. He stares at me before handing me the daisies in his grasp.

"Storm, I love you. I have loved you for as long as I can remember. I'm a hard-headed fool and I almost lost you because of it." He takes my face in both his calloused hands and plants a kiss on my lips. "I want you and only you. I want us to be a family and I want you to be my old lady. I need you by my side or I won't be able to survive. You, me, and Brogan belong together."

He stops speaking and stares at me, waiting for me to say something.

"Please say something?" he pleads.

"Yes."

"Yes?" He looks confused for a moment.

"Yes. I want us to be a family. I want to be your old lady. Yes, I love you."

He plants his lips on mine again, kissing me until I feel dizzy.

"Good thing. I just bought this house off Bishop and don't know what I would have told him if you said no."

We both burst out laughing

Epilogue
Pope

Nothing is the same anymore. Some things are better and some things not so much. After I finally got Storm to take me back, we moved into the new house and Bishop took over the lease on Storm's apartment. He has also decided to stay on at the club and is currently our newest prospect.

These last three months have been the happiest of my life. We spend every second we have together, as a family, and I couldn't ask for more.

Brogan has blossomed into a brilliant young man. We got him a rescue pitbull and the two have been inseparable since that first meeting. They spend their time roaming around the farm or at the clubhouse and Scraps—which is what he named the dog—has become a mascot to the club. He is always being fed, or scratched by someone, and simply lives for the attention.

Storm has opened a bakery. She has an incredible hidden talent for baking that none of us ever knew about. She has gotten so busy at the bakery that she even had to hire help. My mum was the first person she asked, and the old woman hopped a plane and moved back to the States, surprising the hell out of me. I shouldn't have been, though, Storm is one of my mum's favorite people and she wants the chance to get to know her grandson better.

I had forgotten that my mum used to be part of the MC lifestyle when she was still married to my dad, but that all came rushing back pretty quickly the first time we took her to the clubhouse. I may have to keep an eye on her and Viking, though.

The part that made our journey less than stellar

was Sparrow. After killing Riot, he couldn't stay in Gypsy Falls anymore. He sold what was left of the house he had with Luna before packing up Gage and moving six hundred miles away from us.

He wanted to hand in his patch and formally leave the club, but he got his ass outvoted. He is officially our first nomad member. Hopefully, time will heal his wounds and he will be able to return to us sooner rather than later. But I get why he left. Everything and everyone reminds him of his loss. He was made for Luna and Luna was made for him. This isn't going to be a quick fix.

The rest of our family and friends are happy and healthy. The club is flourishing and we haven't heard anything from King or the Iron Disciples since that day, so I am cautiously optimistic. All we can hope for is that tomorrow will be as good, if not better, than today.

The End

Gypsy Bastards MC–The Pope Playlist

Usher ft Alicia Keys – My Boo
Thomas Rhett –Marry Me
Selena Gomez – Love you to love me
Miranda Lambert – Vice
Chris Jansen – Drunk Girl
Five Finger Death Punch – Jekyll and Hyde
JP Saxe ft Julia Michaels – If the world was ending
Gabby Barette – I Hope
Kelsea Ballarini – Homecoming Queen
Maddie & Tae – Die from a broken heart

JADE MARSHALL

Shane West – What could have been
Claire Bowen and Sam Palladio – I will fall
30 Seconds to Mars – Stay
Florence and the Machine – Addicted to love
Cory Marks – Outlaws and Outsiders
Five Finger Death Punch – I Apologize
Kane Brown ft Laura Alaina – What Ifs

ACKNOWLEDGEMENTS

I have so many people that I want to thank. First off Stacey, Audrey and all the other Evernight Publishing staff members. Without you all, none of this would have been possible. My husband for having a ton of patience and supporting my dream. My daughter, for encouraging me when I feel like quitting.

My lovely beta readers Surita van der Merwe, Jessica Kuhn, and Celia Moolman. I love your feedback and enthusiasm. You make even my darkest days brighter. To Mr and Mrs van Zyl, for enjoying my work so thoroughly and pimping me out to all your friends. Even if you did call me graphic…

To Angie C Cody, Madhuri Palaji, and all the other lovely reviewers for taking a chance on a new author. Thank you to each person that purchased a copy of my first novel, and a special thank you to anyone who left a review. Each person brightened my day and gave me insight into what they would like to see going forward.

Lastly, to each and every friend, new and old, for your tremendous support. I love giving my stories to you.

Enjoy.
LHR
Jade

JADE MARSHALL

EVERNIGHT PUBLISHING ®

www.evernightpublishing.com